THE THIRD PHONE CALL CAME JUST AS I WAS STEPPING OUT OF THE SHOWER

"Emerson Ward?"

"Yes, this is he." I didn't recognize the voice.

"Remember this number," the strange voice said, and rattled off a seven-digit number. "Have you got it?"

"Yes, I have it."

"Get to a pay phone and call me in fifteen minutes."

The line went dead before I could reply. I gently cradled the receiver, and watched curiously as my hand began to shake.

It was just one of those days.

" . . . a major step forward for Michael W. Sherer—an exceptionally good read with its own voice and style. A fine and enjoyable book."

—Ed Gorman, *Mystery Scene*

Also by Michael W. Sherer

An Option on Death
Little Use for Death

Available from HarperPaperbacks

MICHAEL W. SHERER

Death Came Dressed In White

HarperPaperbacks
A Division of HarperCollins*Publishers*

This is a work of fiction. The characters, incidents, and dialogues are products of the author's imagination and are not to be construed as real. Any resemblance to actual events or persons, living or dead, is entirely coincidental.

HarperPaperbacks *A Division of* HarperCollins*Publishers*
10 East 53rd Street, New York, N.Y. 10022

Cover illustration by Earl Keleny

First printing: August 1992

Printed in the United States of America

HarperPaperbacks and colophon are trademarks of HarperCollins*Publishers*

❖ 10 9 8 7 6 5 4 3 2 1

To Phil,
friend and inspiration,
and to Mel and Gina
for putting up with us.

I

IT WAS ONE of those days that started and ended badly, and was made worse by the fact that I was nearly strung out from lack of sleep, too much booze, and a massive case of self-doubt. I know, that's a little like being damn near pregnant—either you are or you aren't. But I lie to myself a lot less now than I did then. The first call came a few minutes after eight on that August Saturday morning. The strident, chastising ring of the phone brought me out of an uneasy sleep. We had been in bed barely an hour. A band of dark purple against the black night sky had shown faintly when our plane had taxied to the gate at O'Hare, and had grown perceptibly lighter during the drive to Chicago's near north side. The sky had been filled with bright diffused light when we had tumbled yawning into bed. Now, outside the window, the sun burned fiercely through what was left of the morning haze, threatening to bubble the asphalt of the streets later. The day would be a hot one, made less bearable by the cloying humidity of mid-August unless a breeze kicked up off Lake Michigan.

The phone rang again, sounding strangely insistent. I rolled over to pick up the receiver.

"Emerson?" said a female voice. "Emerson, this is George."

I came fully awake; the voice of Georgia Grant sounded much more urgent than had the ringing of the phone. The lanky body of the girl in bed next to me stirred gently, then settled in sleep.

"Good morning, I think," I rasped, clearing my throat. "What's up?"

"Have you seen or heard from Morgan?" Her voice held worry along with the urgency, for which I was almost glad. My friends know better than to attempt a conversation with me before ten on Saturday mornings.

"I saw him just yesterday," I said, frowning. "What's wrong?" I swung my long legs over the side of the bed and reached for a cigarette on the night stand.

"Did he say anything or act funny in any way?" she asked, ignoring my question.

"He seemed fine to me. What in hell is going on?"

"He's gone. I got home at six last night, and he wasn't home. He didn't come home at all last night. Where did you see him ?"

"At your house. Yesterday afternoon about three." I lit the cigarette that dangled from the corner of my mouth and took a drag—it tasted terrible. "He seemed perfectly normal," I said, squelching the impulse to cough. "At least he didn't drop a hint that anything was wrong. Did you two have a fight?"

"No, nothing like that." Her voice quavered a bit. "Help me find him, please. I need your help."

I was annoyed that the worry in her voice did not cause me more concern.

"Look, he probably went out drinking with the boys and ended up spending the night with a friend."

"I don't think so. I've made a few calls already. No one has seen him. Please help me look for him. I think he may be in trouble."

"Okay, okay, George. Calm down. I'm sure he's all right." Of course, I would help, but exhaustion rolled over me in waves. I stifled a yawn. "Can I call you back in an hour or so? We just got back in from Reno a little while ago and haven't had any sleep all night. Let me catch a little nap. When I wake up I'll give it some thought and buzz you back, okay?"

"Oh, thank you," she said, her voice husky. She sounded near tears. "I'm worried to death."

"It'll be all right," I said soothingly. "I'll get back to you later this morning. Until then, stay calm and don't worry about it. We'll find him."

"Okay."

I cradled the phone gently, rolled over, and brooded before falling into the same uneasy sleep. Morgan was a good friend, and while nothing had seemed amiss when I'd seen him the day before, I suspected that perhaps he had an even bigger problem than the one I was just beginning to admit I had.

The second phone call came just an hour later, a few minutes after nine. It was Brandt.

"Sorry to wake you," he said gruffly when I answered the phone. Brandt Williams was one of those who knew not to wake me on Saturday mornings; not only am I bearish, I'm usually incoherent.

"Apology accepted." I was surprised to hear the voice of my oldest and best friend. Teddy Bear Brandt, with his kind eyes and broad smile, who put up with just about anything, especially from me, was mad at me for some reason, and had been stubbornly silent about it for weeks. In fact, he had avoided me.

"I've been trying to get hold of you since last night," he said. "Tom Blanchard was mugged. He's been asking for you. You weren't home, so the hospital called me at his insistence."

"What the hell went on in town last night?" I exploded. The sleeping girl next to me stirred again, but didn't wake. Silence, then a confused stammer came over the line. "Never mind," I sighed. "It just seems to be a day for bad news." I briefly explained the phone call from Georgia Grant.

"That doesn't sound like the old Morgan," Brandt said when I was done. "But neither one of you has been predictable lately."

"What the hell is that supposed to mean?" Suddenly I felt defensive.

"Just what it sounds like."

I was silent for a moment, then decided not to pursue it. "Tell me what happened to Tom. How badly was he hurt?"

"Pretty bad. Apparently, he was getting his car out of his garage when somebody jumped him. He was badly beaten. The doctors say he has a severe concussion, and they're afraid of hemorrhaging."

"What hospital is he in?"

"Highland Park. A neighbor stopped by and found him, and took him straight there."

"Thanks. I'll get up to see him as soon as I can."

"Emerson? Room 247."

"Thanks. Talk to you later."

I yawned, then got up and stretched to my full six-foot four. Sleeping in late on this Saturday morning, it appeared, was out of the question. I walked naked into the bathroom and relieved myself, then stepped in front of the mirror to confront a haggard visage, replete with tousled brown hair flecked with grey, washed-out, red-rimmed, pale blue eyes the color of a hazy summer sky, long face with a nose that was just a tad too big, and a mustache that helped hide the fact. The face in the mirror looked disgusted with me, and I turned away quickly before I saw what lay behind those eyes.

I found the jacket and slacks I'd worn the night before draped over a chair in the living room downstairs. The left pants pocket yielded up a crumpled wad of bills, some change, and a five-dollar blackjack chip from the MGM Grand in Reno—a souvenir of a crazy impulse to fly to Nevada, gamble for an evening, and fly back on a red-eye. Pulling my car keys out of the right-hand pocket, I patted down the jacket and felt my wallet, sunglasses, and the envelope for the airplane ticket. The little pewter hip flask was in a side pocket. I pulled it out and washed down two No-Doz tablets with a swig of single-malt Scotch. Might as well be a wide-awake drunk, and one with style at that, I thought cynically.

As the alcohol slid warmly down my gullet, I felt marginally better, but the ringing in my ears and the metallic taste in my mouth told of the exhaustion that would not be overcome by the stimulant, no matter how many tablets I swallowed or how much coffee I drank. One of these nights, I would have to get some sleep. One of these days, I would have to quit drinking—if it wasn't too late. Despite its familiarity, this depression and self-pity didn't suit me.

There was movement at the edge of my vision, and I looked up to see the lady who had warmed my bed leaning in the doorway of the hall. She was naked, and stood in a relaxed pose, weight on one leg, the other crossed in front. There was a sharp delineation between the dark tan of her smooth legs and stomach and the white triangle that framed the smaller dark pubic vee. Her arms were crossed over her small breasts, each slender hand loosely grasping the opposite shoulder out of some lingering sense of modesty because it definitely wasn't cold. The air conditioning, turned on low, already was having a hard time beating the day's heat.

Her face was slack, the sea-green eyes unfocused, then her jaw trembled as she stifled a yawn. It was an intriguing and beautiful face; round, squared off at the jawline, and enough cheekbone so that it looked as much American Indian as Irish. A small, straight nose pointed to a round mouth with full lips that could pout almost as well as they could smile. Her elfin face was at the same time both young and old, and it was framed by waist-long, wavy light-brown hair with bangs cut short, all streaked with sun-bleached strands of blonde. The eyes were what made her look older, more worldly-wise.

I'd met Catherine McCrae at a benefit fashion show down at the Palmer House. Local boutique owners and designers had donated their chic wares, time, and energy to putting on the show on a sleety Thursday afternoon in late February. Elegantly coiffed and expertly made-up thoroughbreds had twirled and slunk through their paces on the runway, showing off lines of summer clothes to best advantage, luring wealthy socialites to reach deep into their pocketbooks and adopt the latest fashions. I don't remember who had benefited, but it all had been for a good cause.

I am not a clothes horse who is interested in the latest fashions. Clothes to me are meant to be utilitarian, and are an evil necessity at best. But my friend Brandt Williams had convinced me to go. Brandt is always talking me into going to one charity function or another, saying that it's better to give than to receive. "It will do you good," he says. "It will give you perspective." He's on the boards of so damn many organizations—the Lincoln Park Zoological Society, Santa Claus Anonymous, Chicago Symphony, the Art Institute, Infant Welfare Society, et cetera—that it's hard to avoid going to his functions at least once in awhile.

Actually, watching all of Chicago's elite meet and greet between sets had been fun. I had skirted the outside of the crowd, preferring to stand and walk around rather than to sit among the heavily perfumed and furred matrons, even though many of them were young, yuppified, and very, very pretty. And I had seen a handsome double-breasted seersucker suit to buy after the show, figuring I'd find some occasion on which to wear it—after all, it was for a good cause. I had worked my way over to one side, off to the left of the runway, when Brandt found me.

"Enjoying yourself?" he said in a low voice, leaning close.

"As a matter of fact." I glanced at him, then turned back to watch the show.

"I want you to meet a friend."

When I turned back to face him, a lithe and lovely lady magically appeared at his side. She loosely held Brandt's arm, and seemed draped on his shoulder, like a contented tabby. She was tall in heels, almost even with Brandt's five-eleven or so. The round mouth had pouted, but the green eyes had smiled and sparkled. A mild shock went through me, like an electric current tingling through my fingertips and toes.

"Emerson Ward, this is Catherine McCrae."

Her long fingers pressed warmly into my palm,

amplifying the spark running through me. Our eyes locked.

"Call me Cat." Her voice was breathy.

"Charmed," I murmured.

"Catherine is the best designer in this show. Oleg and Bill and Diane and Yves have got nothing on this girl." Brandt was beaming, as if he'd created, not merely discovered, her talent.

"A designer?" I repeated.

"Yes, and I've got to run," she said in the same breathless tone. "I'm up next."

"Sure. It was nice to meet you."

"Would you like a drink after all this is over?"

"Yes, I'd like that," I stammered, somewhat taken aback.

"Good." She smiled and turned, striding briskly away.

The breathlessness in her voice, I discovered later, was because she had been frenetically pinning up models backstage, preparing for her set, when Brandt had pulled her away to meet me. He looked at me with a smile of amusement as I stared after her.

"Cat got your tongue?"

"I think she does," I grinned. "But Brandt, really. A fashion designer?"

"You'll love her, I promise. Now I've got to run. You know—got to butter up these old biddies and tell them how 'mahvelous' they'll look in these clothes so they'll buy more. All for the cause." He laughed—at himself, because he loved them all, young and old, each and every one. Then he left with a sly look on his face.

I wandered, paying close attention to the next set of models traveling the length of the runway from a number of vantage points. Catherine McCrae's clothes were clean and bold, with straight, no-nonsense lines. They were attractive and flattering, yet sensible and suitable for everyday wear. It was nice stuff, and as I thought of the lady backstage, the stereotype of a clothing designer I'd formed in my mind began to dissolve a little around the edges.

She found me when the show was over, took my arm as though we were old friends, and led me off to one of the hotel bars. I liked the way her hips swung when she walked, and the way she walked with purpose—no dawdling for this woman.

"You're the writer, right?" she asked when we had gotten settled and had ordered—a vodka and soda with lime for her, and a Bass Ale for me.

"One of many, many writers in the world, yes. How did you know?"

"I thought I recognized you. You were pretty obvious wandering around the room when almost everyone else was sitting. I asked Brandt to introduce us."

"How do you know Brandt?" Silly question. Brandt knew everyone, and just about everyone seemed to know Brandt.

"I met him through a friend of a friend. I was opening my shop on Halsted, and needed some help setting up the books, that sort of thing. Brandt sort of came to my rescue."

"He's good at that," I laughed.

"Which? Setting up books, or saving ladies in distress?"

"Both." Her mind was as quick as her smile. I liked that.

She had two shops, it turned out. The one in the hot

neighborhood around Halsted and Armitage had done so well in its first year that she had quickly expanded the business with another boutique down on Oak Street in the high-rent district. She carried other lines besides her own, and had hired and trained good people to run the business so she would have more time for designing. She'd done damn well for herself, considering she hadn't yet hit the big Three-Oh.

After finishing our drinks, we headed north, deciding to have dinner together. We settled on Yvette's, just a short walk from the brownstone I called home on the near north side. Dinner was good, and the company was even better. I liked this woman. She was smart, attractive, and sensible. I felt comfortable with her and was flattered that she had singled me out as someone she wanted to get to know. I sensed that her time was at a premium, and that she didn't have many friends as a result.

We ordered champagne with dinner, and when we'd finished eating and drained the second bottle of Taittinger, it was nearly eleven. Time, and the conversation, had flown by. She declined dessert and coffee, so I asked our waitperson, as they like to be called these days, for the check.

"Where to, ma'am?" I asked when we were out on the sidewalk, bundling up against the cold, damp night air.

"Your house for coffee, sir. I'm having too much fun to call it quits just yet. You do know how to make coffee, don't you?"

I nodded. "Damn good coffee, too."

"Then let's go," she laughed.

I took her arm as we walked down the slick sidewalk. She had a hard time keeping her footing, and I'd had enough champagne so that it was difficult to keep her steady. It was a short, but treacherous walk, and we were giggling like schoolkids by the time we arrived at my door. I turned on a single lamp and took her coat, then went to the fireplace, shoved some crumpled newspaper under the logs, and lit it. She kicked off her wet shoes and sank to the carpet in front of the flames with a sigh of contentment. I excused myself to go back to the kitchen and start the coffee. When it was done, I served us both, then turned off the lamp, and sat on the carpet next to her.

"Mmm, this is good."

"Glad you like it."

She reached out and put her hand on mine, and her touch was electric. There was a long moment of silence. We stared into the fire, unable to meet each other's gaze. Then she leaned into me, and when I turned to face her, she reached up with her hands and pulled my face to hers, tenderly brushing her lips against mine. The soft contact and the scent of her perfume set my heart thumping and my head spinning. I put my hands on her shoulders and gently separated us.

"Whoa, girl. Easy now."

She pulled back slightly, fingers still tracing the line of my jaw, and her eyes searched my face.

"I know this is damn forward of me to invite myself here for coffee," she said softly. "I'm not drunk. A little tipsy, maybe, but not drunk. And I'm not easy." Her voice had turned into a whisper. "I'm just so damned alone. I didn't want to go home by myself. You understand?" Her eyes glistened with wetness in the firelight.

I nodded. A lump in my throat prevented me from

answering. Instead, I pulled her close and put my arms around her tightly. I understood all too well.

Her skin was hot to the touch under the satiny texture of the silk blouse. I sniffed her hair and my head swam. She tilted her head back, and I bent to brush her lips with mine. We kissed tenderly, for an eternity, making the slightest contact, then pulling apart for just fractions of an inch, feeling the current running through us. Pressing her weight into me, I felt the heat of her hardened nipples burn into my chest. She pushed me back onto the carpet and straddled me, working her way up until she could press her mouth hotly onto mine, greedily sucking my tongue into her mouth. Her long hair cascaded around our faces, creating a warm, soft cave that was humid with our breath, scented with her perfume.

Her hands played lightly across my chest, and I felt her fingers work at the buttons on my shirt, then a gentle rush of air as the skin was exposed, and finally the cool touch of her hands. I pulled the loose filmy fabric of her blouse up over her back, and she broke the kiss long enough to raise her arms and let me pull it over her head, exposing her smooth skin to the glow of the fire.

My fingers felt the bumpy ridge of her spine, the little indentations on either side, and the strong back muscles under the soft skin. I worked my fingers into her flesh, kneading gently from shoulders down to the dimples at the base of her spine just above the hips. She sighed, melting into me, nuzzling my neck and nibbling my ear, sending a tingling through me that travelled like lightning from head to toes and back up through my groin to my chest. I was on fire, and her body absorbed the heat and reflected it back.

She rolled off me so that she lay snugged in tight next to me, one bent knee resting across my legs, her face pressed into my neck, long hair splayed out across us both. She caressed my chest and stomach with her fingertips, making me feel all fluttery inside.

"You know, I've had a crush on you for the longest time," she murmured in my ear.

That was it—a little appeal to the male ego, and she had pushed me right over the edge. My heart pounded, and my senses were full to the brim with her—the sight and smell and feel of her. I lightly traced the outline of her breast with a forefinger, and gently pinched the nipple. She gasped and bit my earlobe, then put her hand on my cheek and turned my head to lock us into another soul-stirring kiss. We grasped at each other with a need to fill the loneliness in each other's soul with something other than emptiness. Our hands groped for the catches that would loose us of the clothes that came between us. Slowly, we undressed each other, but with panic in our need to get as close as two people can possibly be. When we were finally naked, our haste disappeared, and we luxuriated in the feel of each other's skin and the warm glow of the fire.

We stroked each other gently, and it both soothed and increased the tension between us, causing the tiny, downy-soft hairs on her arms and thighs to stand up, and goose bumps to ripple across my upper arms. We hardly dared to breathe. In one smooth continuous motion, she rose up and rolled onto me, straddling me with her knees, then lowered herself until she was sitting on the top of my thighs. And as we joined, I felt all of me rush into her, and she back into me.

We both groaned involuntarily at the same time,

and it was if I spoke with her voice, and she with mine. She arched and threw her head back, and I marvelled at her beauty, the strong line of her jaw and the soft curve of her breast silhouetted in the firelight. Her head rolled on her shoulders, and she leaned forward, locking her arms on either side of my rib cage and hanging her head so that her hair brushed across my chest. I reached up to tenderly stroke her face, neck, and shoulders, and lightly squeeze her soft breasts. She moaned, and began moving her hips in a slow circular motion. Energy flowed between us until our bodies were so charged that the current passing back and forth was almost painful. She moved slowly, and I let her set the pace, feeling the blood flow into every open capillary, filling me. Finally, we exploded. Like an overloaded transformer, we sparked and smoked with a crackle and pop and hiss, and finally burst into flames that melted us together and fused our souls.

Much later, when both the fire between us and the one in the hearth had flickered out, we found the energy to move. We shifted position and held each other tenderly.

"This is so much better than being alone," she murmured.

"So much better," I agreed. "What did you mean, you've had a crush on me?"

She turned her head to look at me and smiled. "I've seen you around. You spend more time in my neighborhood than you do here. I've seen you hanging around Blue Mesa a lot."

She was right. I ate there often. I liked the heat of the New Mexican food, and the cool tingle of Corona beer with lime. "I'm flattered, but you don't even know me."

"I probably know more about you than you think."

"Brandt?"

She nodded. "I'm not some starry-eyed teenager. I'm a big girl who can take care of herself."

"I'll say," I murmured. "Well, you caught me. I hope I'm what you wanted."

"Mmm, yes, exactly," she purred, stroking my chest. "Now, if we could just try that again . . ."

She had split what little free time she had between her condo in the Willow-Dayton area and my house. I couldn't tell if it was too much time, or too little. It probably didn't make much difference. I liked her. The problem was I hadn't liked myself much in recent months, and I don't think even she would have been able to save me from myself.

I'd tried to talk to Brandt about it one afternoon, to explain the malaise that seemed to afflict me. "I have this terrible feeling of not belonging," I told him, "of being somehow misplaced in time. I look around at my generation, at its attempts at gentrification. It's just one huge mass of postwar boomers grasping for the brass ring, snapping up half-million-dollar town homes and turbo Saabs like they're rolls of paper towels, to be used and discarded. I just don't know what what it's all for."

"You're just mad that you can't afford a new BMW instead of that old beater you drive," he said in his soft Texas twang, a smile on his face.

"I'll have you know that car's becoming a classic," I retorted. I thought for a minute. "But I guess that's the point. I live in a ritzy neighborhood because I was lucky enough to buy a fixer-upper a long time ago when the price was right. Now I can barely afford the taxes. I drive a ten-year-old car because a new one costs as much as a small bungalow in the suburbs.

"There's not enough good in the world, Brandt, and the yuppie philosophy of doing good is to make and spend more money. Our parents wanted more for us, wanted us to be better than them. And so we are—better educated, better informed, better qualified. But there are too many of us, all grabbing for a piece of the pie, and somehow, it seems to me, everyone's values have gone askew. We're just fucking things up for the next generation."

He looked at me curiously. There was nothing wrong with his values. He came from an old, monied San Antonio family, had rebelled for a time and shed the weight of familial responsibility to find himself and make his fortune. The foundation of refined breeding still remained, mixed with an understanding of the ways in which society was changing. Philanthropy was now his strong suit.

I hadn't felt a part of what my generation seemed to stand for. I'd almost had a woman who would have rooted me in a little world we could have created for ourselves. But she had died. And so everything seemed off kilter, a tad to the left of center for me, and colored in dull earth tones. The writing had stopped almost entirely. The words had shriveled and dried up at the base of an enormous writer's Block, with a capital *B*. And writing, in my strange world of self-imposed solitude, was my only consolation, my only vent.

Writing is what saved me from a life of cold calls and stock market corrections. At some point during my junior year of college, my classmates suddenly found themselves on one of three paths—pre-law, pre-med, or business. By the end of the following year, campus career counselors found most of them spots in graduate schools or positions in New York investment banks. Armed with a degree in English and no burning desire to be anything in life other than comfortable, I decided at the last minute to interview with one of the big brokerage houses, and squeaked into a broker training program. I ended up living in Denver, and hating the brokerage business. I wasn't that good at it, but a couple of wealthy clients and a few lucky breaks had provided me with an old GMC motor home and more than enough of a cushion to roam the country for a few months while trying my hand as a writer. I discovered that not only was I pretty good, but by the time I eventually settled in Chicago, writing had become the burning ambition I'd lacked. I made a living freelancing articles and writing newsletters and annual reports for corporate clients.

This disinterest in writing probably would have been no more than a mild case of the mid-winter doldrums when even Brandt usually makes a point of steering clear of me. But I had gotten a little too far out of control at a party one night, trying to force a jocularity I didn't feel. And someone had passed me the little vial of cocaine and a tiny silver spoon that looked as if it had come from an antique doll-house place setting. Under any other circumstances, I would have let it pass, and reserved judgement on those who accepted it. But in my self-destructive mood, I was suddenly fascinated by its effects on others.

I did let it pass—a good Scotch or cold beer had always sufficed—but in a stupid attempt to gain acceptance from people who didn't matter that much to me, I'd gone and made myself another drink instead, and then had insinuated myself into the clique, emulating the affectations of those in the know, learning the buzzwords, even getting to know the dealers who occasionally showed up at parties to spread more chemical cheer. No one seemed to notice that I never put the white stuff up my nose, substituting snorts of Scotch or tequila instead.

At first, I'd been the life of the party. I was sociable, charming, outgoing—so loveable that even Brandt marveled at how I'd pulled myself out of my February funk. The words had started flowing again for a time, and they were wonderful, well-crafted works that I never even got around to sending out to my list of editors. Instead, they'd gone into a drawer, usually not quite finished because I had gotten a flash of inspiration for another article or essay or book chapter. They too, went unfinished. The more I drank, the faster the words came into my head, too fast to get down on paper, and too disjointed to make sense. I collapsed into silent introspection. Something had compelled me to think that like Faulkner, a bottle of booze a day would inspire me. My muse was soon forgotten in the driving need simply to stay drunk.

It had taken Brandt a while to figure out what was happening, but I think he knew, and now he was avoiding me. It had taken Catherine a while also, but enough time had gone by so that she didn't have a prayer of stopping me from sinking into the abyss of my own self-pity. I hadn't let her get close enough. Something in me was afraid of staying in her sights for too long.

Now, her eyes focused. She stared at the table in front of me for a long moment.

"Oh." She said it quietly, matter-of-factly—a perfect "oh" from that perfectly round *O* of a mouth. But it set off my defenses.

"It was a long night last night," I said a little too heatedly, trying to justify, "and it looks like I'm up for the day already. Why don't you just go back to bed."

"Damn you, Emerson." Now she looked at me, and her green eyes bored into me, making me squirm with guilt. "I've been patient, and have tried not to pass judgement, but you're screwing yourself up."

"I can handle it."

"No you can't."

"I can handle it!"

"Then just give it up. Pour it down the sink. You don't *need* it!"

"You're right, I don't need it. I just like being buzzed. It makes it easier to deal with life."

"Damn your eyes, you stubborn S.O.B. I've loved you since the first time I laid eyes on you, and you hardly even let me get close. I just want to help, damn it!" Her eyes glistened, and she bit her lower lip, but she would not cry. She was tough.

"Don't worry about it. I'm okay." I knew I was lying to myself.

She was silent for a moment. "Who was on the phone?" she asked quietly.

"Georgia Grant called. Morgan is missing. And Brandt called to tell me a friend of mine is in the hospital." My voice was sullen.

"I'm sorry. Can I do anything to help?" She spoke softly, hesitantly. We'd never been angry with each other.

"No." I sighed. "Why don't you try to go back to sleep. There's no reason you should ruin your day. I'm going to take a shower and call Georgia back in a little while."

"Okay." She gave me a long look before turning and disappearing down the hall.

I sat back for a minute, listening to the soft tread of her footsteps up the stairs, then pushed myself out of the chair and headed up to the bathroom. The shower helped, rinsing away some of the staleness that hung on me, and easing the tension in my shoulders. The third phone call came just as I was stepping out of the shower. I cursed and grabbed a towel, then ran to catch it before it rang again. I picked up the receiver in mid-ring and said hello.

"Emerson Ward?"

"Yes, this is he." I didn't recognize the voice.

"Remember this number," the strange voice said, and rattled off a seven-digit number. "Have you got it?"

"Yes, I have it."

"Get to a pay phone and call me in fifteen minutes."

The line went dead before I could reply. I gently cradled the receiver, and watched curiously as my hand began to shake.

It was just one of those days.

II

I WENT BACK to the bathroom to towel off and comb my hair, then found clean shorts and shirt and a pair of Topsiders to wear. It didn't take long enough to dress; my watch said I still had ten minutes. I prowled the house, stalking silently from one room to another, trying to sniff out anything amiss. There was nothing wrong in the house. I looked in on Cat. She had drifted back to sleep and I padded to the bed to bend over and kiss her head and snuff her hair. It was time to go.

The city had become a summer sauna under the hot August sun. There was a pay phone in the basement of the Ambassador East across the street. It was only half a block's walk, but my shirt stuck to me damply by the time I spun through the revolving door into the coolness of the hotel lobby. The phones were at the bottom of the stairs to the left. I lifted the receiver of one, looked at my watch, then dropped a quarter in the slot and dialed.

"Ward here," I said when the voice answered.

"Good. Here's what you do. There's a sandwich place on Wells called Nookies'. Take a taxi—an American cab so I'll know it's you—and come alone. Meet me there as soon as you can."

"Why should I?"

"Because you're Morgan's friend." Again, the line went dead.

Nookies' was a public place, and at this hour of the morning, it would be packed. I didn't think I'd be in danger. I walked across the street to the cab stand outside the Ambassador West and got lucky. There was an American cab third in line. The driver was reading a newspaper and had the engine running with the windows rolled up. I walked up to his door and rapped on the window. He lowered the paper to look at me, and motioned toward the other cabs in front of him. Ignoring him, I opened the back door and climbed in. The drivers in front of us leaned out their windows and yelled. The driver of my cab looked at them, shook his head, and just shrugged his shoulders.

"This better be good." He put the paper on the seat beside him.

"I want to go to 1746 North Wells."

"Shit. That's as far as you're going?" He yanked the gearshift into drive, savagely twisted the wheel, and pulled away from the curb, tires squealing.

The cabbie made the trip in less than five minutes. He dropped me across the street from the restaurant, and brightened only marginally when I handed him a five and told him to keep it. I waited for some cars to pass, then walked across the street, scanning the entrance and front window of the restaurant. I'd been right; the place was jammed, with five or six people squeezed in the tiny foyer waiting for tables. Set in the middle of the city, it was a little greasy spoon with classic truck-stop food. Spiro, the owner, had been so successful dishing out omelets, pancakes, and patty melts, that he had two other restaurants up on Halsted, both clones of the original in the food department, but with a little nicer decor.

I pushed past the people in the front entrance, thinking that perhaps I had beaten the caller to the meet. A short bald man waved from the back of the room. I started to make my way back when someone jostled my elbow, and a tall blonde with short spiked hair and too much makeup squeezed past me. I watched as she waved back at the bald man and made her way through the tables with a smile of greeting on her face. I was surprised when the man who had taken her place at my elbow leaned into me and tapped my shoulder.

"Ward?" he asked in a low tone.

I turned to face him. He was a head shorter than me, with neat, light-brown, blow-dried hair and a bushy mustache, probably in his mid-thirties. He wore baggy, gray cotton pants and a gray satin windbreaker over a white sports shirt. It was too hot for the jacket, but he didn't seem to notice.

"Yeah, that's me."

"I've got a table right here." He motioned behind him. He'd picked a deuce set back a little from the front windows, but with a good view of the street. He turned and stood behind the chair facing the window, waiting until I sat in the opposite chair. When he sat, he played nervously with his water glass, turning it around and around. He would not meet my gaze, and he was silent while the waitress came over and asked me if I wanted anything. I ordered coffee and a bagel with cream cheese. The waitress poured coffee in my cup and left.

"Not eating?" I stirred cream and sugar into my coffee.

"I already had something," he said, finally glancing up at me. "Look, what I'm about to tell you is just for your information. You don't know me, and you didn't get this from me, okay?"

"All right." I paused. "You're a friend of Morgan's?"

He nodded and swallowed. "Morgan asked me to do him a favor. I owed him." He leaned across the table and spoke in a low voice. "He asked me to tell you if your phone was ever tapped. It is."

I sat in stunned silence for a moment. "How do you know?"

"I work for the phone company. I've been checking your line every couple of days or so."

"For how long?"

"About two weeks." He paused. "Look, I don't know what's going on, and I don't want to know. I'm just doing what Morgan asked me to."

"Because he's a friend." I watched him nod, and thought for a moment. "His wife says he's disappeared."

"Shit," he whispered.

"Why would he disappear?"

"I told you, I don't know anything. I haven't talked to Morgan since he asked me to do this favor. If he's in trouble, he's on his own, and so are you. I've done my thing, man. Okay?"

"Sure. I appreciate it."

"Well, okay then." He pushed himself away from the table. "I'll be seeing you around. Or better yet, I won't."

"I'll get the check."

He walked away without a word, then turned and paused, looking me up and down. He came back to the table and sat down, fidgeting for a moment.

"Look, Morgan got me out of a jam in 'Nam way back when," he said slowly, staring down into his lap. "I owe him a lot more than this favor, and I like him a lot. He wouldn't have asked me to tell you about the tap unless he trusted you, so I hope you're not into whatever it is that's got him scared. Maybe then you could help him. Because when I talked to him, he was about out of his mind with paranoia. He was real scared of something. Well, so am I. I've had enough of bad guys for one lifetime. So, if you're Morgan's friend, I hope you can help him."

"I'll try." His little speech sent my mind reeling.

"Look, I've got to go," he said. "Good luck, man."

"Yeah, thanks." I watched him leave, then turned and stared into my cup of coffee.

The waitress brought my bagel, and I asked her for the check. The bagel tasted gluey and bland, like damp cardboard. My stomach roiled from drinking Scotch on an empty stomach and from the uneasiness that washed over me. After two bites, I pushed the plate away, drained the coffee, and got up to pay the check. Morgan had been watching out for me. Why? What had I been doing that warranted a tap on my phone? What had he been doing that he might think it would be connected to me? And who the hell had a tap on my phone?

There was a pay phone on the wall in the restaurant's little entryway. I dialed the Grants' number and impatiently waited for it to ring.

"Georgia, this is Emerson," I said when she answered. "Stay put for awhile. I'll be up there as soon as I can. We've got to talk."

"What is it? Something about Morgan? Do you know where he is?"

"No, no," I interrupted hastily. "I don't know where he is, but don't worry. I just need to ask you some things. I'll see you soon." I hung up before she could ask me anything else. Then I sat on the little bench next to the phone and thought for a moment, oblivious to the people coming in and out of the restaurant. The entryway was like an air lock, only half as hot as it was outside. There was a hum in my ears. My palms were sweaty, and my shirt was damp.

I got up and stepped back outside, looking both right and left, then briskly started walking south. When I reached North Avenue, I hailed a taxi and directed the driver down Wells, and told him to make a right on Schiller. A white BMW turned the corner behind us. I told the cabbie to take a right into an alley and wait for a minute.

"You feel okay, fella?" he asked, peering into the rearview mirror.

"Sure," I mumbled, looking out the back window. The white car drove past. "Just thought I forgot something. Take me to State and Goethe, okay?"

"Whatever you say, mister." He shrugged, and backed the cab out of the alley.

Everything in the house was as I'd left it. I moved quietly from room to room, double checking. Cat was still sleeping, her long hair splayed across the sheets. I went back into the living room and began cleaning up the clothes strewn all over the floor. Like other bad habits I'd picked up, sloppiness was part of life as a drunk, I'd discovered.

Cat was awake when I went upstairs to stuff dirty clothes into a hamper. I heard the shower running. I waited until she was out, then told her I was going up to Georgia's house.

"Will I see you later?"

"I don't know. I've got to open the store in twenty

minutes, and I don't know when I'll be through this evening." She put on her makeup in front of the bathroom mirror as she talked. Then she paused and looked at me. "Will you be all right?"

"Fine, I think." I hesitated, then decided to tell her. "I just found out somebody's put a tap on the phone. I don't know why, so it's probably better not to use it for awhile."

"Good God, what have you gotten into now?"

"I don't know. But it's enough to sober me up."

"Good." She walked over to where I stood in the doorway and kissed me lightly on the lips. "I worry about you."

"As long as you're going to be tied up at the store, I think I'll go visit Tom Blanchard after I talk to Georgia."

"Maybe I'll see you later tonight, then."

I went back to the garage, opened the door, and started up the squat, red, snub-nosed Alfa Romeo coupe that sat parked next to the motor home. The day was too hot to even think about turning on the air conditioning. In city traffic, it would have overheated the engine, so I just rolled down the windows and headed toward Lake Shore Drive to get some lake breeze. It was not yet eleven in the morning, and the beaches were already jammed. The traffic was terrible, and it got worse when I turned off on Fullerton and headed up to Diversey through the park.

The Grants had a new, brick townhouse off of Diversey a block or so west of Halsted. I found a place to park on the street out front, but made my way through the courtyard around to the back. George met me at the door when I rang the bell. She let me in, and we settled in the kitchen. I accepted her offer of coffee, but declined anything to eat.

"I'm so glad you could come over," she said as she brought coffee to the table. She was a striking woman, tall and sinuous, with sharply chiseled features. Shoulder-length hair the color of burnished teak framed a long, oval face. She wore baggy, gray sweat pants and an oversized, short-sleeved, pink Lacoste chemise that accentuated her pale, lightly freckled skin. Her feet were bare, her toenails stylishly painted with a coral polish.

"Thanks," I said as she handed me a cup of coffee. "George, I think we've got a problem. Are you sure Morgan is gone?"

"He left a note. Here." She handed me a piece of note paper.

"You don't know anything," it read. "You don't know where I am. I'm leaving. It will take the heat off both of us, I hope. If anyone bothers you, call Michael."

"Michael Lansing?" I asked. She nodded. Lansing was a mutual friend, a lawyer who had done favors for all of us on occasion. "What else have you done since you discovered he was gone?"

"Just called friends to see if anyone had seen him." She reeled off the list of names she had called.

"And nobody knew anything about where he might be, right?"

"No, nobody."

"I don't think anyone would tell you, even if they knew."

"Why? Why wouldn't they tell me?"

"Look, I don't think any of the people you just named would know where he went, anyway. He didn't tell you, and he didn't tell me, either. I think he's trying to protect us from something or someone. But if someone did know where he was, they wouldn't tell you, at least not over the phone. I think it's tapped."

I told her what had happened just an hour earlier.

"A tap on the phone?" She looked incredulous. "That's spy stuff. Who would put a tap on the phone?"

"Depends on what Morgan has been up to lately. Has he been acting strangely?"

"Well, yes. He's been nervous. He hasn't been sleeping well. I just thought it was because of his job."

Morgan was a big handsome man, an inch or so taller than my six-foot four, with about fifty more pounds of meat on his big-boned frame, and had a deep, mellow bass voice. When he'd been drafted to serve in Vietnam back in the late sixties, he'd ended up based sixty miles northwest of Saigon as a meteorologist for the artillery. He'd used his Army experience and his voice when he'd come back to get a job in radio, working his way up from town to town until he'd gotten a job in Chicago working for a network affiliate radio and TV station. He'd doubled, working on both the FM station and the daytime television newscasts. The station had recently been victim of a strike by the engineers' union, and Morgan had had to put in even more time than usual. He'd sympathized with the strikers, but hadn't walked.

"What about the station?" I asked. "Have you talked with anyone there?"

"He quit. Yesterday afternoon. His contract was up for renewal, and he submitted a letter of resignation, saying the station's offer wasn't good enough." She paused. "God, Emerson, I'm so worried about him."

It seemed he'd really tied up loose ends, as though he'd been planning to leave for some time.

"Shit," I swore softly. I could think of nothing that would have made Morgan suspect a tap on my phone—except drugs. Despite being in a semi-stupor for the past few months, I knew that Morgan was probably involved in the trade somehow. But despite the fact that I'd cozied up to an odd collection of yuppie cokeheads, I'd never touched the stuff, and I wondered why Morgan would be watching my back.

"George, was Morgan into cocaine?"

"I don't think you can be in his business and not be exposed to it. Sure, I suppose he used it socially."

I knew Morgan had used cocaine. I'd seen Morgan at a few of the gatherings I'd been to. He'd even suggested someone I could talk to about scoring if I ever decided to take the plunge. "No, I mean was he dealing it?"

"I don't know. I don't think so. Why would he?"

"Money. A favor to friends in the business. Maybe somebody coerced him into it?"

"We don't need the money. We're doing all right."

Something had scared Morgan enough so that he'd planned a way to skip town without a trace. But I was implicated somehow, and as much as I hated to admit it, drugs seemed to be the only connection that made any sense.

"Okay, here's what I want you to do," I said calmly. "First, call the travel agency you usually use to book trips. See if he's made any reservations. Does he have an Avis or Hertz card?" She nodded. "Call the rental agencies. See if he took a car. Let's see. Okay, then—"

"Wait a minute," she interrupted. "Let me write this down." She got up to find a pencil and note paper.

I waited until she sat down again. "Next, find your most recent phone bill. Check the numbers you recognize, and list those you know and who they belong to. Then write down the ones you don't recognize. If you have recent credit-card bills, check them to see what he's bought in the last month. It might give us a clue. Most importantly, don't make any of the calls from here. Use a pay phone, or use the phone at work. There wouldn't be anyone in your office today, would there?"

"No. That's a good idea."

"What did he take with him?"

"I'm not sure. I hadn't thought to check."

"Who knows if it'll do any good, but it might tell us something. Okay, have you got enough to keep you busy?"

"Yes, thank God. I don't think I could have stood just sitting around here waiting for something to happen. Thank you, Emerson." She leaned over the table and kissed me on the cheek. "You're a dear friend."

Perhaps a dead friend, too, if I didn't find out what happened to Morgan. I stood up and stretched. The exhaustion I'd kept at bay was beginning to seep back into every pore.

"I've got to run up to Highland Park. I didn't want to tell you, but Tom Blanchard got mugged last night."

"Oh, no! What happened?"

"I don't know yet."

"Was he hurt?"

"Brandt says it's pretty bad."

"That's terrible. Please give him my best, and tell

him I'll try to get up to see him, maybe tomorrow. He's in Highland Park Hospital?"

I nodded. "He'll appreciate that. I'll check in with you later and see what you found out." I smiled. "Don't worry. Morgan's a big boy. He can take care of himself."

"I know," she sighed. "I'm just so damn mad he didn't tell me. I'm his wife!"

"Whatever the reason," I said quietly, "Morgan thought it was serious enough to want you out of it. I want you to be very careful."

"I will be."

It wasn't evident how much of Morgan's concern had been real and how much had been imagined. There was no way of telling what he was running from. But Georgia could take care of herself. She was strong-willed and smart, and no one could have persuaded her not to look for Morgan. But I trusted her to be cautious.

I took Lake Shore Drive, then Sheridan Road up to Highland Park. It was longer than taking the expressway, but I needed the start and stop of traffic and the twists and turns of the route to keep me awake. It took more than an hour to make my way through the northern suburbs. I thought about Tom Blanchard, wondering why bad things happened to good people.

I'd known Tom since college. We'd been buddies, though I'm not sure why, since he was a few years older. He'd always been quiet and reserved, and though I'd been more outgoing, I'd been enough of a loner to attract his curiosity. I'd run into him again when I'd moved back to Chicago years later. He'd started his own business on the near north side, a small florist's shop that did a good side business in contracts with downtown businesses. He was a smart businessman, with a flair for arranging, and competed head to head with the big chains. We'd picked up our friendship where it had left off. I'd referred a lot of my acquaintances to him, and he'd become a fixture in my small circle of friends. He had no family, and had never married.

It had taken me a while to figure out that he was gay. It was Brandt who'd made reference to his sexual leanings one night when he and I had been having drinks on my patio. I supposed I'd known all along, but Tom had always been discreet, and had never made a big deal of it. He'd never given me reason to feel uncomfortable around him, so I'd never treated him as anything but a good friend. Eventually, he'd bought another shop in the suburbs, and had moved to Glencoe, preferring the quiet, slower-paced life there. He'd worked his ass off, had made a decent living, and deserved to take it easy, but we didn't see much of him anymore.

I wheeled into the hospital parking lot and found a slot that was less than a mile away, locked up, and headed for the admitting entrance. The asphalt was hot under the soles of my shoes, and the heat and humidity made me feel even more logy. Inside, the air conditioning revived me, evaporating sweat that ran down the sides of my face. I stopped at the desk and got a pass, then found my way up to Tom's room.

It was dim and quiet in the ward. The smell of antiseptic hung heavily in the damp air despite the air conditioning, and the white walls took on a greenish pallor under the fluorescent lighting. An old man shambled aimlessly down the corridor, pulling an IV tree behind him, his spindly, hairless legs sticking out from the bottom of a hospital robe. A nurse's crepe-soled shoes squeaked softly on the linoleum floor as she wheeled a patient past.

Room 247 was private. The shades were pulled to help keep it cool. Tom lay in the bed with his eyes closed. What little of him was visible looked like shit. Most of him was covered with bandages. His right arm was in a cast. His face was a massive bruise, all swollen and purple. Both eyes were black, and his nose was taped. The bandages on his head almost looked like a full turban covering the shiny balding head. The sheet covering him only came up just past his navel. A wide swath of gauze was wound around his ribs.

A nurse had stepped into the room, and spoke in hushed tones. "Don't stay too long, okay? He needs lots of rest."

I nodded and turned back to look at Tom. The beating had been vicious, sadistic. I hesitated, then looked around the room for a chair and pulled it over close to his bed. He seemed to be asleep, but when I sat down, his eyes fluttered open. His face grimaced with pain, but when he saw me, he tried to smile.

"Emerson. Good to see you," he mumbled through puffy, cracked lips.

"Hello, Tom," I said softly. "You look like hell. Hurt bad?"

"More than that fucking kidney stone I had a few years back." His smile was wan.

"What happened?"

"Got the little faggot shit beat out of me." His tone was mocking, self-derisive. "Couldn't even defend myself."

He probably wouldn't have even if he could. He was

one of the gentlest men I knew. "Who was it?"

"Don't know. Came up from behind. First thought it was that little houseboy I threw out last week." He spoke haltingly, in half sentences, as though saving his strength. "Thought if he sucked my cock he wouldn't have to work. But the guy who did this was bigger, much bigger. Maybe one of the little shit's friends." He lapsed into silence, and his eyes closed. It was a long minute before he opened them again and looked at me wearily.

"Wanted to talk to you about something else. Can't remember." His eyebrows knit in concentration. "Thought of it just before I got clobbered." He was silent again for a minute. "Oh. Yes. Something about the farm. God, my head hurts." He stared at the ceiling.

"What about the farm, Tom?" I prodded gently. He'd bought a big piece of property up north, near the state line about twelve miles from Lake Geneva, Wisconsin. When he'd moved to Glencoe, he hadn't spent as much time up there, so he leased it out.

He turned his head slowly and looked at me. "Something's not right there. Something about the tenants." He paused, and I thought I saw fear on his face. "I need a favor, old friend. Find out what's going on up there?"

"Are they paying the rent?"

"Yes, yes," he said impatiently. "That's not the point. Need your jaundiced eye, lad. Check it out. Things are not what they seem."

"Why are you telling me this?"

"Because you're good at fixing things. And because you never know what might happen to me. I'm not in very good shape, they tell me."

"I don't want to hear you talk that way. You'll be

fine." He *was* scared, holding something back, but I didn't think I'd get much more out of him. The drugs were making it difficult for him to track. "I'll drive up one of these days and look the place over. Okay?"

"Thank you. Knew I could count on you." There was relief in his voice. He yawned, and his eyelids drooped. He started, and opened them one last time. "Sorry I'm so tired. Come back later and visit?"

"Sure, Tom." His head rolled laxly in sleep before I got to the door.

I stopped by the nurses' station on my way out to find out how he was really doing. They ran down the list of injuries for me—broken arm, three broken ribs, broken nose, multiple bruises and lacerations, lacerated kidney, and so forth. It made me wince. But what they were most concerned about, they said, was the concussion, and the fractured skull. They were afraid of bleeding—subdural hematoma I think they call it. The rest would heal; bleeding in the brain case could kill him.

"What time did they bring him in?"

The nurse checked her chart. "About ten last night."

"Does it give the name of the reporting officer?"

"Yes, Officer Robert Webster, Glencoe police."

"Thanks. Take good care of him."

Was it just me, or was this paranoia spreading? I did not want to do another favor. I had no desire to drive up to the country and talk to strange people on the basis of a vague uneasiness. I sighed. I would do it for Tom, but not today, and maybe not this week. I had my own problems. I didn't want to talk to the police either, particularly in my current state of exhaustion and nervousness, but something told me to follow through. Maybe it was instinct, or past experience, or just plain curiosity.

My watch said it was about two-thirty. If I hurried, I could probably catch Webster just before his shift started. Pushing aside the exhaustion, I walked a little faster.

I took Sheridan Road back down to Glencoe and found the police station. I'd been right; the shift was just changing, and when I asked for Officer Webster, the desk sergeant said to sit and wait and he'd point him out to me. It wasn't long before he yelled to a young officer who was heading out the front door, and the sergeant motioned me over at the same time. Webster stepped back to the desk, and then turned and looked in my direction as I ambled over. I stuck out my hand.

"I'm Emerson Ward. You took a friend of mine to the hospital and wrote up the report. Tom Blanchard?"

"Oh, sure," he said, recognition sparking in his eyes. "He even asked for you. What can I do for you?"

"I wondered if you could tell me what happened. I just came from the hospital, and he was pretty groggy."

"Sure, come on back, and I'll get the report." He told his partner to wait a minute, and escorted me back into the heart of the station. I waited while he pulled a copy of the report, opened it, and scanned it while walking back to where I stood.

"Not much here, really. He managed to give us a general description of the guy, but not really enough to go on. Said he had just gotten out of his car after putting it in the garage. He closed the door, and somebody jumped him from behind."

"He had no idea of who it might have been?"

"No. He told us he thought it could have been someone his former houseboy hired. Some bad blood there, I guess. We're looking for the kid now. Whoever it was took his wallet, but the house hadn't been broken into. Could be he surprised a burglar, or it was just a simple mugging. Who knows?"

"Would you call me if you find out anything?" I pulled a card out of my wallet.

"Be happy to." He took it from me and put it in his shirt pocket.

"Thanks. Sorry to have bothered you." I left feeling better and worse at the same time. I was sorry that it had happened. It was senseless, and had put a good friend in the hospital in serious condition. But I felt relieved that it seemed to be just a coincidence it had happened on the same day that everything else had gone wrong in the world. Maybe it was something in the water, or a full moon.

I pulled into a gas station on the way home, and stopped in front of the full-serve pumps. While the attendant was filling up the tank I found a phone and called George to see if she'd found out anything. There was no answer. I plodded across the hot pavement to the car. The young attendant, dressed in cutoffs, T-shirt, and loosely tied high-tops with no socks leaned across the hood, cleaning the windshield.

"Christ, it's hot," he muttered. The humid air was close, stifling. "It ain't supposed to let up for days." Sweat plastered curly tendrils of dark hair to his forehead and the back of his neck. A bead rolled down his nose and dripped on the hood of the car. He hunched up his shoulders and rubbed his eyes on the grimy T-shirt sleeves, leaving streaks of dirt on his face.

I handed him a credit card, and climbed back into

the Alfa. The steering wheel was hot to the touch, and I stuck to the leather seats as soon as I sat down. After signing the chit, I wheeled the car out into Saturday traffic. I took Willow Road out to the Edens, and as the little car accelerated, I caught a glimpse of a white BMW merging into traffic behind me. Black, metallic gray, and gun-metal blue are the BMW colors of choice in Chicago. A white one is rare. I tried to keep it in sight in the mirror. It stayed with me down the Kennedy, but I lost it in the traffic on North Avenue. Coincidence, maybe, but I didn't like it.

The house felt big and empty. It was full of furniture, and memories that I would not acknowledge—not now—but it was empty of life. The living room still smelled of the stale cigarette smoke that had clung to my sports coat and slacks, a memento from the casino.

The den smelled musty from disuse, and the keyboard and screen of the word processor were coated with a thin film of dust. I found a dust rag and spray polish under the sink and cleaned off the desk, rubbing it to a sheen.

The kitchen smelled of overheated, ripening garbage. I tied up the bag of trash and took it out through the back gate to the alley, then sprayed the garbage can with a deodorizer and put in a fresh bag.

The bedroom and master bath smelled of Catherine, her powder and perfume, her essence. But almost overpowering that was the smell of me, sweaty and slightly sour, like spoiled milk. I took another shower to rinse away the sweat and grime, then air-dried in the dim coolness of the living room. I dropped a tape in the stereo and put on the headphones, turning the volume up to drive the thoughts out of my head. The music reverberated through me, pulsing and pounding my tired body, hypnotizing me. Before the tape was over, I had fallen asleep in the chair.

The ringing phone startled me awake, sounding distant and muffled through the headphones still clamped over my ears. It hadn't been restful sleep. Above all, I was cranky and irritable—I was sober. It was Georgia on the phone. I said I was right in the middle of something, and asked if I could call her back. She told me she was still in the office. I looked at my watch as I hung up. It was after six. I put on my shoes, locked up the house, and walked across the street to the hotel.

"What's up?" I asked when George answered her phone.

"I wanted to tell you what I've found out so far. He rented a car out at O'Hare. I checked the charge card bill we got recently, too. There was a charge from Eddie Bauer, so I called the store to ask if the bill was right. He bought camping gear —a sleeping bag, ground cloth, knapsack, that sort of stuff. What is he doing?"

"I don't know." I thought a moment. "Listen, do me a favor. Don't file a missing person report with the police."

"I hadn't planned on it. I thought we should give him some time first."

"Good." She was thinking the same way I was. Better to see if we could find out what was going on before we brought in the police. "Is the car rental agency going to call you back to let you know when the car is dropped off?"

"Yes. I've been going through phone bills for the last couple months."

"That's fine. I think that's about all you can do for the time being."

"How's Tom?"

"Not good. He was pretty well banged up."

"Can he have visitors?"

"Yes, but not for long. You might want to wait until he's a little stronger before you visit."

"Thanks, I guess I will. I'll call you tomorrow?"

"Sure. Better yet, I'll come up, say around noon."

"Fine. Tomorrow, then."

I hung up and decided to walk down to Yvette's for a beer. Hungry, finally, I ordered an appetizer at the bar. When I'd had my fill of the carpaccio and a decent buzz on from a few beers, I paid the bill and walked slowly home, hoping I'd be able to sleep. I puttered around the empty house, not quite ready to turn in, wanting the exhaustion to completely overtake me so I would be oblivious to the dreams I knew would haunt my sleep. Shortly after nine, I heard the sound of a key in the lock.

Cat let herself in with the key I'd given her. I was sitting in the living room, reading a magazine, and looked up to say hi. She walked past without a word, heading upstairs for the bedroom. I sat puzzled for a moment, then got up to follow her. I found her in the bathroom, packing makeup in a small toiletry bag. I stood in the door frame and watched her.

"I just came by to pick up a few things," she said, refusing to look at me. Her mouth was drawn tight at the corners, jaw set firm.

"Staying at home tonight?"

"I have to pack for L.A. Or had you forgotten I have to fly out there tomorrow?" There was anger in her voice.

"I'm sorry. Yes, I'd forgotten." I paused. "What's wrong?"

She turned to face me. Her green eyes flashed. "Us. We're wrong. And we can't go on like this."

"What do you mean?"

"You lied to me, didn't you?"

I reddened, feeling like a kid caught with his hand in the cookie jar. "What? I had a beer down at Yvette's with some dinner."

"See? I knew it. I don't know what your problem is, Emerson, but it's not me. I love you, the real you. I fell in love with the man you are, somewhere in there. But the drinking has turned you into someone else. I can't go on living with the little lies, the excuses. You don't need that crap. All you need is me, and you won't let me be there for you."

Her eyes brimmed with wetness, and a single tear rolled down the side of her nose. She swiped at it with the back of her hand. I felt a rush of guilt flow through me.

"You're right. It's not you. I don't know what it is."

"Damn it! I know you were in love with someone else once. Were you hurt that badly that you can't let me into your life?" I was squirming so much with my own embarrassment that I could give her no answers. "Look, I don't want to leave. I have to." Her voice was pleading. She stared at me for a long minute, then turned away.

"Call me if you ever find yourself," she said, pushing past me.

I stood numbly in the doorway, hearing the sound of the front door closing and latching tightly. The anguish welled up in my throat, choking me. I'd let her walk. And what hurt the most was that she was right.

III

I SLEPT FITFULLY, soaking the sheets with sweat in the sticky atmosphere. The air conditioner hummed from the depths of the house, trying to keep up with the warm air assailing the walls. The mercury had refused to dip below eighty-two degrees during the night. The cool air spewing out of the vents just made my skin feel clammy, and I climbed toward consciousness every half-hour or so. Visions of a lady I'd once known drifted in and out of my dreams. She seemed to be saying it was all right, that she approved of this new one called Cat. But I couldn't tell for sure. I kept reaching out to her, beseeching her to come closer so I could talk with her, just one more time. We hadn't had enough time, she and I. And even though there could never be time for us again, I felt guilty for having let Catherine love me, as if somehow I could have prevented it. I'd done almost everything possible not to live up to the image she had of me.

I started out of the surreal world between sleep and wakefulness a little before noon, feeling as though I'd slept for only a few minutes. I desperately wanted a drink but I resisted. I would show Catherine—and myself. I wanted her back. After making coffee, I cooked eggs and bacon and toast for breakfast, and ate half a cantaloupe to go with it. When I was finished, I washed the dishes and cleaned the kitchen, first wiping down all the counters and scrubbing the sink, then deciding to sweep and mop the floor.

I took a second cup of coffee with me to the den, and looked over the stacks of mail that had gone unopened for weeks. I sorted it into piles, and when that was finished, I looked at everything else that lay unattended on my desk and made a list, setting priorities. Before getting started, I realized that I had promised George I would come visit. I dialed her number.

"Hi, it's me. I'm not clear."

"Oh," she replied after a moment. "I understand."

"Anything new?"

"No, not really."

"Then I think I'll just hang around here, if you don't mind. I don't think I'd be very good company today."

"That's fine. There's probably not much we could do today, anyway. It's Sunday."

"Thanks. I'll try to call you tomorrow."

I started on the list as soon as I hung up, forcing myself to take care of each piece of mail as it was opened, either sending a reply, writing a check, or tossing it, depending on what action was called for. About halfway through, I found myself yawning and staring at the wall, procrastinating. I gave myself a break, went to the bathroom, and got a drink of juice from the kitchen. Then I stripped down to my shorts, pulled the weights out of the closet, and pushed and pulled them until I was drenched with perspiration, going through the whole routine twice—military presses, stomach pulls, neck pulls, bench presses, and curls. When my arms felt as if they were on fire, and my breath came in short pants, I quit and took a cold shower. After towelling dry, I went back to the den and finished the pile of work.

At five, I pushed in my desk chair and left the house in search of a bite to eat. It had cooled off to the high eighties, and the heat, for once, actually felt good after being in the air conditioning all day. Joints that had stiffened after lifting weights in the cool air thawed out in the sauna outdoors. I walked down to a deli on State, ordered a sandwich, and watched all the people on the street through the plate glass storefront while waiting. Clothing was at a minimum out there, and the cars that rolled slowly by in the bumper-to-bumper traffic either had tops down and windows open, or windows shut tight against the heat.

Cat had flown to Los Angeles to negotiate with the owner of an exclusive chain of boutiques on the West Coast to convince him to take on her line. I knew she was staying at the Century Plaza, probably in one of the nice, newer tower rooms, the ones with the huge double beds and oversized bathrooms with double sinks and soft terry-cloth robes hanging on hooks behind the door. I smiled at how appropriate the luxury of the hotel room would be for Catherine. I finished my sandwich and walked slowly home. It was two hours earlier in California—I would wait until six to call.

The hotel operator connected me with Cat's room. She picked up on the fourth ring, giving me a chance to hear her voice again.

"Hi. How was your flight?"

"Emerson. I'm so glad you called. I hate being angry with you. I hated leaving knowing there was something between us."

"I know. But there is something between us."

"Yes, there is." She paused.

"Look, I won't promise you anything, but I want to try to make 'us' work. I don't want you out of my life."

"That's all I wanted to hear. I just wanted to know if it was worth sticking around."

"I know I'm not what you expected—"

"You're not you," she interrupted. "You're someone else, some stranger. I'm still waiting to get to know the real Emerson."

"I'll see what I can do about that."

"That's okay. Don't push it." She paused again. "I was about to hop in the tub. I've got drinks at seven and dinner at eight. Let me call you back in fifteen minutes when I'm out of the bath."

"Sure. It's good to hear your voice."

"I'm glad you called."

I felt better. Maybe she would have the patience to stick with me until I grew up enough to figure out what was awry in my life.

She didn't call back in fifteen minutes. In twenty, I called her. Her phone was busy. I called again in thirty minutes—still busy. I paced for another ten minutes and called again. The hotel operator connected me, and all I heard was the incessant buzz-buzz of the busy signal.

She'd probably gotten hung up in a conversation with one of the people she was doing business with. I went to the kitchen and opened a beer, then tried again on the kitchen phone. Still busy. Now I was worried. She couldn't still be on the phone. I nursed the beer and waited a full half-hour before trying again. Now I needed to know that she was all right.

I called the hotel operator back, and explained the

situation. I gave her my name and told her I was a close friend of Miss McCrae's and that I had been talking with her earlier, and could she please send someone up to the room to check on her phone. I told her I would wait on the line. She sympathized and promised that she would have the bell captain send someone up right away. I told her again how urgent it was. She assured me that she would take care of it, and then she put me on hold. I waited forever. I'd never hated being put on hold so much in my life. It was a full seven minutes before the operator came back on the line. Her voice was hesitant, confused.

"Mr. Ward, I think there's been an accident. I'm not sure yet what's happened. Would you please give me your number? I'll get back to you as soon as I can, I promise." Her voice had a pleading quality to it.

I was frantic with worry. An accident. My mind reeled with the possibilities—she'd slipped in the tub, or had dropped a glass and had cut herself. There were too many of them, and they were driving me crazy. It could be something minor, or she could be badly hurt, and if so, I suddenly realized, I wanted to be there. I sat back down at the desk and called the airlines. American had a flight going out at 9:40. I booked a reservation and hoped I would hear back from the hotel in time. I hung up and paced some more. The phone still did not ring. I changed clothes, putting on slacks, starched shirt, seersucker sports jacket and tie, then packed a small overnight bag with a toilet kit and clean shirt, socks, and underwear. When the phone finally did ring, a few minutes after nine, I snatched up the receiver savagely.

"Ward here," I snarled.

"Mr. Ward, this is Benjamin Coleridge, assistant

manager of the Century Plaza. One of our operators promised you a callback."

"Yes, yes. What happened?"

"This is difficult to say." He paused. "Miss McCrae is dead."

It wasn't what I'd expected to hear. As often as I'd heard the words, they were never really expected.

"Mr. Ward? Are you there?"

"Yes," I choked, then cleared my throat. "I'm still here."

"When one of our bellboys could get no response, I went up personally and let myself in with a passkey. We tried CPR, but couldn't revive her. I'm sorry, Mr. Ward. There was no sign of anything amiss in her room, but we had to call in the police. Is there someone we should notify?"

"You just did," I said dully. "I have reservations on a flight to Los Angeles tonight. I will be there by twelve-thirty your time. I'll want to know who to talk to. I may need a car, and I suppose I'll want a room. Do you understand?"

"Yes, Mr. Ward. If you'll tell me the flight number, I'll have a car waiting for you. You can ask for me as soon as you arrive."

"Thank you." I gave him the flight information, then hung up and took a last look around the house. There was nothing I needed. I had close to two hundred dollars cash in my pocket and credit cards in my wallet. It would be enough.

I grabbed the little valise and ran out the front door, slamming it shut behind me. At the hack stand outside the hotel, I clambered into the back seat of the first cab in line.

"O'Hare," I snapped. I held up two twenties so he could see them in the rearview mirror. "They're yours if you make it by 9:30."

It was 9:32 when we pulled up with screeching tires in front of Terminal three at O'Hare. The cabbie had more than earned the tip. I ran into the terminal, didn't bother standing in line at the ticket counter and went straight to the gate. They wouldn't want to sell me a ticket there, but I had a reservation, and was paying full fare.

They gave me an aisle seat in the back. When I made my way to the back of the wide-bodied jet, I collapsed breathlessly in the seat. It just didn't seem possible. Benjamin Coleridge had made a dreadful mistake, had let himself into the wrong room. Cat couldn't be dead. Pretty women in their late twenties who are enjoying good health do not just drop dead in hotel rooms. There was some other explanation. And I was on my way to Los Angeles to find out what it was.

I tried catnapping on the plane, but could manage no more than twenty minutes of a trancelike stupor. There were too many thoughts running through my brain. I half watched the movie, but couldn't concentrate. About two hours into the flight, I dug my toilet kit out of the overnight case and found two Valiums. I washed them down with what was left of the Scotch on ice I'd gotten from the flight attendants, wondering why it was so easy to break my promise to Cat. I settled back again and closed my eyes, letting the thoughts tumble through my head, listening to the dull roaring hum of the big engines driving us through the inky night sky.

Cat had no family that I knew. Her mother had died when she was about eleven, she'd told me, and her father, an Irish immigrant, had walked out, unable to cope with raising her by himself. She'd been sent to foster homes, and no one had wanted to adopt a girl that old, so when she'd turned sixteen, she'd struck out on her own—and had been lucky. She'd stayed with some friends for awhile, sleeping on the couch and working part time at a fast-food restaurant. In her free time, she'd modeled nude for evening art classes, and one of the instructors had taken her under his wing, giving her a place to stay. His interest had been platonic, and he'd given her some financial help so she could finish high school. When she'd shown a flair for design, he'd even helped with tuition to a design school. She'd worked her way through school, and when she began to make good money by selling her clothes to offbeat boutiques, she'd paid him back. Eventually, she'd moved out, getting her own place. Now, all she had was me, and I hadn't been as good an investment so far.

Coleridge indeed had a car waiting for me. A man holding a sign with my name on it met me at the gate and escorted me down the escalator onto the people mover that led to baggage claim. Outside, he opened the rear door of a big Cadillac that was parked in the "white" zone. The trip to the hotel took only twenty-five minutes. Even at that hour, the freeways were full, but it was a straight short run up the San Diego Freeway to Santa Monica Boulevard, then the familiar turn up Avenue of the Stars past the fountain to the hotel entrance. I tipped the driver and went straight to the desk to ask for Coleridge. He came out of his office immediately.

"Mr. Ward," he said, coming around the desk with his hand outstretched, "I'm so sorry about what has happened. It was quite a shock to all of us here. I'd let you get settled, but I'm sure you'll want to find out what's going on." He took my arm and drew me a few steps out of earshot of the people at the desk. "The police have been here to conduct a preliminary investigation. They want you to identify Miss McCrae's remains, of course. A Lieutenant Ramirez will meet you downtown. A driver will take you there. In the meantime, I'll have your bag taken up to your room. You can ask for the key when you get back." He motioned to the bell captain.

He'd taken complete charge. The bell captain took the overnight bag out of my hand, and Coleridge steered me toward the door with a gentle hand on my shoulder. I walked back outside, and the same driver held open the door of the Caddy for me. The cool night air was a relief from Chicago's heat. I pushed the button on the armrest and the electric window slid down silently. I asked the driver if he minded. He shook his head and put the car in gear. He obviously knew where we were going, so I leaned back into the soft cushions and watched the lights of L.A. slide by.

After almost half an hour, we ended up outside the county morgue, the building immortalized by *Quincy* on television. The driver said he'd wait for me. Inside, I was given directions, and found my way down the sterile hallways to the right office. A medical examiner took me to one of the vaults where they keep bodies in refrigerated drawers. When we got there, we waited. I was about to ask why when the door opened. A small, handsome Hispanic man on the shy side of forty walked in. He was neatly dressed in a navy worsted suit, had short dark hair starting to gray at the temples, perfectly even white teeth, and hard black eyes that seemed to say they'd seen it all. He carried a paper bag in his left hand.

"Mr. Ward, I'm Lieutenant Ramirez, L.A.P.D." The soft baritone voice belied his size. He stuck out his hand, and his grip was firm. "Would you mind if I saw some identification?"

I pulled out my card case, and handed him my driver's license. He looked at it carefully, then nodded to the medical examiner, and handed it back. The medical examiner walked over to the bank of drawers and pulled open one down near the bottom and to the left. I took a few hesitant steps toward the shape under the sheet. He pulled it back. Her skin was so white with the long hair flowing around it. The eyes were closed.

"Damn," I heard myself swear softly. I was suddenly aware of the antiseptic smell, the cold air, the sounds of the medical examiner's nasal breathing, the heat of the flush in my face, the sting of salty wetness in my eyes, the pain and the taste of blood in my mouth as I bit my lip to fight back the emotion that welled up from deep inside. There wasn't a mark on her. She was as beautiful in death as she had been in life, and I suddenly realized how much I had loved her. Too damn late, I thought, hating myself and the self-pity I felt.

"How did she die?" I whispered.

"We're not sure, yet," the examiner said. "Looks like a heart attack. We'll have the autopsy done before morning."

"That's Catherine McCrae."

"What did you say?" Ramirez asked sharply behind me.

"It's Catherine McCrae," I repeated, turning to face him.

"What relationship were you to the deceased, Mr. Ward?"

"Good friends. We've been seeing each other for about six months."

"And how well would you say you knew her?"

"Pretty damn well. She was in love with me. She didn't hold back much. Why?"

He reached into the paper bag and pulled out a lady's handbag. "Do you recognize this?"

"It looks like one of her purses."

"Her name is Gillian McCrae, not Catherine, according to this." He pulled a driver's license out of the purse.

I stepped closer to look at it, confused. It was a California license issued to Gillian McCrae. The picture on it was that of the girl who lay dead in the drawer. She didn't give a damn what her name was anymore, but I did.

"I don't understand."

"Maybe you didn't know as much about her as you thought you did." Ramirez shrugged his shoulders. "We checked the address. It all fits. Do you know if she has any relatives?"

"No, none that I know of. No, that's not true. She said her father ran out on her when she was eleven. He might still be alive. He was from Ireland. There might be relatives there, too." Something was not right, but this wasn't the time.

"The manager at the Century Plaza said you flew in from Chicago?"

"Yes. Catherine—or Gillian—has a place there. She owns a couple of boutiques. Designs her own clothes."

"What did she tell you she was doing here in L.A.?"

"She's—she was meeting with some people to talk about representing her line."

"I guess it's not too unusual for someone who spends a lot of time in two places to have two residences, two drivers' licenses." He looked at me with a raised eyebrow for a moment. "Could be that Gillian is her middle name."

"I suppose that must be it."

"Well, I think we'll hang onto her personal possessions for a time, to see if anybody who might be a relative steps forward. Unless you have objections?"

"No, no, that's fine." I didn't like the suspicion in his voice.

"Well, I just have a few more questions, then, and you can go."

The medical examiner pulled the sheet up over her face, closed the drawer, and left the room. Ramirez asked me more questions about where I lived, and what I did for a living, writing down my answers on a note pad he'd pulled out of his coat pocket.

"Thank you, Mr. Ward," he said with a nod when he was satisfied. "There's probably nothing more you can do here. If no one comes forward within a few days, we'll probably be in touch with you."

"I want to know how she died," I said softly.

"I'll have the coroner's office give you a call when the autopsy is complete." He gave me a sad look, as if he suddenly felt sorry for me. "Why don't you go back to your hotel and get some sleep. You look bushed." He looked as if he'd wanted to say something else.

The limo driver was waiting outside right where he'd dropped me off. I climbed in the back and sat silently staring out the window for a minute. The driver didn't say anything.

"Have you got anyone else to pick up?" I asked.

He looked into the rearview mirror. "No, sir."

"Then take me to the beach. Venice, I guess. Or Malibu. Take your pick."

I wanted to see the ocean, the stars.

There was a bar in the back of the limo. I broke out a bottle of Scotch and a glass. I didn't care that there wasn't any ice or how much it would cost. I poured three fingers into the glass and sipped slowly while the big car glided through the city streets until we found a freeway entrance. My world was crashing in on me, and I had no answers, no reasons for it. Nothing that had happened in the past two days had made any sense.

The driver found a deserted strip of beach along the Pacific Coast Highway between Santa Monica and Malibu. I sat out on the sand by myself, watching the waves roll in, just able to see the white froth in the dark. The sky far behind me glowed from the lights of the city. I finished almost a third of the bottle of Scotch, welcoming the numbness, and then I walked blindly, not thinking. The glow in the sky was perceptibly brighter when I finally found the limo. I was surprised it was still there. The driver stood leaning against the front fender, smoking a cigarette. My watch said it was well after six in the morning, which meant it would be dawn soon here in Los Angeles. I wordlessly climbed into the back of the limo. The driver threw away the cigarette, got in and took me back to the hotel.

The hotel lobby was finally quiet. There were no foreign dignitaries, no celebrities, no beautiful people milling about. It was too bright after being out under the night sky. I got the room key from the desk and took the elevator up to the fifth floor. The room was not in the new tower, but it didn't make any difference. It looked out over the wide avenue. The sky was turning pink in the east. My bag was on the floor next to the desk. I picked it up, dropped it on the bed, and took my toilet kit into the bathroom. I took a long, hot shower, and then turned it icy cold for a moment to try to sober up just enough to function for a few more hours.

There was nothing more I could do. I'd identified the body. The police would figure out who it belonged to, and if they didn't, I would take care of it, and find her some peaceful place to rest. After I'd dressed in clean clothes and had shaved, I called American to see when I could get a flight out. There was one leaving a little before seven. I booked a reservation, then called room service and ordered coffee, juice, and an English muffin. My watch said it was now about seven-thirty in Chicago, so I called Brandt.

"It's me."

"You're up awfully early," he said with a yawn.

"I never went to bed last night."

"Somehow that doesn't surprise me." I heard the sarcasm in his voice.

"Where are you, anyway? You sound so far away."

"Los Angeles. Catherine's dead. She came out here on business, and just dropped dead in her hotel room. I flew out last night to identify the body." My voice sounded flat, lifeless.

There was silence on the line. "Just like that?"

"Just like that. They don't know why."

"Are you okay?"

"No. I'm half drunk, overtired, cranky, and very confused. And there's this hollowness in the pit of my stomach." I paused. "Brandt, you helped her set up the business. I assume you know some of her people—the managers, at least. Someone ought to tell them. And maybe you know something about how to handle her estate."

"I'll take care of it," he said softly. "Thank you for telling me. When are you coming home?"

"I'm getting on a plane in about an hour or so. I think it gets in sometime after noon."

"I'll come by later."

"Sure. Later, then."

Room service delivered breakfast. I paid in cash and finished it quickly. Then I went downstairs to the desk to check out. They would not let me pay for the room, or for Catherine's. It surprised me. I did not even have to pay for the limo or for the bottle of Scotch I'd dented. I told the desk clerk to express my gratitude to Benjamin Coleridge, and left one of my cards in case they needed to get in touch with me, writing a quick note of thanks on the back to Coleridge.

I slept on the flight back to Chicago. When I got home around one-thirty, I slept some more. I woke up in the early evening. The sun was still high and hot. I didn't want to be up. I felt low, hang-dog tired, and mean, and I didn't want to feel anything. I found a bottle of rum in the kitchen, then sat in a living room chair and proceeded to drink myself into oblivion.

The doorbell rang sometime around nine. I stumbled to the door and pressed my eye to the peephole. It was Brandt. I let him in, and fell back into the chair in front of the television. The house was dark except for the blue light emanating from the TV screen.

"You're in a fine state, I see." There was a note of

disgust in his voice. He turned on a light and walked over to turn off the television, forcing me to look at him. There was anger on his face.

"What difference does it make?"

"Plenty," he snapped.

"Why? I'm not hurting you, or anybody else, for that matter."

"You're a recalcitrant, stubborn fool. Yes, you are hurting me. It hurts me to think you're this stupid. I know you. I can't believe you'd do this to yourself. And you hurt Cat. She couldn't even get close to you. Lord knows, it wasn't for lack of trying."

"Catherine's dead! She doesn't give a damn what I do or don't do."

"You're an ass, Emerson." He said it with such contempt that his words slapped me across the face. Brandt had never been this angry with me. "The rationalizations, the lies, the self-righteousness are all so much easier after a half a bottle or so, aren't they?"

"What the hell do you know about it?" I demanded.

"You sit there, swimming in a sea of self-pity," he continued, ignoring me, "thinking that nothing you do touches anyone else. That everyone and everything is out to get you. It just isn't true. But I'll tell you something, as long as you keep drowning yourself in liquor, nobody much wants to have anything to do with you. I don't know why you think you have to go on these binges. You're like a child desperate for attention."

I squeezed my eyes shut against the flood running through me, mind whirling, set aflame by the giddiness of too much alcohol. It came bursting out of me in a wail of despair and water running down my cheeks. "What the fuck do you know about it?" I cried, feeling anguish and pain and loss. I rocked in the chair, feeling small and sad and alone. Brandt knelt beside me and put a big arm around my shoulders.

"I know enough," he said gently.

"Do you really? Do you know what it's like? Oh, Christ, Brandt. I measure out my life in fingers of Scotch, bags of trash, envelopes of cancelled checks, cups of laundry detergent, and ashtrays of cigarette butts." The words tumbled out of me incoherently.

"It's not you. Don't you understand? I can't tell you to stop. I won't tell you to stop. No one can, except you. But it's the drinking. It's not you. There's nothing wrong with you. Shit, you're not even a certifiable alcoholic. You just get to feeling too sorry for yourself sometimes."

"Christ, I wish I could believe that. I don't know what's real anymore. Nothing seems to work." I'd hit bottom.

"It's okay," he murmured, patting me gently on the shoulder. He held me like a small child for a long time while I rocked back and forth. Finally, I calmed down and sank back into the chair in exhaustion. After a minute, he helped me up and put me to bed.

I slept the sleep of the damned, going from one nightmare to another, haunted by faces of the dead—faces I'd known. I woke up just after dawn, and went to the kitchen to gulp down aspirin with lots of ice water. Then I put on shorts and running shoes and slipped out the front door into the calm, humid morning air and ran to pump the poison out of my system and to exorcise the demons that had haunted my sleep. I was afraid I'd pour a drink if I didn't have something to do with myself.

Moodiness is one thing, but I'd never broken down like that, not even in front of Brandt. He had made it clear that he'd had enough of my childish shit. I'd had enough, too. I'd lost Catherine, and was losing the best friend I'd ever had. I pushed myself hard, over to the lake, up the beach to Fullerton and then under Lake Shore Drive for the leg up to Diversey, and finally back down through the park. I huffed and puffed, doing a series of wind sprints on the way back, driving myself to sweat it out and make it hurt.

The sun had risen high enough to make it hot already. I slowed to a trot down Dearborn, then turned the corner on Goethe and walked toward my house with my hands on my hips, trying to catch my breath. The side streets were still quiet. I took small notice of the businessman ambling toward me until he stepped in front of me, blocking my way as I turned up the walk to my door. When I tried to sidestep, he stepped with me. Feeling a sudden presence, I whirled to see another man in a suit not more than six feet behind me, hemming me in. He'd come out of nowhere. My heart leaped in my throat, and I took a deep breath to calm myself. The man in front of me took a short step forward. His tie was loose, the top button of his shirt was undone, and his suit was rumpled.

"We'd like you to come with us, Mr. Ward," he said quietly.

I looked up and down the street. There was no one within a hundred yards in either direction. And if I made a scene, passersby would probably side with the suits before they'd side with someone in shorts and a torn T-shirt.

"What for? Who are you?"

"We need to talk."

I didn't want to talk. I was too damn paranoid. These guys didn't want directions to the Art Institute. They were both a shade over six feet, athletically built, but not chunky, with nondescript looks. There was only one choice. They'd gotten a little too close. I pivoted backward on one foot and stamped down hard with the left foot on top of the instep of the man behind me. And in almost the same motion, I swung the leg forward and up, aiming for the groin of the man in front. He'd seen it coming, and had started to move, so he only caught a glancing blow, but I bulled right through him, knocking him over as I started to run.

"Jesus Christ!" one of them swore as they scrambled after me.

I headed east and ducked around the corner at the end of the block, then right into the alley, pumping my legs as fast as they would go. But they felt heavy after the long run through the park, and I could hear footsteps close behind me. I was halfway up the alley when one of them barked out behind me.

"Hold it right there!"

The authority in the voice stopped me dead in my tracks. I turned around to see the man who'd had his foot stomped walking slowly toward me with a gun in his outstretched hand. The sight of it drained all the fight out of me. I quivered involuntarily, waiting for the muzzle flash and the sharp crack that would register just before the bullet smacked into flesh and bone, turning out all the lights, forever.

IV

"SHIT," HE SAID as he walked up to me, "you're a lot better than I thought you'd be." There was a small grin on his face.

The other one was coming up behind him with a slight limp. I'd probably bruised his thigh pretty good. "Naw, we're just not awake yet. We didn't get much sleep on the plane. He just got lucky." He grimaced, and I could hear the annoyance in his voice, embarrassed that he'd been caught off guard.

"Look," the first one said to me in a friendly voice, "we do need to talk. I'm going to put this gun away, okay?"

I nodded, and he slid it into a holster under his coat. I stayed on my guard, edgy and nervous. "What about?" I asked.

"Gillian McCrae. You wanted to know how she died." The astonishment must have shown on my face because he looked at me with a peculiar expression. "You okay?"

"Yeah, I'm fine." I shook my head, trying to clear it, feeling as if I were in a dream. A sudden hunch made me shrug my shoulders. "Okay, so let's talk."

"Some private place," the second one said. "Some place around here."

"Sure. Have you got a car?"

They nodded in unison, and we all trooped around

the corner to the car that was parked at the curb in front of a fire hydrant about fifty feet from my door. It had rental car plates on it. The one with the limp had sandy hair. He climbed in the back seat. The other one, with dark hair, slid into the driver's seat, and I got into the front seat. I directed him onto the inner drive, through the underpass to the other side of Lake Shore Drive, and into the parking lot near the North Avenue beach house. We got out and walked. I led them out onto the promontory looking south toward the top of Michigan Avenue. They sat on a bench. I sprawled on the grass in front of them, heart still pounding from the running and the adrenaline.

"Y'know, that was a dumb move back there," said the sandy-haired one when we had settled. "You could have been shot before you'd gotten ten feet." He rubbed his thigh with a rueful look.

"True," I admitted. "Look, it would help to have names."

"I'm Ed," said the dark-haired one, "and he's Steve."

"That's it? That's all I get?"

"For now. Look, we've got a lot of questions, and we don't have a lot of time. Let's start with how you happen to know Gillian McCrae."

"Her name was Catherine," I insisted. "At least that's what she called herself here. What are you guys, anyway? L.A.P.D.?" They exchanged looks. "I don't think I want to say anything until you tell me who you are, so we might as well relax and soak up the sun." I leaned back on my elbows.

"All right," Ed said slowly. "I'm DEA, and Steve is with another agency. You don't need to know which one. We're working together on something. And we need answers from you."

His words sent a chill through me, and fired up the paranoia that had been lurking in the back of my head. I took slow, deep breaths. The Drug Enforcement Agency—what on earth did they want from me? They weren't going to arrest me, that much was obvious. I slowly relaxed. "How could I help you?"

"Gillian McCrae died of a massive overdose of cocaine."

They looked at me with funny expressions when they heard the small sound, like a cat mewling, that bubbled involuntarily from somewhere inside.

"Not possible," I said when I could talk. "She would never go near the stuff. She abhorred drugs. She didn't really like people who do drugs. And stop calling her Gillian. Her name was Catherine." My Cat, who had given herself to me as totally as she had dared. And I had not been prepared to accept her, had turned her away through my neglect.

The two of them looked at me with puzzled expressions. "You'd better tell us what you know about her," Steve said quietly.

After thinking for a moment, I started with how we'd met, how Brandt had introduced us, since he'd known her fairly well. I told them about the time we'd spent together, that we'd never been apart for more than a day or so since we had first met. I explained about her business and told them I'd never seen her take drugs of any kind. Then I recalled the trip she'd taken to Los Angeles, what I knew about her purpose there, and the details of what had happened the night she'd died.

Steve had taken out a little dictation machine when

I'd started to talk, and when I'd finished, he switched it off. "Your friend Brandt—that's Brandt Williams?"

I nodded, surprised that he knew. He looked at Ed. "It could fit," he said.

Ed nodded, then turned to me. "We never said she used drugs," he said softly. "The McCrae girl was known to us as Gillian. She died because she'd swallowed balloons filled with cocaine. They burst in her stomach. When they cut her open, they found two that had holes eaten in them from the acid in her stomach. There were four others that were intact. All told, there had probably been about an ounce of dope in those balloons, and it was 88 percent pure—damn near pharmaceutical quality."

"I don't get it. Why?"

"Look, we haven't had much time on this thing. Very early yesterday morning, when L.A.P.D. found out what had killed the girl, they called me, and I verified that ID they had. They told me about you, and we started running checks. We know your mother's maiden name, where you went to school, what you do for a living, and who your friends are. We didn't find anything that made us think you were anything but clean. We did find some things that suggest you may be a little more than you pretend to be, but not enough to worry us. So we are taking a risk and talking to you because we don't have much else to go on.

"I have one problem, and Steve here has another, and we think they're related, so we've joined forces for the time being. My problem is a new source of near pharmaceutical-grade coke that's coming into the country in very large quantities. We think it's being distributed from two locations—L.A. and Chicago. We're not sure where it's coming from or how it's getting in.

"What we know about the McCrae girl is that she was a model, and that her assignments sometimes took her out of the country—to Mexico, for example. We think she was a mule in this pipeline, not for major amounts, but for samples of each batch that was being readied for sale and distribution. We were trying to get close to her because we think we could have made her turn evidence and help lead us to the source.

"One of our operatives was deep undercover in L.A. posing as a dealer. He made contact with the McCrae woman and got a sample of the coke from her. He arranged a small buy, then tried to arrange a bigger buy. He was trying to get the woman to lead him to her source. He told us she was scared, that she wanted out, and he was pretty sure we were close to moving in on the whole operation. Last week, he turned up dead, floating face down in the ocean with a bullet in his brain. And what he was onto could have helped us solve Steve's problem."

I looked at Steve. "What's your problem?"

"Mine is a little bigger than his, and probably not that relevant right now." He made it clear that he wasn't going to say more.

"If you already know so much, I don't understand what you want from me."

"Verification of what we know," Ed said. "Any information you can give us on the McCrae girl."

"I've told you what I know. And I can't believe that she was even remotely involved in cocaine smuggling."

"Believe it. We have it on good authority. We've been trying to find an inside track on this thing for months, and she was it. Now we have to come at it from another angle, and that may take a few more months."

"No, I don't buy it." I couldn't believe that I had

been so out of touch with reality that everything Cat had told me had been a fabrication.

"How well did you really know her?" Steve asked.

"Well enough," I snapped.

"She couldn't have been dicking you around?"

"Me, maybe," I admitted, "but not Brandt."

They exchanged looks again. "We'll look into it," Ed said. "I don't think we're wrong. I saw her twice on stakeout. It's hard to forget that face. And you can't deny the fact that she had an ounce of coke in her stomach."

He was right on both counts. She'd had a face that might dim in my memory, but would never be forgotten. And somehow, for some reason, she'd swallowed six balloons filled with nearly pure cocaine hydrochloride. When the balloons had broken, the white crystalline powder had dissolved, entering the bloodstream like lightning, overloading her system and bursting her heart, indirectly breaking mine.

My mind suddenly switched gears. "Someone put a tap on my phone," I said quietly, waiting for a reaction.

It was Steve who glanced at me sharply. "We know," he said after a moment. "It's not ours. We'll try to monitor it. Something might shake loose."

"I want to know what your role is in this," I said, leveling my gaze at him. "Everything you've told me is news to me, but obviously someone thinks I know more than I do. I have to watch my flanks. I need to know what to watch for."

He thought for a minute, rubbing his chin. "We live in a complex world," he began slowly. "There are too many people with too many self-interests in too small a space. And it's all beginning to bubble around the edges.

A whole lot of those people are willing to blow each other up, to get what they want, or simply to make a point. Sikhs in India stop three buses hundreds of miles apart and riddle them with machine-gun fire, killing a hundred or so, mostly women and children. IRA terrorists throw a bomb into a department store in London, and it kills whoever happens to be unlucky enough to be passing by at that moment, no matter who they are or where they're from. The PLO massacres innocents in the airport in Rome. Most of it is senseless, but it makes sense to those who are doing the violence. And half of it wouldn't be possible without still more people who make a great deal of money by selling guns and bombs and bullets. We try to control who gets the ammunition, the firepower, by at least trying to limit the underground movement of arms. We can't stop France from selling arms to whomever it wants, for example, but we can try to stop the black market sales from within our own borders. And that's a piece of what I do."

I hadn't wanted a lesson in geopolitical science. I didn't understand it, and didn't want to because it made me so angry. "What about our own 'legitimate' arms sales?" I snapped. "Some of Uncle Sam's own deals seem a little dubious."

"The world is not about to stop making guns and bombs and bullets, Ward, despite the fact the cold war is over. I try not to think of the shades of gray. Is an arms-for-hostages deal in Iran right or wrong? I don't know. But the private, under-the-table sale of *plastique* to a cell of Italian Red Brigade terrorists is a clear-cut, black-and-white issue with me."

Silence fell on us for a minute. The world seemed a strange place where a pretty girl could sit in a hotel room and vibrate from the rush of a drug before dropping stone-cold dead.

"I think we've gotten everything we can," Ed said quietly, breaking the stillness.

"How do I get in touch with you?"

Steve looked at me with a hint of amusement on his face. "Why would you want to do that?"

"Catherine died two days ago. The day before that, I found out there's a tap on my phone. You tell me that Catherine was not really Catherine at all, but a dope smuggler named Gillian. Everybody seems to know a whole lot more than I do about what's going on in the world. But somebody thinks I know something, or have been told something, and that makes me very nervous."

They both looked at me for a minute, then at each other.

"Someone could try to make contact with him," Ed said. Steve hesitated, then nodded. "Okay," Ed said, turning to me. "What you do is call the number I give you and say to whoever answers, 'I got a message that Ed wants to talk with Emerson Ward.' They'll tell you they don't know, but that they'll check. You say that if Ed wants to get in touch, he can call you at such and such a number. Use a phone where you won't be disturbed. It may take some time before someone gets back to you. Got it?" He'd scribbled a number on a piece of scratch paper and handed it to me. I took it and nodded.

"We're done here," Steve said.

"I'll walk back, thanks," I said.

They both got up from the bench and walked casually back to the lot where their car was parked, leaving me sitting on the grass, wondering how many people in the world were dying in that moment and at whose hands. The sun was too damn hot. I got up and walked slowly home, trying to stay in the shade. In the coolness of my own living room, I walked to the bar and stared down at the rows of bottles. I picked up an armful, took them to the kitchen and tipped them over the sink so that the clear and amber liquids ran down the drain.

It was not the hardest thing I'd ever done. I thought it was tough to look at a blank sheet of paper every time I sat down to write, struggling for the moments when the words would come out the way I wanted them to, in the right cadence and sequence, with the right melody, and most importantly, mood. But I realized that probably the most difficult thing I'd ever done had been to let go, to say goodbye to a girl I'd loved, a girl who'd died. And now I had to say goodbye to another one. It made me wonder why I hadn't stopped pickling myself a long time before.

I showered and shaved, then dressed for the day in baggy cotton slacks, oversized short-sleeved cotton shirt, and deck shoes with no socks. I walked down to the corner to get a paper, then came back, made coffee, and sat at the kitchen table to read and catch up on what had been happening in the city, in the world. All had gone on without me. The world had not missed my presence while I'd exiled myself. It had not missed me, nor would it miss those I'd lost. But I mourned, sitting there at my kitchen table. I missed them all—Jessica, and Cat, along with the others—and I began to feel a little indignant that they had all been taken away. The dead could not be brought back, but I could at least look for the living.

I walked down to the hotel to use the pay phone to call George. I caught her just as she was leaving for work. We made a date to get together at her house after she got home. Then I spent the rest of the day puttering, moving from one little task to another to stay busy, to keep my mind off Catherine. I cleaned up the yard, moving slowly in the day's heat, sweeping the brick patio, then hosing it down, and spraying off the lawn furniture. Then I watered and weeded the little garden along one wall, marveling at what had remained alive despite my neglect.

I made myself lunch, and while I was still in the kitchen, I opened and closed cupboards and made a grocery list. After cleaning up, I busied myself in the den for a while, doing some reading and sorting files I'd left unfinished a few days before. About three-thirty, I fixed a tall iced tea and went out onto the patio to bake in the sun and sweat out the remains of the hangover that still nagged me. It wasn't long before I heard the tinkle of the bell at the back gate. I got up to answer it —it was Brandt.

"No one answered the front door. I thought you might be back here." He stood outside the gate in the alley.

"Well, come on in." He hesitated a moment, then walked past me onto the patio. "Refreshments?"

He looked at the iced tea on the patio table and nodded. I went into the kitchen and quickly fixed him a glass, then joined him back on the patio.

"How do you feel?" he asked when I was settled.

"Better than I probably have a right to."

There was a pause. "Someone has been making discreet inquiries into my background."

I looked at him, startled, then wondered why I was surprised. "How do you know?"

"My friends downtown are very loyal." He paused.

"That's not all. Michael Lansing tells me he's received an official request to audit the books of Catherine's business."

This time, I was even more surprised. "Why?"

"I don't know. Michael's listed as legal counsel on the corporate books, so they served the papers on him. He told me because I'm the executor of Cat's will." He saw my look of bewilderment. "I know. I didn't find out until just now. I did her a favor when she first got started—introduced her to a few people who could help her, reviewed her business plan. I never expected that she would want me to handle her affairs. And the problem is, according to Michael, that the will is nowhere to be found."

"That is peculiar. Why not just have Michael handle it?"

"As executor, even without a will, I'm obliged to get involved. I probably would have anyway—for Cat." He paused. "Emerson, what's going on?"

"Cat died of a cocaine overdose," I said bluntly.

He harumphed. "She couldn't have."

"She did."

"I don't believe it. She didn't get it from you, did she?"

I held up my hand, shaking my head. "No, I'm not that deranged. I've been sauced for the better part of the last two months, but I never did drugs. Let me finish. Two men confronted me this morning. One was with the Drug Enforcement Agency. The other was with a government agency that he refused to identify. They told me that Cat had an ounce of cocaine in her stomach in balloons. Two of them had burst. They identified her as *Gillian* McCrae, and said that she was smuggling a sample batch into the country to deliver to potential buyers." I told him the rest of the story. When I finished, he had a somber look on his face.

"They were looking for verification, you said?" I nodded. "Then that's why the background check on me. And the audit of the books is to see if she's been laundering any cash through the business. I find all of this a little implausible."

"Yet it's happening, Brandt. And they've moved very quickly. I only talked to them this morning, and already they've got the papers to look at Cat's books."

"But I know Catherine. She's incapable of anything like this."

"I thought I knew her, too," I said softly.

"What have you gotten us into?"

"Us?" I looked at him sharply. "I got myself—*me*—into something. I'm not sure how, but I'll get myself out of it, thank you, whatever it is."

"I'm involved. I don't like the thought of government agencies snooping into my background."

"Why? You've been there before, haven't you?"

"That's the point. I know how the system works, and I don't trust it."

I thought for a moment. "No, I don't think so. Right now, you're nothing more than a name on a piece of paper in a lawyer's office. I've had enough trouble lately taking care of myself. I won't take the responsibility for you, too. I don't want you any more involved than you are. I have to live with myself, and with the guilt I feel."

"Fine." He set down his drink and got up to leave.

"Look, I haven't liked myself much for the past few months. And that hasn't made me very good company. I may never find out why Cat died. Or I may get sucked up into whatever it was she was involved with. In any case, I need to look for answers on my own. You can't do this one for me, Brandt. You said so yourself."

"So be it. You're on your own."

He let himself out the back gate, and I sadly watched him go. He'd taken a certain delight over the years in being a part of the world I inhabited. He'd lived vicariously through me and had actually taken part in some of the strange situations in which I'd found myself while doing favors for friends. Now I was excluding him. For both our sakes, I hoped. The last time—the time I was trying to find out who killed Jessica Pearson—he'd gotten hurt because I didn't take enough precautions. This time I didn't have the faintest notion of why my world was crumbling in on itself.

Around six, I took the car out of the garage and drove up to George's. She was home, and had already started puttering around the kitchen, fixing a light supper of soup and salad for both of us. I hadn't expected to be fed, but I realized I was hungry, and I sat at the kitchen table while she worked, savoring the smells emanating from the pot on the stove. She served us both, then joined me at the table. She had a file folder with her.

"Morgan turned in the car at the airport yesterday," she said after she'd taken a spoonful of her soup.

"Damn. That means he could have gone anywhere."

"But it also means he's still all right."

"You're right. You might try to call your credit card companies to see if he charged a ticket somewhere. Did you find out anything else?"

"I don't know. I've been going through the phone bills to see what numbers I recognize. I know most of them, but there are a few that I don't. What should I do with them?"

"The friend at the phone company—do you know his name? You know, the one who told me my phone was tapped."

"I'm thinking. Wait, I've got it—Keith Graham."

"Call him tomorrow from the office. Tell him if he wants to help, he should find out who those numbers belong to."

"You know, it's strange he never called me. Why would Morgan expect a tap on your phone? Apparently there isn't one on ours."

"That is strange." I mused for a moment. "What else have you got?"

"When we finish dinner, I want to show you something I found."

We ate in silence, occasionally remarking on how hot it was and how things were going at George's office. When we finished eating, George cleared the dishes from the table, then led me downstairs to the basement. George turned on the lights as we came down the stairs. Most of it had been finished as a comfortable rec room. The laundry room was the only area that still had a bare cement floor and cinder-block walls. There was a big cardboard box in the middle of the floor.

"I found this stuffed in the back of the laundry room."

I squatted down beside it and started pulling out the contents piece by piece. There was a triple-beam Ohaas balance scale accurate up to small fractions of a gram, a *Merck's Reference Guide*, a copy of the *Physician's Desk Reference*, old copies of *High Times* magazine containing articles on various chemical substances, cocaine among them, a large jar of Inositol, some sort of ledger, and other assorted junk and paraphernalia.

"What is all this stuff?" George asked, kneeling on the floor next to me. She picked up the jar of Inositol.

"That," I said, pointing to the jar, "is what's commonly

known as 'cut.' It's what's used to step on cocaine."

"What do you mean?"

I couldn't believe she was that naive. I thought everyone had watched "Miami Vice" at least once. I sighed. "Major dealers bring relatively pure cocaine into the country. They sell to distributors who add something like Inositol to it—usually about 10 percent. That cuts the strength of the coke a little, but not enough to make it any less effective. And it gives them more to sell, a greater profit. They sell it to small dealers who step on it again to make an additional profit. By the time it gets to the average user in the street, the stuff is only about 40 or 50 percent cocaine, but no less dangerous."

"Does all this stuff mean what I think it means?"

"That Morgan was dealing coke? It sure looks like it. But I guess we won't know for sure until we ask him. He could have been holding this for someone."

I opened the ledger, hoping it would tell us something, but the dated entries consisted only of numbers that meant nothing to me. There were no names, no places mentioned, no record of what the transactions were for. I reached back into the box and pawed through the remaining contents, peering in to see if anything looked interesting. It seemed to be mostly junk, more drug paraphernalia—plastic freezer bags, razor blades, that sort of thing. Suddenly, I came across a set of keys, and held them up.

"Any idea what these might be for?" George shook her head. I handed them to her. "Hang onto them. Maybe we'll find out later."

I put everything back into the box, then carried it into the laundry room and put it back where George said she'd found it. Morgan had been dealing, but it was difficult to tell on what scale. Something had scared him enough to want out—the heat had been on from somewhere. But why had he been concerned about me?

"Let's go," I said, shivering. George led the way up the stairs, and I turned out the lights as I followed. "You have no idea what Morgan was up to?" I asked when we were back in the kitchen.

"None." She shook her head. "I just knew that things weren't quite normal."

"What about acquaintances from Vietnam? Has anybody made contact with Morgan recently?"

"No." She hesitated. "It's hard to tell. He hasn't been home that much. He's been keeping odd hours lately."

I switched gears. "Do you know anybody who drives a white BMW?"

"No. Why?"

"No reason." I shrugged. "Thanks for dinner. You'll let me know if anything unusual happens?"

"I'm fine, Emerson. I'll be fine." She saw my hesitation. "I'll call you if anything happens. Really."

She put a hand on my shoulder, but her touch didn't give me much reassurance.

V

THE FOLLOWING SATURDAY, a week to the day after everything had started going to hell, I got a rent past-due notice in the mail.

I'd spent most of the week in hiding, nursing the anxiety attacks that sprang without warning from the depths of my subconscious, rocking in a chair until the desperate desire for a drink passed, leaving me trembling and sweaty. The nights had been sleepless, full of tossing and turning and staring at the ceiling in the dark. But each day had been a little better than the one before. The depression could not last forever—my system was slowly ridding itself of poison.

There had been no strange phone calls, no nocturnal visitors, no letter bombs in the mail. Nothing had seemed out of the ordinary except that I was alone. I missed the lanky girl with the long wavy hair and sea-green eyes. But knowing how she'd died, shuddering and trembling horribly, had made it both easier and more painful to deal with my own withdrawal.

The letter threw me. I didn't pay rent. With the stake I'd saved from the brokerage business, I'd been lucky enough to pick up a run-down brownstone on Chicago's Gold Coast a few years before real estate prices went through the roof. The investment I'd made in refurbishing it had been well worth it, though I could now barely afford the taxes. I looked at the envelope again, thinking there must be some mistake, but it was addressed to me in care of something called Copious Productions. I frowned and read the notice. It named me, Copious Productions, and somebody named Burt Antoly as lessees of a space over on Clybourn.

It had to be a mistake. I called the realty company that managed the property and explained the problem. The woman on the other end of the phone was polite and efficient, and after putting me on hold for a moment, she came back on the line and assured me that no mistake had been made—the rent was, indeed, past due, and the name and address on file were correct. I took down her name and asked her to pull a copy of the lease. I would be there in ten minutes, I told her.

"I'm sure we can clear this up, Mr. Ward." The woman I'd spoken to on the phone led me back to her desk. "Here's a copy of the lease you signed."

I took the document from her and looked at it. It was a standard preprinted agreement, naming Copious Productions as the lessee. I turned it over. There, at the bottom, was my name in ink. Typed neatly below it was my name and the title, "President, Copious Productions." Burt Antoly was a co-signer.

"This isn't my signature." I handed the lease back to her. "It isn't even a good forgery. Here, look." I pulled out my driver's license and a credit card and showed them to her. "This is someone's bad idea of a joke."

She compared the two signatures, then looked at me with a confused expression. "Well, you're right, but I don't quite know what to say."

"Let me see what I can find out about this. Do you have an address for this Burt Antoly?"

"Yes, I'm sure we do. We would have sent him a notice, too."

"Would you get it for me, please, and make me a copy of this lease?"

"Of course." She was back in a moment with the copies. "I really don't know how this could have happened." She looked apologetic.

"That's all right. I'll get it straightened out, and I'll call you Monday. You have my address and phone if you need to reach me."

"Thank you, Mr. Ward. I'll wait to hear from you."

The address she'd given me for Antoly was up on Broadway. It took me less than ten minutes to find it. I found an illegal spot at the curb and parked. The building didn't look promising. A sign out front proclaimed it a transient hotel. I pushed through the glass doors into the lobby. An old man in a checked shirt and dirty blue cardigan sat watching television behind the registration desk.

"Can I help you?" He looked up when I stopped at the desk.

"Does a Burt Antoly live here?"

"He did."

"You mean he moved?"

"Don't know. Haven't seen him in a week."

"Then he could be back?"

"Checked his room. His stuff's all gone. He's paid up through the week, but if I don't see him tomorrow, I'm renting his room."

"Thanks." The little bit of information I'd gleaned only added to my list of worries. I was suddenly leaseholder of a property I knew nothing about, and president of a company I never knew existed.

I got a call from the hospital on Sunday morning.

Tom Blanchard had slipped quietly into a coma. The two times I'd driven up to see him, he'd looked pale and fragile, shrinking under the swath of bandages that covered him. Both times, he'd been reserved and quiet, as if saving his strength because the effort of talking was too much for him. During my visits, he'd put on a brave smile and a fixed look. I bantered inanely about the weather, which refused to cool down except during the occasional violent afternoon thunderstorm that just made everything more steamy when the sun came out again. I talked about the general craziness of summer in the city, the parking problems, the bare-skinned natives driven to plain rudeness by the heat. Both times I'd assured him that I would get out to the farm as soon as I could, but that I'd been awfully busy working on a couple of articles—a small white lie to assuage my guilt. He'd seemed unconcerned, murmuring his thanks, saying he knew he could count on me, that there was no hurry.

I'd told the duty nurse to call only if his condition changed. It had, and now there was nothing they could do but stick tubes in him and keep him alive until he found the strength to come out of the coma.

The weather had cooled to the low eighties, and a high pressure system had pushed in some drier air from Canada, making it feel much more pleasant outside than it had for weeks. It probably wouldn't last long. I used it as an excuse to get out of the house. Armed with a book and a blanket, I spent the rest of the day on Oak Street Beach, determined to put reality on hold for a few hours.

When the sky out over the lake turned deep purple and the streetlights on Lake Shore Drive flickered on, I looked up from the book. The beach bunnies and the hunks had packed it in for the day, leaving the beach empty save for joggers and bicyclers. I shook the sand out of my towel and headed for home.

Late that evening, I drove up to George's. She answered the door in a pale blue sundress and white leather sandals.

"Emerson, come in." She looked surprised to see me.

"I just wanted to check in. I hope you don't mind my dropping by this late."

"Not at all. Come in the kitchen. I've got coffee made."

She poured and served two mugs while I got settled at the small, round table, then rummaged through her handbag. "I got another phone bill in the mail." She pulled out an envelope. "There are calls charged on the credit card that were made from Indiana on Monday and Kentucky on Tuesday."

"I guess that means he didn't take a plane. He's headed south, that's for sure." I thought for a moment. "If he bought camping gear, then he's probably hitchhiking. Anything from the guy at the phone company?"

"No, I can't get ahold of him, and he won't return my calls."

"Keep trying." I paused, sipping coffee. "This probably won't make any sense, but something weird happened yesterday, and I can't help thinking it might have something to do with Morgan." I told her about the past due notice from the realtor. "Do you have any idea what Copious Productions is?"

"I'm not sure."

"How about Burt Antoly? Ever hear of him?"

"Oh, sure. Burt Antoly is someone Morgan met years ago. They were acquaintances through the business, I guess. Burt is a small-time record producer. I met him a few times and never liked him. You know the type—a small man, balding, wears gold chains around his neck and likes to keep his shirts unbuttoned almost down to his belly button. Loud and obnoxious, always bragging about who he knows. The kind who pinches cocktail waitresses in a bar as if he thinks they enjoy it. I don't think he actually knew many of the people he talked about. He always seemed to be broke—I heard him ask Morgan if he could borrow some money once." She paused.

"Copious Productions, you said? Sounds like a record label. You know Morgan thinks he has a pretty good eye for local talent. The only thing I can think of is that he and Burt got together to produce records. Maybe Burt talked him into it."

"Did Morgan have the money to set up a recording business?"

"I don't know. Not enough. In fact, I think I remember Tom Blanchard giving Morgan a loan. Maybe that's what it was for."

"Tom Blanchard? Why on earth would he loan Morgan money to start a recording business?"

"I don't know. Maybe he fancied himself a record mogul. He's always been generous to his friends."

"But this doesn't make sense." A thought suddenly dawned on me. "The keys, the ones in the box—you still have them?"

"Of course." She got up to take a key ring off a hook on the wall.

"George, you know what this means if Morgan's

running Copious Productions." She looked at me blankly. "If these keys fit that space, it means he set me up."

"Morgan wouldn't do that." She put her hand to her mouth.

"Then why is my name on the lease?"

"He wouldn't do that to you. It just isn't like him. He must have had a reason for it."

"Come on, George. Don't you think if Morgan wanted to produce records, he'd be aboveboard about it? If Antoly is as sleazy as you say, would Morgan get involved with him?"

"I don't know. I don't know what to believe anymore." For a moment, she looked ready to cry.

"I'm sorry," I said gently.

"Where is the space?" She was composed now.

"On Clybourn, somewhere between Armitage and Fullerton."

"Let me come with you. I want to see for myself what Morgan was up to."

"I don't think that's a good idea, George. Between the tap on my phone, those two jolly government fellows who visited last week, and the white BMWs I seem to see everywhere I go, I don't know what kind of trouble is following me."

"Then call me and let me know what you find. The waiting, the wondering is starting to drive me crazy." She dabbed an eye with a slender finger.

"I know," I said softly.

The Clybourn Triangle was an up and coming neighborhood. The area had been zoned for business and light manufacturing. Most of the buildings were old warehouses and small factories. As Chicago's taxes on businesses had risen, a lot of smaller manufacturers had moved out of the city, leaving them deserted and in disrepair. Smart developers, seeing the yuppie movement westward to the el tracks at Sheffield and beyond, had snapped up the abandoned buildings, rehabbed them, and were selling them as fashionable condo lofts or leasing them to chi-chi stores, both for a hefty price. Everybody had gotten into the act.

I came down Clybourn from the north, driving slowly, looking for the numbers on the buildings. The street was quiet, the buildings dark. Despite the area's yuppification, there were still factories and warehouses that had shut down for the day, and the occasional deserted, boarded-up shell waiting for someone to come up with the cash to give it a face lift. When I spotted the address, I swung the wheel and nosed the car alongside the curb.

The building was in the middle of the block, a tall three stories, with big windows of frosted glass. There was an alley to one side, and a fenced-in vacant lot on the other. It looked deserted—one that had not yet gone condo. The front door was heavily padlocked. None of the keys I had fit. I rounded the corner of the building and went down the alley. There was no streetlamp in the alley, but there was enough light from the street to let me find the side door. This time, one of the keys fit the lock. I sucked in my breath and eased through the door.

There was a steel and cement staircase on my right. I took it to the third floor, listening for sounds as I climbed silently. The stairs opened out onto a long corridor at the back of the building, running the full width. A light of some kind behind the building filtered through the frosted glass windows in the wall on the right. On my left, there were big steel fire doors that had been drilled to accommodate new lock cylinders that glinted in the half light against the dull gray of the doors.

The key fit the third door I tried, turning smoothly in the new lock. The big steel door opened with a groan. My fingers groped the wall for a switch. Bright bulbs under metal shades hanging high overhead bathed the room with light. I blinked against the glare. It was a big room, about thirty feet square, with a cement floor painted a glossy grey. The room was pretty bare, but looked as if it had been cleaned out in a hurry. On the floor, there were open cardboard boxes full of wire and audio cables. A big electronic audio mixer sat on one table. Another long, tall table was bare. There were a couple of comfortable stools scattered around. The space had never been turned into a recording studio. I could see where someone had started to put cork tiles on the wall in one corner to create some soundproofing. But the walls to separate the studio from the control booth had never been built.

I wandered around, sifting through the boxes of junk. Everything was covered with a thin layer of dust, and as I ran my fingers along the bare table, I saw traces of white powder spilled on it. I wet my finger and touched one of the spots, then put my finger to my tongue. I knew enough from hanging around those who used the drug to know that this was cocaine. Someone once may have intended to turn the loft into a studio, but its walls probably had never heard a note of music. Judging from the box of stuff George had found in her house, the loft had been used to break down, weigh, and cut quantities of coke.

There was nothing else there to explain where

Morgan might have gone. Taking a last look around, I flipped off the light and opened the door. I stood for a moment in the doorway, trying to let my eyes adjust to the sudden darkness. There was a rustle and a rush of air, and before I could move, two powerful hands grabbed my shirt and slammed me back into the door and through it. Somebody smashed a fist into the side of my face, snapping my head back and setting off fireworks in my brain. I fell backward in slow motion, feeling the floor rise up to meet me, then bounced hard, jarring every bone I had.

Hands reached down and pulled me up. I struggled to my feet, and now someone else reached around me from behind and pinned my arms in a hammerlock. Instinctively, I sucked in my breath and twisted, tensing, trying to avoid the next blow that landed squarely in my midriff, doubling me over. My head was yanked up savagely by the hair, and someone punched me twice in the face, splitting my lip, and sending the room spinning. My knees buckled, and I slid to the floor in a heap. There was a dull roar in my ears and spots in front of my eyes. A light shone in my face. I squinted against the sudden glare.

"Shit, it's not him," someone said.

"So what? He's here, isn't he?" a second one said. "Where's the money?" he demanded, prodding me in the ribs with a shoe.

"What money?" I mumbled. My lip already felt numb and puffy.

"The money, man! The money!" the first voice said.

"I was just looking for a friend."

"Look, asshole, don't give us that shit. We want the money." It was the second voice again.

"I don't know what you're talking about."

He kicked me in the ribs. I groaned and rolled into a ball, feeling the pain shoot through my brain.

"How'd you get in?"

"Door was open," I gasped.

"Bullshit!" He kicked me again, and now my side ached dully. "Roll him over," he said, putting his foot into my side and pushing. Hands grasped my shoulder and pulled me over, then one of them reached into my back pocket and pulled out my wallet. There was silence for a minute, then they grabbed my arm and rolled me onto my back. There were two shapes behind the light that shone in my eyes.

"I don't know what you're doing here," the second voice said, "but you take this message back to whoever sent you. You tell your friends that 'The Man' is not happy about being ripped off. You tell them that they should give the money back. You tell them that and be thankful we didn't kill you." He tossed the wallet at me, and they turned and left.

Their footsteps receded down the corridor. I lay unmoving on the floor in the dark for a long time after the sounds had faded. Christ, it hurt. I slowly moved everything, testing to see if it all worked, then sat up, and finally managed to get my legs under me. I put a hand on the wall to steady myself down the corridor. The stairwell was a yawning black pit. Clutching the bannister with both hands, I walked down hesitantly and cautiously opened the bottom door. No one lurked in the alley, but I hugged the wall of the building, staying in shadow. There was no one in sight on the street. My car was still at the curb, untouched. I unlocked it and slid gingerly into the driver's seat, still feeling woozy.

They hadn't said much of anything, but they'd

spoken volumes. Thoughts tumbled through my brain, and I shook my head, trying to clear it. Damn, that guy had hit me hard. Nobody had been watching me for the past week, despite the tap on my phone, but somebody had been watching the loft, waiting for its tenants to return. There'd been traces of coke in the loft, and 'The Man' had been ripped off. I couldn't believe that Morgan would be that stupid. He was in a hell of a lot of trouble, if what I'd stumbled into was any indication. And he'd managed to suck me into it without much difficulty.

I drove slowly, afraid that the car would get away from me if I let it go the speed limit. The city traffic made me nervous. Nothing like a couple of good sucker punches to make you feel vulnerable as a kitten. I wished the little Alfa were armor plated. Cabbies honked at me irritably, flashing the finger at my grandmotherly driving as they roared past. Even so, it didn't take long to get home.

The encounter at the loft had made me jumpy. Rounding the corner into the alley, the Alfa's headlights briefly illuminated movement in the shadows halfway down. Slamming on the brakes, I peered into the darkness nervously, but saw nothing. Letting the car roll slowly down the alley, I pushed the button on the garage door opener, and pulled the Alfa in next to the bus, then killed the lights and turned off the ignition. I closed the garage door and walked through the garage onto the patio. A burned out floodlight left the patio dark. Something didn't feel right.

I took four steps toward the back door, then paused, trying to identify the gnawing presence. Turning slowly, a sudden movement caught the corner of my eye. I whirled to see a dark figure bolt from the corner of the house toward the back gate.

"Hold it!" I barked, tensing, ready to fight this time.

The figure froze, then turned slowly toward me. The dim light from the alley silhouetted a tall, slender person in long pants, a trench coat, and wide-brimmed fedora pulled low so the face was entirely in shadow. It was too hot to be wearing a coat.

"Who are you?" I demanded.

"Emerson?" It was a woman's voice, spoken softly and hesitantly, and it sent a chill through me, rooting me to the spot. "Emerson?" she said again, taking a step forward and lifting her head so that the light hit her face. "I need help."

A groan bubbled up from deep inside as I watched her lips speak the words, and heard the voice that had been so familiar. A dread fell on me, turning all my muscles to jelly. I sank to my knees and groaned again.

"No," I whispered.

"I need your help, Emerson," she said again, plaintively, appealing to me. It broke my heart.

It was the ghost of my Catherine. I'd been whacked in the face too hard, and now I was seeing things. I'd pickled my brain with booze, and now I was going loony. I'd lived my life just a little too recklessly, taking a few too many chances, getting bopped on the head one too many times, and now I was going off the deep end. It was Cat. Even in the dim light, I knew it was Cat. And I knew that the girl I'd seen lying in the morgue in Los Angeles could never be a warm, feeling, living being again.

I sat on my haunches, immobile, eerily frozen by

the emotion that washed over me. She moved toward me, and I shivered involuntarily, staring at her in disbelief. She knelt on the bricks in front of me, and reached out her hand to touch my face. Her touch was real—warm and electric.

"You're hurt," she said, gently touching the bruised lip.

"Who are you?" I managed to choke out the words, enthralled by the face of the girl who'd lain pale and unmoving in a drawer of cold steel.

She looked into my eyes. Hers were sad and afraid. "I'm Gillian," she said softly. "I need your help."

"You're dead," I whispered.

"No, Catherine's dead—I'm Gillian." Her voice, too, held a note of sadness, but she spoke so matter-of-factly that it startled me.

My brain began to thaw, and the gray cells started going back to work, asking questions, yet not quite ready to accept the apparition in front of me.

"How'd you get in?"

"I climbed over the gate."

"How'd you get here?"

"I hitched. Look, could we go inside? I feel kind of nervous out here in the open. And it's been a long trip."

She got up and held out her hand. I took it, still a little dumbfounded, and let her help me up. She walked over to the corner of the patio where she'd been waiting for me, and brought back a small nylon duffel.

"Okay, now?"

"I think so." I led her into the kitchen and clicked on some lights, then turned to look at her.

Under the light, I could not believe it wasn't Catherine. She took off the hat, peeling it back off her forehead, then tossed her head, letting the long hair cascade down her back. Then she took off the coat and tossed it over a chair. I just stood and stared at her.

"Have you got a drink? A Scotch or a beer? A beer would be better, I think. I'm thirsty."

"Sure. Just a second." I got a bottle of Corona out of the refrigerator—at least I hadn't poured those down the drain—uncapped it, and handed it to her. Catherine would have asked for wine. She took a long pull on the bottle. "Twins?" I felt foolish as soon as I asked.

"No, I'm her mother," she snapped. There was an awkward silence. "I'm sorry," she said softly. "I've been through a lot."

"Why don't we go in the living room? You can tell me about it."

She turned to look at me, and I saw sudden concern in her eyes. "But your face . . ."

I touched my fingers gently to my lip and felt the dried blood. For a moment, I'd forgotten the pain.

"Do you have a first-aid kit?"

"In the bathroom, right around the corner down the hall."

"Come on, then." She took charge.

I followed her down the hall and into the bathroom. She wet a washcloth with warm water and daubed the lip and chin where the blood had trickled down, then wiped the rest of my face gently. She held my chin and turned my head, first one way, then another, looking at me. I was astounded by her resemblance to Catherine.

"What happened to you, anyway?"

"Two guys didn't like the way I dress." She didn't laugh. "No big deal. It's nothing you should worry about."

"You should put ice on that mouse," she said. "Other than that, you're fine."

I went back into the kitchen and wrapped some ice in a towel and held it to my cheek where the bruise was swelling. I opened a beer for myself, then went to see where she'd gone. She was in the living room, looking at some of the Oriental prints on the wall that had been a gift from a friend who collected Chinese antiques.

"I like your house. It's cozy." She turned to look at me.

"How did you find me?"

"Cat told me about you."

"How come she never told me about you?"

"We never told anyone about each other." She walked toward me and sat on a couch. She even moved like Cat. "She probably told you our father ran out on us after Mother died. We were separated and sent to foster homes. We didn't know where the other was for years, and when we finally found each other a few years ago, we vowed we'd never be split up again. We just never told anyone that the other existed. It seemed safer and simpler that way." She had a fierce, protective look on her face, like you'd see on a bitch guarding a newborn litter.

"Tell me about Catherine. How did you know she was dead?" It seemed as good a place as any to start.

"I found her," she said quietly. "I went up to her room. I was going to surprise her. I got her room key easily enough by telling the front desk I'd lost it. They thought I was her. I let myself in and found her dead."

A light suddenly went on in my head. "*You* switched IDs. But why?"

"I was scared. Look, it's a long story, and I guess

you deserve to hear the whole thing." She paused. "Have you got anything to eat? I'm starved. I haven't eaten since yesterday."

I could see that she wasn't going to say anything until she'd been fed, so I led her back to the kitchen, showed her where things were, then sat at the table when she insisted on making something for herself. She found the fixings for a huge sandwich, pulled out mustard, pickles, potato chips, celery sticks, and carrots, and munched as she puttered around. I watched her in fascination. She had gotten out enough food for three people, and with slow determination was devouring it all. She opened another beer, then brought beer, sandwich, condiments, and chips to the table and sat down. When she started slowing down, she began her story between mouthfuls.

Like Cat, she'd been shunted from one foster home to another. When she'd finally gotten away, she'd headed for California with the notion, she said, that she'd break into movies or something like that. She'd had visions of stardom, success, big bucks, a Hollywood lifestyle. She'd found disillusionment and a lot of hard work just to stay alive. Eventually, she'd been discovered—not in the way she'd planned, but in a way that had helped pay the bills. She'd been approached by a photographer who'd said he could do things for her. She'd figured that she could use him to get what she wanted, so she'd let him use her. And it had worked. She'd had to sleep with him, but she'd started to get modeling assignments, and the money had gotten better. Finally, she'd gotten really plum assignments—fashion shoots in Mexico and Hawaii, a couple of magazine covers. She'd broken off with the photographer, but they'd done some shoots together afterward, and as much as she'd thought she could control their relationship, he'd kept a kind of hold on her, even after she had the money to stay free of him.

It was at a party he'd taken her to that she'd discovered coke. From then on, she'd always had it. He'd never given her any, but whenever she ran out, someone had made sure she'd gotten more. And once, on a shoot in Mexico, she'd been asked to carry something home for a friend. She hadn't known it was cocaine, hadn't asked, and hadn't found out until the second time she'd been asked to carry another bag. By then it was too late. She'd gotten paid the second time, and the hook was in deep. She didn't think she could refuse the third time, but then she began to get very nervous. She hadn't wanted to be a mule, and her own drug habit made her paranoid and confused. She decided she wanted out.

Listening to her talk, I could see the difference between her and Catherine. It wasn't just her choice of words or the expressions she used. Her whole outlook was darker than Cat's had been. She spoke with a certain bitterness, as though the world owed her for the travail she'd been through. Cat's life had been no less hard, but she'd aggressively pursued a dream, a way out of the basement and into the mainstream. I got the sense that Gillian had looked for the easy way out, and had been surprised when the world had bitten her on the ass. It had given her a different perspective—a more realistic, but drearier view of the world than Catherine had had. I was both annoyed and empathetic at the same time. Lately, I'd been nursing the same grudging feelings that the world was out to get me.

She finished talking at about the same time she

finished eating the last pickle spear in the jar, and she sat back with a faraway look on her face.

"What about Catherine?" I nudged her gently. "How did she get mixed up in this?"

"Oh, God, I don't know," she sighed. "I didn't want her anywhere close to this mess. She always worried about me, tried to protect me. She was the one who found me. I'd given up even looking for her. She saw my picture in a magazine and tracked me down." She paused for a long minute. "She called me," she said finally, "to tell me she was coming into town. She told me where she would be staying. I was supposed to meet a contact to set up another run from Mexico, so I told my contact to meet me at the hotel. It was stupid, too much of a risk, but it was convenient. When I found Catherine dead, I panicked, but I also saw a way out of my problem. If I switched drivers' licenses and credit cards, then maybe everyone would think I was dead, and I could get out of this mess."

"You mean you didn't get Cat mixed up in your smuggling?" I was confused.

"No." She looked startled. "I knew I was in trouble. I didn't want her in trouble, too. Why?"

"You don't know how she died?"

"No. I just switched the contents of our purses and got the hell out of there. I was scared. She was dead, and there wasn't a mark on her. I didn't know what to think. And then I remembered her talking about you. I thought maybe I could hide out here for a while."

"Damn you," I said quietly. It was all beginning to fall into place. She started again, looking a little frightened and confused. "Did your contact know you wanted out of the business?"

"Well, yes, but I tried to keep it low-key. I was just looking for a way to break off cleanly and get out."

"Catherine died because of you, damn you!"

She looked at me, wide-eyed and open-mouthed. "What are you talking about?"

"Catherine had an ounce of cocaine in her stomach, damn it!" My anger grew, bringing a flush to my face that fortunately masked the revulsion I felt, for now I knew how Cat had died. "Someone wanted you dead. They thought you were going to talk. They mistook Catherine for you, and they got into her room and forced her to swallow six balloons filled with coke. And then they watched her so she couldn't move, couldn't call for help. They watched until the balloons burst in her stomach and the coke sent her into a frenzy, a rush so intense it burst her heart."

She shook her head in disbelief even as the words registered, and she put her hands over her ears and asked me to stop. But I couldn't. The anger I felt made me want to reach out and slap her.

"They probably pricked the balloons to hurry up the process. But they caused her a slow and agonizing death. Do you see what you've done? You killed her, damn you!"

She was as tough in a different way, as Catherine had been. But now the guilt and anguish washed over her in waves, and she let loose with a wail that was as primitive as nature. It pierced my being, but I hoped she hurt as much as I did.

"Oh, no," she moaned. "Oh, God, no." She fought back tears and put her hand to her mouth, gnawing on a knuckle. "No, it's not true."

"Yes, it is." I said it more gently as my anger faded. I didn't want to admit that her loss was as great as mine, but they'd been sisters—twins—and there was a piece of Catherine in her that I didn't want to hurt.

"I flew to L.A. to identify her," I said, trying to explain. "Two days later, I got a visit from the DEA. They think it was you."

Her eyes widened. "But how?"

"They were watching you. They know you were running coke for someone. They were going to try to turn you. You met with a dealer a couple of times to deliver samples and set up a buy. Maybe you saw him somewhere else, too."

"Sure, that was part of what they made me do. I was the go-between."

"No, you don't understand. You met him recently. Someone who asked you if you wanted out. Someone who you may have wanted to confide in."

Awareness dawned in her eyes. "There was a guy, a nice guy. We even went on a couple of dates, if you could call them that. He took me to a drive-in for a hot dog, one of those places where the waitresses wear skates. I thought it was a little strange. Nobody in this business is that nice."

"He was an undercover cop. DEA. And now he's dead. His cover was blown. He wanted you to lead him to your source."

"God, no. I can't. Then they'll know I'm alive. They'll kill me. You've got to help me." She looked frightened, and she swiped at the tears in her eyes with the back of her hand.

"I want to know who killed Cat," I said quietly. It brought her up short.

"Digger," she whispered after a moment. "Digger Graves. It could only be him." She shuddered.

"Who is he?"

"My contact. His name's Stan Graves, but they call him Digger. And he looks the part—real creepy, a thin, sharp face with lots of pits from acne when he was young. High cheekbones and sunken eyes and cheeks. Thin lips. He looks like Death. And he's mean. I think he likes to hurt people. I mean, I think he really takes pleasure in it, like it was almost sexual." She shuddered again. "I was supposed to meet him at the hotel. He must have seen Cat and thought it was me."

"And then followed her up to her room and killed her. He knew you'd met with the DEA agent. He probably thought you were passing information."

"But I didn't know he was a cop. How the hell was I supposed to know he was a cop? Damn it?"

"Too late now, isn't it?" I paused. "Tell me how it worked. Who ran the operation?"

"I don't know. Digger was always the one who told me where to be and when. One time it meant carrying a makeup bag back from a weekend in Puerto Vallarta. Sometimes it was just a matter of driving down to Tijuana and meeting someone at a shop. I'd buy some trinket, like a doll, at a specific shop, and when I got back to L.A., I'd deliver it. There were no other names and no other faces I saw more than once except Digger."

Never the same people, never the same route. No wonder Ed and Steve had had such a hard time getting a handle on it. But if they couldn't find the source, I don't know what made me think I could find the person who had ordered Gillian's death, killing Catherine by mistake. I probably couldn't find this Digger fellow if he didn't want to be found. As the hopelessness of it sunk in, the lust for vengeance ebbed, leaving me empty and angry, impotent and helpless. I sat and fumed, incensed by the futility, the senselessness of it all.

"What about the photographer? Who is he?"

"My Svengali?" Her short laugh was bitter. "Peter Harriman."

I thought for a moment. "The name sounds familiar."

"It should. He's pretty well-known. His work's right up there with the guys like Skrebneski. In fact, he has a studio here in Chicago, too."

"Maybe that's it." I had the nagging feeling I'd heard the name somewhere recently.

"We have to do something about you," I said after a moment. "I don't like the thought of you staying here."

"Why not?"

"Somebody could be watching the place. There's already a tap on my phone. I don't know who put it there."

"What the hell are you mixed up in?" She looked surprised.

"I don't know yet. Some personal problems. Nothing to do with you, but I'm not sure that those fellows from the DEA won't be back. And if they spot you, they'll have a lot of questions for you, and for me. I'd rather not answer them."

"What do you want me to do? Sleep on the street?"

"You can stay in the spare bedroom upstairs for a day or two, until we figure out a safe place for you."

"Thanks. That's real generous." She got up and paced. "You wouldn't happen to have any blow, would you? I've been climbing the walls all week."

"What are you, crazy?" I couldn't believe my ears. "Haven't you been listening? Your sister died from coke! You're on the run because of coke! Every goddamn thing wrong with the world right now is because of coke!" I heard myself yelling and stopped to calm down. "Look, there are three rules if you want to stay here. First, no cocaine. I don't want to be around it. I don't want to hear about it. Second, no phone calls. And last, I want you to stay out of sight. I don't want you to risk being seen."

Gillian looked at me for a long minute, her jaw clamped, chin set like a recalcitrant child. "Shit," she said finally. She turned and grabbed her duffel off the counter, then stalked out of the kitchen without another word.

VI

THUMPS AND BANGING came from upstairs—the sounds of a child throwing a tantrum when told to go to her room. We were both on edge. Living without a drink every couple of hours or so had not been as difficult as I'd thought it would be, but I'd been a lot moodier than usual, if that was possible, and easily irritated by even the small inconveniences. If Gillian had been as hooked on coke as I had been intent on self-anesthesia, then I had a good idea of what she was going through.

It was late. We'd talked past midnight, and I was tired. I checked all the downstairs doors and windows, turning out lights as I went. When everything was locked up tight, I headed up the stairs. There were still noises coming from the guest bedroom, but the door was shut. I turned the corner down the hall to the bedroom with the king-sized, empty double bed. I stripped and threw the clothes over a chair, then went to the bathroom to brush my teeth and splash my face. The lip was puffy and sore, and there was an egg under the right eye. All in all, though, the face in the mirror didn't look too bad. I sighed and turned away, clicking off the light as I headed for the cool sheets on that big bed.

It was sometime much later that her touch woke me. I hadn't heard or felt her slide naked under the sheet next to me. And I was so used to the light touch that it almost didn't wake me. Still half-asleep, I rolled over into her arms, and for a long moment, I didn't know where I was.

"I'm sorry," she whispered, stroking me gently. "I'm really not a bad person."

I responded to her touch, knowing I must be dreaming. The feel of her was so familiar. My fingers knew every nook and cranny, soft curve and velvet inch of that body. And I knew how to touch her in a way that made her gasp and wriggle. As I felt the heat grow between us, I gradually awoke and became aware that I was not holding Catherine. God, how I ached for her. The soft lips that kissed mine, the long, silken hair that brushed my chest, the fingers that softly caressed my cheek, so frighteningly familiar.

"God, no," I moaned, pushing her away.

"Don't. Please don't," she said softly.

But it was no use. My mind knew it wasn't Catherine. I fell away from her and squeezed my eyes shut tight, trying to dim the memories that played in Panavision against the big movie screen in my mind.

"God, I loved her." I held my arms tightly across my chest, afraid of everything else in there that wanted to get out. It was the first time I'd said it aloud. I'd tried to suppress it, but now the ache in my heart felt like a knife tearing up my insides.

"I loved her, too."

The words registered slowly, and I heard my grief echoed in them. She rested her head on my chest, and I felt her tears, wet and warm, on my skin. My hand went out tentatively and softly stroked her hair.

"When Cat told me she met you, I was so envious, so jealous. All we really had was each other. And then she had you. I was happy for her. I really was. But I was so jealous." She wept silently, and I pulled her close. "I want to kill the man who did it," she said after a moment. "I want him dead. Will you help me find him?"

I stared at the ceiling in the dark and stroked her hair. "Yes," I murmured, even though I knew it was probably futile. I understood her need for revenge. It was to assuage the guilt. For Gillian and I were both accessories—through our neglect, for not loving Cat as much as she'd loved us. So we took comfort in each other's arms, and fell asleep cradling each other like small children.

In the morning, I walked over to the hotel and used the pay phone to call Lieutenant Lanahan down at the Chicago Avenue police station. He'd sat in my living room one cold February afternoon, warming himself with an Irish coffee, trying to explain to me why young women sometimes get killed for no apparent reason. Since then, he'd called me from time to time to hit me up for one police charity or another. I liked him. He was a big, bull-headed, tenacious Irish cop, the kind you could count on if he was your friend. We weren't exactly friends, but we knew each other well enough to have established a degree of mutual respect and trust. I didn't call him to see if he could explain away Cat's death. I had a different question for him this time.

"What can I do for you?" he asked after we'd exchanged the requisite pleasantries.

"Peter Harriman, lieutenant. Does the name ring a bell?"

There was silence on the line, and I could picture him rubbing the chin of his ruddy face. "Sure," he said finally. "Fashion photographer. Well-known around town—in society circles, too. Originally from here, but spends most of his time in Los Angeles now."

"Has he been in any trouble with your people lately?"

"I don't know. Let me ask around and get back to you."

"Thanks. I appreciate it."

I dropped another quarter in the slot and punched in a different number. A familiar voice answered in an efficient tone.

"Hello, Nell. Is Brady in?"

"Emerson? Is that you?" Nell's voice warmed in recognition. "Where have you been? Let me see where Brady is." She put me on hold for a moment. "He'll be right with you. How have you been?"

"Fine, thank you. How's Darlene?" I held my breath, hoping I'd gotten her daughter's name right, remembering that Nell was divorced.

"Growing like a weed. She started high school this year, if you can believe it. You're nice to ask."

"I'll bet people think you're her sister."

"That's sweet of you." I could practically hear her blush.

"Emerson," a voice boomed over the line, "it's good to hear from you."

"Hello, Puppy. How are you?" Brady Barnes was a commercial photographer, one of the best, and an old friend. He was a giant of a man—six and a half feet and close to three hundred pounds—but generous and gentle with big, sad eyes that turned down at the corners, making him look like a St. Bernard. His third wife, Kitty, had given him the nickname, and it fit.

"We're on a tight shooting schedule—clients in

town, you know—but I've got a few minutes to talk. What's up?"

"I wanted to get your take on a guy—Peter Harriman."

"Good photographer. Fashion mostly. Has an eye for form, for lines. He can elicit a look from his models unlike anyone else. Anything else he's tried is for shit. He can't do set pieces. That's why guys like me are still in business. Why?"

"Do you know him? Personally, I mean."

"Not really. He runs around in a faster, more fashionable circle than I do. You know me. I'm a homebody. I don't get out much. Kitten and I like to cozy up in front of the television and waste our minds. Harriman's got a house in Bel Air and keeps a condo up on Walton east of Michigan Avenue. But he spends most of his time on the coast. I don't know how he does it—so much fashion photography is done in New York—but he's in demand a lot, and his fees are high. They have to be to support his lifestyle. Your turn."

"I've got an acquaintance who lived with him. They broke up. Now she's up to her eyeballs in something both illegal and dangerous. I was just wondering if Harriman could have had anything to do with putting her there."

"I don't know. Harriman's is a world of fast cars and fast women. High fashion can be like that. But it doesn't mean that everybody in the business is into kinky sex and has a monkey on his back." He sounded thoughtful. "What's the something? Drugs?"

"My, uh, friend was a mule. Small stuff. Samples mostly. By the time she found out she was carrying, it was too late. The hook was in, and she didn't see a way to back out."

"Any reason to think Harriman was involved?"

"Only the fact that they lived together for a time, and she was his model on some shoots in Mexico when she was forced to carry."

He was silent for a moment. "I don't know, Emerson. It's possible. But I hate to bad-mouth someone in the business. I just don't know him well enough. He's got a good rep, and his work's solid—a little flashy for my taste, but solid. I wouldn't want to suggest he was into anything like that unless I had some evidence."

"I see your point. Well, thanks. Sorry I've been out of touch. I'll have you and Kitty over for dinner one of these nights, I promise."

"Sure. Don't be such a stranger around here. And do call Kitty. Let's not put off this dinner thing or it'll be another six months before we see you."

I laughed. "All right. I will."

"Good. Take care of yourself."

I sauntered back across the street, thinking of Gillian. Her presence posed unknown dangers that I didn't even want to think about. She was supposed to be dead. Whoever had wanted her out of the way probably wouldn't be happy to learn she was alive, and I wondered how to make her stay dead. As I strode up the steps, I realized that the safest place for Gillian might be Cat's apartment. I still had the key.

Gillian was in the kitchen having coffee. She was wearing one of my cotton dress shirts. It was big enough, barely, to cover the tops of her thighs, and I felt an involuntary flush of desire as I looked at the mirror image of the girl who'd spent six intense months of her life with me. It was spooky.

"Hi. Did you get something to eat?"

"No, I'm not hungry, thanks. Coffee's fine."

"Suit yourself." I shrugged. "I thought about where you could stay, and I figured Cat's place would be about as safe as any."

"You thought about it? What about me? Don't I have a say in this?"

"Well, you can't stay here. Have you got any better ideas?"

"I guess not." She sighed and pouted, looking like a little girl.

"Look, why don't you get dressed, and I'll take you over there." I was exasperated. She ran hot and cold, first cuddly and warm, then bitter and frosty. If this is what addiction did, I felt ashamed of what I must have put my friends through in the past few months.

She stalked out of the kitchen. I poured myself a cup of lukewarm coffee and sat down to wait for her. Gillian was ready in less than ten minutes with packed duffel bag in hand, dressed in jeans that snugged her hips and ass, accentuating her figure. She was still wearing my shirt, with the collar turned up. It looked good on her. I suggested she wear the hat she'd had on the night before, so she pulled her hair up and wound it up on the top of her head, then pulled the hat down tight over it. She took a pair of black-framed dark sunglasses out of her bag and put them on.

"Am I sufficiently disguised?"

"You're fine," I replied, annoyed that she couldn't take this seriously.

Cat's apartment was a loft on Seminary just south of Armitage, a short five-minute drive. We pulled into the alley around back, and parked up close to the rear entrance. I got out and opened up the back door with the set of keys Cat had given me, then motioned to

Gillian to get out of the car. I held the door open for her, and when she was inside, I strode past her and led the way down the corridor to Cat's apartment.

It was on the ground floor, facing the street. I worried about how obvious it might be that the place was occupied, but it would have to do. The loft smelled musty from being shut up. I found the thermostat and turned on the air conditioning. Then I turned on some lights in the kitchen and the track lights in the loft-bedroom area, feeling a little like a burglar. Gillian moved into the living room and threw her duffel on the couch, then went to the windows to open the Venetian blinds.

"Don't touch those," I said sharply.

She froze, then turned and gave me a withering look. "Oh, Christ," I heard her mutter. She flopped on the couch.

I went to the kitchen to check on supplies. There were strange green things growing in the refrigerator, so I found a plastic garbage bag under the sink and cleaned out the moldy food, then made out a list of staples that needed to be restocked. I opened the cupboards and checked those, too.

"I'm making a grocery list," I called. "What do you like to eat?"

"I'm not a very good cook. Frozen stuff is fine. Anything I can just heat up, okay?"

I finished up the list and went into the living room. "I'm going to the store. I'll be back in half an hour. I want you to stay put."

"I'm not a dog, Emerson. I do not sit and stay on command."

"Oh? You could have fooled me. If you ask me,

you're acting like a first-class bitch. Pedigreed, with AKC papers and everything. What do you think this is? A game or something?"

She burst into tears. She clasped her arms across her chest and rocked on the couch with great sobs and little mewling sounds that made me think of a tiny kitten frightened by some monster dog. I suddenly felt small and mean. Maybe I hadn't needed to snap at her, but I couldn't figure her out. I sat next to her, put an arm around her shoulders, and pulled her close.

"It's all right," I murmured, stroking her hair. "I'm sorry. I'm not really a bad person, either."

The sobbing suddenly stopped, and she turned to look at me. She giggled and snuffled at the same time, swiping at the tears under her eyes.

"I don't know what's wrong with me." She looked embarrassed.

"I think I do. You're getting a nasty drug out of your system. Your body has already thanked you for it, but your mind is still playing games."

"I never thought I was hooked." She shook her head slowly. "Maybe that's it." She was silent for a moment. "How long will I have to stay here?"

"I don't know. Until I find out who's watching me and why. Or until the feds find out who your source was."

"I don't understand why someone is watching you. What happened to you last night?"

"It has something to do with a friend of mine who's disappeared." I told her how Morgan had left suddenly, but not without first devising a way to warn me that somehow I was involved. And I told her what had happened when I'd gone to check out the loft space he'd leased using my name.

She was frowning when I finished. "Why are you the center of attention all of a sudden?" she murmured.

"I don't know, and I don't like it. Is that supposed to be a joke?"

"No, it all just seems so weird. Tell me again what happened when you found out Cat was dead."

I looked at her in surprise. She was on a different tack. I started in again, and she made me go through it all, day by day from the morning I got George's first phone call. This time, she sat lost in thought when I'd finished, and it was my turn to frown. I wasn't sure what was on her mind.

"I'm going to go get those groceries now."

"Sure," she said, not really paying attention.

It took close to an hour to get to the store, buy everything on the list, and get back. Gillian was on the couch, reading a book. I'd picked up three more for her at the store—thick trashy paperbacks. When the bags were empty and the shelves restocked, I picked out some things for lunch, putting a can of Senegalese soup and two bowls in the freezer. I made sandwiches while the soup was chilling—smoked turkey, cream cheese, sliced cucumber, watercress, and a little dill on cracked wheat bread. I found a tray, and carried Gillian's lunch to the living room table. I took mine to the table in the dining area. Before I sat down, I went out into the hall to get Catherine's mail.

I sorted through the bills while I ate. Phone, gas, electric, credit card companies, they were all there, waiting to be paid, not caring if Catherine was alive or dead. I wrote out checks for the utilities, and stuffed them in return envelopes to be mailed later. I would give the others to Michael Lansing. Stretching, I got up and used the kitchen phone to call Brandt. When he answered, I asked him if Catherine had been covered by mortgage insurance. He was surprised to hear from me. But he told me that yes, Catherine had been covered, and that the payments on the condo would be made until the estate was settled. I thanked him and hung up.

Gillian had brought her lunch to the table, and I sat down next to her to finish my sandwich.

"Well, the bills are all paid, so nobody should come knocking at the door looking for money."

"Thank you," she said simply.

"I'm worried, though, that someone might come looking for you."

"Why?"

"I can't believe that the feds won't somehow figure out that you and Catherine are not the same person. There must be birth certificates or something."

"Don't you think they would have thought of that already? Besides, there's not much they can trace without a great deal of difficulty. I know."

"What do you mean?"

"Catherine and I were born in Ireland. We were brought over by our parents under an Irish passport. I had a hell of a time getting a copy of my birth certificate so I could get a U.S. passport. And most of our early medical records and papers got lost or shuffled when Cat and I were farmed out to foster homes. A lot of the records just never followed us."

"Sooner or later, they're going to figure it out. I know it's going to be difficult to stay shut up here, but everyone here thinks Cat is dead. This apartment is supposed to be empty. You've got to keep it that way. If you have to get out just to take a walk, use the back door, and make sure you wear the hat or something so you're not so damn recognizable. You're just too damn beautiful not to be noticed."

"Thank you," she said, a little taken aback. "You really did love her, didn't you?"

"Yes, I did."

"She was never really sure. It made her crazy."

It was too late to tell her now. "I have to go," I said after a minute. I got up and cleared my dishes from the table. "I'll come by later and see how you're doing. Don't call me at home unless it's an emergency. It's too risky. If I call you, I'll let it ring twice, hang up, then call again." I walked back over to the table. "I'm sorry about all this precaution. I just don't like not knowing what's going on. I'd rather be safe." I leaned over and kissed her on the cheek. "It'll be all right. You'll be fine."

She nodded, and I left, going out the back door. I wondered how long she would stay put. I hoped she'd gotten it through her head that someone had wanted her dead. The paranoia was back, sneaking in at the edges of my consciousness, and I wondered why everything seemed to be happening to me.

When I got home, I checked my own mail, and went to the den to read it. I remembered to send a check to the realtor for the rent on the loft, so they wouldn't hound me. I would take it out of Morgan's hide later, and I would talk to Lansing at some point to see if I could break the lease. There was a note in the mail from a magazine editor reminding me that I'd promised a rewrite of an article he'd bought from me. I put everything else out of my mind, and pulled the file out of the desk, suddenly realizing that I really looked forward to doing some work. I spent the rest of the day at the word processor, enjoying the feel of the keys under my fingers for the first time in months.

The phone rang just as I was finishing, and I picked up the extension.

"Emerson, it's me." George's voice came over the line breathless and animated. "I found Morgan! He's in Tampa."

"Damn." She'd blurted it out so quickly I couldn't have stopped her. "What's wrong?"

"Nothing. I just dropped something. That's wonderful news." I looked at my watch. It was almost four. "Are you at the office?"

"Yes."

"Can you get away now?"

"Sure. I think so."

"Why don't we meet for a drink to celebrate, then? How about Yvette's in half an hour?"

"Great!"

I hung up quickly, hoping that anyone listening in on the tap had not heard too much. She could tell me the rest over drinks. But I fretted for the next half-hour. A little before four-thirty, I strolled down the street to Yvette's, and found a table near the back of the bar. The late afternoon was beautiful—warm and dry, perfect for sitting at one of the sidewalk tables—but I didn't want to take chances. George showed up a few minutes later, and I ordered drinks for us both.

"Okay, tell me what happened," I said when the waiter left.

She was flushed with excitement. "We figured from the phone calls Morgan's been making that he must be headed south, right? So I started calling everyone we know that lives in that direction to see if Morgan might have tried to get in touch. I talked to Dave Roberts in Sarasota, and he said it was strange that I called because he thought he'd seen Morgan in Tampa today."

"He didn't talk to him?"

"No, not really. He said he saw someone who looked like Morgan on the street."

I didn't want to take the wind out of her sails, but it sounded as if Morgan still didn't want to be found. Otherwise, he would have called himself, or would have contacted Dave if he was in the area. Dave and Sandy Roberts were old friends. Dave had been transferred to Sarasota to head up a bank there about a year before.

"If he thinks it was Morgan, then maybe it was," I said reassuringly. "Look, why don't I fly down and see what's going on. Maybe I can track Morgan down."

"Would you? That would be great."

"I don't want to frighten you, but I think I should leave tonight. If someone's still listening in on my phone, then they'll know he's in Tampa, too."

She went pale and grabbed my arm. "I forgot. Do you think . . . ?"

"Don't worry. You didn't say that much. Why don't you wait here a minute while I call Dave."

I went to the pay phone and called Dave Roberts after getting his number from information. He was surprised to get my call.

"Georgia told me you think you saw Morgan in Tampa."

"It was strange that she called. You know how sometimes you think you see someone you know, but it can't be because the setting's all wrong? But now that I think about it, I'm sure it was him. Is something wrong?"

"Morgan may be in a little trouble. I'm going to fly down tonight to see if I can find him. Would it be all right if I bunked with you and Sandy for a few nights?"

"Of course. We'd love to have you. Tell me when you're getting in, and I'll pick you up at the airport."

"I haven't checked the flights yet. I think I'll just get a car at the airport when I get in."

"Are you sure? You remember how to get to the house?"

"I'll find it. Don't expect me until late."

"We'll be up."

"Thanks, Dave."

I called the airlines to see what was going out. There was a plane leaving in about an hour and a half—enough time to get home, throw some things in a bag, and get to the airport. I made one more call to Gillian to tell her where I was going, and that I'd be back in a day or so. I told her that if she had any trouble to call Brandt, and I gave her his number. I didn't want Brandt involved, but he was the only one I trusted if something came up that Gillian couldn't handle.

George had already asked for the bill.

"It's all set," I said, pulling some money out of my pocket to pay our tab. "There's a plane out tonight, and Dave and Sandy are expecting me. I'll call you as soon as I find out anything. I promise."

"Thank you. Be careful."

"Sorry to run out on you. Can you get home all right?"

"I'll take a cab. Go—don't worry about me."

It took ten minutes to pack a bag—the hardest decision was whether or not to take a sport coat. I went light and opted for a windbreaker in case the evenings were cool. Downstairs, I paused, then walked back to the den. There was a pile of photos in the desk. I shuffled through the stack of pictures until I found an old picture of Morgan and me clowning around at the Grants' house one Christmas. We were both looking into the camera with goofy grins, but Morgan looked only half as silly as I did. I snipped the picture up the middle, put the half with Morgan's face in my pocket, and switched off the light.

The flight was uneventful, almost tedious. The airport was jammed with summer traffic, so the plane boarded late, sat on the runway for a while, landed late in Atlanta, and waited there on the taxiway for a gate to open up. The stopover was brief, and the plane pulled away from the gate only a few minutes after scheduled departure. I weathered it all calmly, amused by the impatience of the passengers who thought they'd get there faster by fidgeting. But I was glad when the plane finally touched down in Bradenton. The airlines try to pack so many people into those long, thin metal tubes that the seats are much too close together for a person of my size. Even in an aisle seat, my knees were stiff and my ass was sore by the time we landed.

Warm, soft, humid night air greeted us when we deplaned on the tarmac. The perfume of the bougainvilleas and azaleas and palms mixed with the salt from the Gulf made Bradenton's air smell exotic. I drank it in and felt it caress my face as I strode to the terminal.

A pert and pretty young blonde at the rental car window asked me questions with a friendly, cheerful voice and filled out the rental agreement. She gave me the keys to a Firebird and asked if I needed directions. I said I didn't, but took a map in case. The white, low-slung Firebird was across the road in the lot, in slot sixteen just where she said it would be. I threw my bag in the passenger seat and eased in slowly. There was plenty of legroom, and when I started the engine, I was pleasantly surprised by the car's muscle and deep-throated rumble after the higher-pitched whine of my Alfa. It accelerated smoothly and quickly out of the lot, hugging the pavement nicely in the turns.

Sarasota lay to the south, down the Tamiami Trail. I drove with the window down, enjoying the breeze. It was a quick four miles down to the waterfront near the center of town. I turned right and headed out the Ringling Causeway to Lido Key. Dave and Sandy had a big house on the water facing toward town on the south side of the key. It took another seven or eight minutes to find it. The lights were still on, shining warmly in the darkness. The sweep of the headlights across the front of the house brought Dave to the front door.

"Emerson, it's good to see you. It's been a while." He took my bag and led me into the house.

"Good to see you, too. Is Sandy still up?" My watch said it was after eleven-thirty.

"She just went to bed a little while ago. Said she couldn't keep her eyes open any longer."

"I'm sorry I got in so late."

"Don't worry about it. Come on in. Tell me what you've been up to." He set the bag down and led me through the living room out onto a screened-in veranda overlooking the water. Floodlights lit the yard and dock beyond, and I could see the small sport cruiser pulling gently against its mooring lines as it bobbed gently in its slip. I sprawled in a chair and sighed as tiredness overtook me.

"Something to drink?" Dave asked.

"Sure. A beer if you've got one." During the week, I'd had a chance to think, and realized that Brandt probably had been right; alcoholism was not my problem, being stupid and stubborn was. Nervously, I decided that one beer would not hurt.

"Back in a flash."

He disappeared, but returned moments later with two open bottles of St. Pauli Girl. He handed me one. It was icy cold, and its carbonated bite felt surpisingly good on my tongue and down the back of my throat.

"So, tell me what the hell's going on with Morgan?" he said, perching on the edge of a chintz-covered ottoman.

"I don't know," I said after a moment. "But I think he's in trouble. How did you run into him?"

"I was up in Tampa today on business. We'd finished our meeting, and I was going to get my car out of the parking garage. I saw a man who looked like Morgan across the street, about half a block away. I shouted at him, but he must not have heard me. By the time I crossed the street, he was gone."

"You're sure it was him?"

"Like you, he's hard to miss, he's so big. He stands out, you know. And after George's call . . ."

"Yeah." I rubbed my chin and frowned. "What was he wearing?"

"Um, jeans and a sport shirt. White, I think."

"Can you tell me exactly where you saw him?"

"Sure. Wait a second. I'll get a map." He got up and went into the living room. He brought back a map of downtown Tampa and spread it out on the ottoman. He peered at it, and after a moment, he put his finger on the map. "Here, on this corner."

I bent down next to him and looked at the spot on the map. "What was he doing?"

"Walking. Why? What do you mean?"

"Had he just come out of a building? Which way was he headed?"

"I'm not sure. I mean, come on, Emerson. How the hell should I know where he came from, or where he was going? He was walking up the street, so I guess he was heading north."

"Sorry." I was silent for a moment. "Was there anyone with him?"

"Not that I could tell. Look, what's going on, anyway?"

"I think Morgan was dealing cocaine and got on somebody's bad side."

"No." He looked incredulous. "You're kidding."

"Afraid not." I shook my head.

"Why? Why would he deal drugs?"

"Who knows? Maybe a last shot at recapturing his youth, a last act of rebellion. We're not getting younger, you know. Maybe he just wanted to walk on the edge again." The words echoed strangely in my head.

"Jesus." He stared at the map in front of us. "So, what's he doing in Tampa?"

"I don't know. He's on the run from someone or something. Unfortunately, he's put me in the middle. And I can't ask him what's going on until I find him. I'll drive up tomorrow and poke around. It's a long shot, but I might come up with something."

We both said nothing for a moment.

"How's Brandt?"

"Fine. Same as ever. Things haven't changed much." I don't know why I lied except that I was too tired to go into a long explanation of what was wrong with my world. "We miss you and Sandy." This time I told the truth.

"We miss a lot of people. Florida has its problems

—too many people, too much development—but it's nice down here. More relaxed. We like it."

We fell silent again.

"Well, I'm going to turn in. Breakfast is at seven-thirty if you want it. I'll try to make sure the kids don't wake you if you feel like sleeping in. You're in the guest room. Remember where it is?"

I nodded. "Thanks. I think I'll sit up for a few more minutes."

"Sure. See you tomorrow."

He left me, nursing the beer. Staring out across the water dappled with reflections of stars and city lights, I wondered how I would find Morgan.

Busy family sounds woke me in the morning. I had breakfast with Sandy and the kids—two good-looking blonds, a boy and a girl, probably six and eight, respectively. They were well-mannered and well-spoken, calling me "Mr. Ward" instead of "Emerson," making me feel older than usual. Their shiny, scrubbed faces and inquisitive chatter tweaked an emotional chord inside, making a part of me wish I had kids of my own. They downed their breakfast quickly and ran off to play, laughing.

Sandy and I chatted for a while. Sitting there, sipping coffee and trading gossip suddenly seemed so normal that it struck me as odd. In the cheery all-American, Anita-Bryant-sunshine of that Florida kitchen, it was hard to believe that Catherine had been dead only a week.

We cleared the table and cleaned up the kitchen, and I sat with a last cup of coffee looking at Dave's map of Tampa while Sandy got ready to take the kids off to town to buy new clothes for school. September was only days away. I rinsed my coffee cup in the sink and went to find Sandy to tell her not to hold dinner for me, since I didn't know when I'd be back. The Firebird beckoned from the driveway. I eased into the driver's seat, already hot from the morning sun, and cranked up the engine.

Reversing the route to the house took me back over the causeway and the bright aqua expanse of water that separated the key from the mainland, then north up the Tamiami Trail, past the airport and up into Bradenton. The highway was littered with strip malls, convenience stores, and gas stations, interspersed with the bigger shopping plazas every three or four miles. Traffic was heavy. Natives all seemed to drive pickups or little Japanese subcompacts. The oldsters, the ones who'd been arrested by leisure police in places like Ohio and Illinois and sentenced to retirement in Florida, all drove big American cars—station wagons, big Chevies, and the omnipresent big old Cadillacs built like tanks. I discovered it best to avoid them after a few near misses. Their drivers were too slow, too hesitant, and sometimes too hard of hearing. I could have taken the freeway, but I wanted to remind myself why I put up with Chicago winters.

The commercialism, the tourist traps wrapped in bright, shiny, thin plastic veneer made me feel a little parochial. All that cheeriness hides the real estate scams, the huckstering and burglaries, nursing home abuse, and violent drug smuggling. Chicago may be no better, but in Chicago we put our crime out in the gritty streets, right where everyone can see it. It's why so many people in Europe who've never been to the States believe that mobsters toting tommy guns still run around Chicago in black sedans. I did not want to be taken in by the happy Florida sunshine. The facade made it too easy to ignore the decay underneath. And that made me uneasy.

VII

THERE WAS NO way of telling where the Tampa city limits started. From Clearwater down through St. Petersburg, all the way around Tampa Bay and down through Bradenton and Sarasota, most of the land is developed. All the towns interconnect, and the urban sprawl is almost as large as Chicago's. Driving north from Bradenton, the concentration of development thinned somewhat. But near Tampa, the strip malls and suburban homes gave way to more crowded housing and businesses that showed their age, looking faded, cracked, and corroded. The humid, tropical air quickly eats away at just about everything, making things look in desperate need of a face lift.

I came up Business 41, across the Twenty-second Street causeway. There were a few cargo ships in the harbor, but no cruise ships. I wondered where they all went when it was off-season. The downtown skyline spread out in front of me, the tall, new buildings glinting in the morning sun. And suddenly I was on downtown streets. Ybor Square and the old Cuban section of town were just a few blocks north. I turned left on Adamo Drive, around Ybor Channel past the banana docks, and down Kennedy Boulevard, toward all the steel and glass that beckoned from the heart of the business district.

The parking garage Dave had used was right across

the street from the Hyatt Regency hotel. I pulled into the garage entrance and found a space on the third level, then walked back down to the street and looked around. The day had grown hot and muggy, with the temperature hovering somewhere around ninety-five degrees. It made Chicago's hot spell seem cool.

Dave's description gave me my bearings. There was the big bank building on the corner of Tampa and Jackson—forty stories of white marble and blue glass. The man Dave thought was Morgan had been heading up the Franklin Street pedestrian mall. I walked around the corner and looked up and down the mall—I had my work cut out for me. I sighed and shrugged my shoulders, then stepped into the doorway of the first shop on the block, a jewelry store. It was empty except for a pleasant-looking woman in her fifties behind the counter. My watch said it was almost ten—still too early, perhaps, for customers.

"Can I help you with anything?" the woman asked with a smile.

"Yes, thanks." I took Morgan's photo out of my pocket. "I wondered if you might have seen this man in the last day or so."

She peered at me closely, suspiciously, looking me up and down. Then her face softened. A pair of half-frame magnifying glasses dangled from a chain around her neck. She perched them on her nose to look at the photo she'd taken out of my hand.

"I know you from somewhere." She turned and tipped her head down slightly so she could look at me over the top of her reading glasses.

"I'm sorry," I smiled. "I doubt it. I'm from out of town."

"Oh? Where?"

"Chicago, actually."

"Somewhere else, then. Have you ever been on television?"

I laughed. "A few times. On talk shows." I'd been on a tour to promote the one book I'd written, but hadn't liked being on TV all that much. It made me uncomfortable to be recognized. The book hadn't quite made my name a household word, but it had been successful nonetheless. I still collected royalties. Promotion had helped, but I preferred anonymity to the glare of the television studio lights.

"Then you *are* someone famous."

"No, not really," I murmured. She didn't press the point.

"This is a friend of yours?" She waved the photo.

"Yes. I'm trying to find him."

"I'm sorry. I haven't seen him."

"Well, thanks for your time."

"Good luck," she said as I turned for the door.

I walked out onto the brick street and went next door to a gift shop, showed the picture of Morgan, and got the same response. I repeated the process at a restaurant, a bookstore, and a clothing store—nothing. I had the same luck in the stores on the other side of the street. Some weren't open yet, and I made a note to come back to them later.

The mall was devoid of life. The city had blocked off this street to auto traffic to entice shoppers to the downtown area, breathe life into the inner city, and help out some struggling downtown shopkeepers. The face lift hadn't had the desired result. The skyscrapers that hemmed in the mall were all bank and government buildings, home to bureaucrats and yuppie bankers, lawyers, and real estate agents. They had no reason to stroll down a pedestrian mall in the heat when they could do all their shopping in the strip malls next to the fitness salons near their homes.

It took the rest of the morning to work my way up the three or four blocks of the street, moving from storefront to storefront, showing Morgan's photo and asking my questions. I was met with indifference and some subtle hostility when it became apparent that I wasn't buying anything. By the time I reached the last store, I was hot, tired, and as grumpy as half the shop-keepers had been. I wiped my face on my sleeve, and headed back down the street to hit the few stores that hadn't been open earlier. A few of the shops had been shuttered for good, unable to survive the competition from the suburbs.

I had no luck on the way back, either. Lunch in some nice, cool place sounded good, so I stepped across the street to the hotel. The little coffee shop next to the lobby looked adequate. The hostess led me to a deuce, and I sat with my back to a banquette so I could watch the entrance. The restaurant was busy, filled with pin-stripe-suited executives, both male and female.

Most of the women, though, were now secure enough to forego the conservative look of the business suit and wear stylish and attractive silk dresses. It didn't make them look any less professional, but it made them look a whole lot prettier. The women in downtown Tampa had a svelte, smooth look that con-trasted with the fuller, Midwestern wholesome look in downtown Chicago. Maybe it's the warmer climate down south that thins them out, making them look more angular, more defined. They made me think of Catherine for an instant, and I squeezed my eyes shut against the vision of her face floating in my mind.

There was a surprising lack of southern twang in the conversations around me. The accent was that nondescript, flat modulation of big-city newscasters, devoid of any regionalization. The slow, drawn-out tones of the Old South can be heard in the small surrounding towns. There is a line just south of the Florida panhandle that's drawn east to west from coast to coast, and in the urban areas south of the line, so many people are from somewhere else that the southern accent has been lost. Tampa was like being in any big city in the U.S. of A. in the summertime.

I had a good piece of fresh-grilled grouper for lunch and lingered over a couple of cold Corona beers with lime, enjoying the cool interior of the restaurant, avoiding the inevitable failure on this wild goose chase. The coffee shop cleared out as the lunch crowd went back to work. When the waitstaff began setting the tables for dinner, I finally pushed myself back from the table, dug some bills out of my pocket for a tip, and went to the register to pay my check.

For the hell of it, I stopped at the front desk and asked the girl at registration if Morgan Grant was or had been a guest in the past few days. He hadn't. I strolled out the motor entrance of the hotel. On a sudden impulse, I stepped over to the doorman standing at the curb.

"Can I help you, sir?"

"Yeah. I'm looking for a friend of mine. I wondered if you might have seen him." I pulled the photo out of my pocket and showed it to him.

He took it and studied it for a moment, frowning. Then he shook his head. "No, I don't think so." He started to hand it back, then looked at it again. "Wait a minute." He called over one of the parking attendants. "Pete, didn't you talk to this guy yesterday?"

A young blond kid took the photo and looked at it, then looked at me. "Sure, I remember him. Big guy. He wanted to know how to get to some place down on MacDill."

"Do you remember where he wanted to go?"

He looked thoughtful, then rueful. "No, sorry. I'm not sure he even told me. He just asked how to get to an address on South MacDill Avenue. I told him where it is from here and offered to get him a cab—it's not far. He said it was okay, that he'd get down there later. Then he split."

I thought for a minute. "Did you see where he came from?"

"Over there, I think." He pointed toward the bank building across the street. "I know he didn't come out of the hotel—I was watching the entrance. He came up from behind me. Sorry I can't tell you more." He shrugged his shoulders.

"Thanks. You've really helped."

"Any message if he happens to come by again?"

I had to stop and think again for a moment. I wanted Morgan to feel safe. "Yeah, tell him Emerson wants him to call Brandt." I fished in my pocket and came up with some bills to give to each of them.

"Sure. Thanks a lot."

I sauntered across the street to the bank building kitty-corner from the hotel—another long shot. I found the building directory inside the cool lobby. Running down the names of the tenants with a forefinger, I paused at the name of a production company with an office on the third floor.

Raised brass letters on blond oak double doors announced the name of the company in the third-floor suite. I turned the handle and walked into a small reception area. Another one of those thin, tanned girls sat behind a big, low oak desk. She gave me an all-American smile as I walked up, and asked if she could help me. She didn't even look to be legal drinking age.

Morgan's photo was beginning to fray at the edges. I pulled it out of my pocket one more time and handed it to the girl behind the desk. Her smile faded and a serious look came over her face as she took the picture and looked at it closely. And for a moment, I thought I saw something else on her face—fear.

"I'm looking for a friend. I thought he might have stopped by here to see someone. Do you recognize him?"

The fear was gone. "No, I've never seen him before." She looked up at me and held out the photo.

I took it back, noticing a slight tremble in her hand. "I guess I must have the wrong place."

"Sorry I couldn't help."

I looked her straight in the eye. She met my stare for a moment with big green eyes flecked with little dots of amber, then dropped her gaze. I couldn't read what lay behind those eyes.

"Thanks anyway." I turned and left.

Weariness seeped into my bones. The weight of the heat and humidity sapped my energy and resolve. Another dead end, and I couldn't focus on what to do next. I retrieved my car, then weaved my way through the city streets until I found the highway down to

Sarasota. I drove without thinking, letting the problem rattle around the edges of my consciousness, watching the palm trees and plastic signs flow past as the car ate up the miles of hot pavement.

It was almost five when the car wheeled into the driveway of the house on Lido Key. Sandy called a greeting from the kitchen as I came through the front door. I called back and told her I was going to go down to the beach for a quick swim, and went straight to the guest room to strip off my sweaty clothes and pull on a pair of swim trunks. I slipped into a pair of sandals and grabbed a big beach towel from a rack in the bathroom, then strode back out to the car.

The late afternoon sun still beat down relentlessly, but the soft, powdery, blinding-white sand was cool under my feet when I kicked off the sandals. I dropped the towel on the beach and waded into the shallows. The water was pale green, gradually turning aqua as it got deeper. It felt great. I swam hard for ten minutes, cutting a swath through its warmth with long strokes, then lolled in the shallows, paddling in slow, lazy circles, reluctant to get out. Finally, I waded to shore, toweled dry, and slipped the sandals back on.

Feeling refreshed and in a much more positive frame of mind, I pulled in the driveway behind Dave's BMW and walked to the house, kicking the sand off my feet. Dave was on the patio, already changed out of his suit, sipping a gin and tonic. I waved and told him I'd be right with him. I took a quick, cold shower to rinse the salt off, then pulled on shorts and a shirt and went out to join him.

"How did it go today?"

"Weird." I flopped into a chair. "Morgan's definitely in Tampa."

"I knew that was him I saw. Where is he?"

"That's the problem. I don't know where he is or why he's here." I told him what I'd done, where I'd been, starting with the shop owners on the mall, and ending with my visit to the production company in the office building.

"The receptionist was lying," I said, convincing myself. "She was frightened for some reason." After all the blank looks and shoulder shrugs I'd gotten that morning, I knew that there had been a flicker of recognition in her eyes when I'd shown her Morgan's picture. And then there had been that momentary look of nervousness. She'd been covering up for someone.

"What are you going to do next?"

"I'm not sure." I thought for a minute in silence, then suddenly slapped my forehead, feeling dumb. "Have you got yellow pages for Tampa?"

"Sure. I'll get them." He looked at me curiously and got up to get a copy of the phone directory.

I thumbed through the pages, looking for the "Entertainment" section and ran my finger down the listings, checking the addresses. There were ads and listings for strippers, balloon companies, party planners, and a bunch of other services. And there, buried with all the other services were a few listings for production companies and studios. I finally found the name of a recording studio on South MacDill Avenue.

"Let me see that map of Tampa again."

Dave brought the map over, and I pored over the cross streets, looking for the location of the address on MacDill. I put my finger on a spot on the map. "There," I said softly. "That's what I'm doing next."

"Emerson, you don't have a drink."

I looked up, startled, as Sandy came into the room. She carried a tray of appetizers.

"You're right. I guess it's about time for one."

"What would you like?"

"A beer's fine."

"A beer it is. Dinner will be ready in about half an hour. Don't fill up too much on cheese and crackers, okay boys?"

Dave laughed. "Yes, dear."

Sandy joined us in a minute, bringing a beer and lighter topics of conversation. I'd missed them. They'd been part of the small circle of close friends who had kept me grounded in Chicago, the folks who had always been there when I'd needed sounding boards, when I'd felt like an odd man out with no roots, no family, no counterpart. They, along with Brandt, Greg and Sally Edwards, the Grants, and a few others, had been my family. I enjoyed their company, perspective on life, conversation, and most of all, their friendship. It felt good when Sandy put an arm around my waist and Dave put an arm around my shoulders to give me a squeeze on the way into the dining room. Their smiles and touch were reassuring, filling the empty hole that Catherine's death had left in my life. After dinner, we put the kids to bed and moved out to the patio and sipped wine, talking late into the night about life and dreams.

I watched the sun pop over the horizon the next morning, casting long shadows outside the window. I showered and dressed quietly, then went to the kitchen to put on a pot of coffee for everyone. After a cup of coffee and a piece of toast, I borrowed a pair of binoculars from a patio table and climbed into the Firebird before anyone else was up.

I headed across the causeway into Sarasota, stopping for gas and another cup of coffee before letting the car have its head on the highway up to Tampa. The morning was still cool, but the sun was already threatening to make the day hot and steamy. Traffic wasn't yet heavy, so I made good time. Instead of cutting off on the Twenty-second Street causeway, I went straight north another mile or so to the Crosstown Expressway, and took that west through town. It wound south, and I got off, taking Bay Boulevard, and then came back east a block to MacDill.

The neighborhood was nice—big old inner-city houses that were coming back in style and being rehabbed. A block or two west was the Palma Ceia Golf Club. The address I wanted was a big, rambling pink stucco house that had been converted into executive office suites. I nosed the Firebird close to the curb on the opposite side of the street. There was an empty parking lot next to the building. It wasn't yet eight-thirty, so I climbed out of the car for a closer look. The brass plaque next to the front door listed only two tenants in the building—the recording studio and an advertising agency. The front door was still locked. I sauntered back across the street to the car and settled in for a long wait.

The lot filled slowly during the next hour. Only a few of the people who went in the building came out again—a couple of messenger service drivers, a man in a suit with an early, short appointment. The sun rose higher, warming the air, turning the interior of the car into an oven. I rolled up the windows and turned on the air conditioning until it cooled down.

A little after eleven, a big sedan pulled into the lot,

and a short, bald man stepped out. He wore pale gray slacks and a pink silk shirt that was unbuttoned halfway down his paunchy middle. There were heavy gold chains around his neck. I sat up and watched him closely as he went up the steps onto the portico and through the front door. I was out of the car and halfway across the street before the door closed slowly behind him.

When I reached the front door, I stopped and waited a long ten-count. Then I opened the door just a crack and peered into the lobby. The fat man was disappearing through a door off the lobby. I waited another three beats, then pushed the door open and stepped through. There was yet another slim, attractive woman behind the reception desk, a brunette this time. In a soft voice, she asked if she could be of assistance.

"I was driving by and thought I saw a friend of mine stop in—the short, bald man?" I was all smiles and eager geniality.

"Oh, that was Mr. Antoly. Would you like to speak with him?"

I let my face fall, even though my heart was racing. "No, that's all right. It's not who I thought it was," I said with a rueful grin. "I'm sorry to have bothered you."

"No problem, sir. Have a nice day."

It might be a good day after all. It was a sure bet that Burt Antoly, one half of Copious Productions—one third if I counted myself in as president—was why Morgan was in Tampa. With any luck, he would lead me right to Morgan. I crossed the street to the car and waited for Mr. Antoly to finish his business. It didn't take long. He came through the door a few minutes later, got into his car, and drove out of the lot, turning south. I let some traffic go by, pulled away from the curb, did a quick U-turn, and fell in four or five cars behind him.

It was easy to keep him in sight. He turned west, south, and west again onto Gandy Boulevard and headed across the long bridge that stretched lazily across the bay. The sun sparkled brilliantly on the turquoise water, and boats dotted the bay, carving white trails in the expanse of blue. Despite the heat, it was pretty, and probably as close to paradise as I'd ever get.

The dark-blue town car turned south on Interstate 275, and I clipped along three cars behind it at about sixty. Ten minutes later, he exited back onto the streets in St. Pete. I closed up the distance between us a little as he took a causeway west toward the beach, winding past man-made keys, all with large, modern houses built on the water and big boats of one kind or another in the slips. Minutes later, the Gulf came in sight, and the road came to a *T*. At the junction was a large, old, stately pink stucco hotel rising high above the ranch-style houses hidden in the palms and hibiscus.

Antoly turned south, passing the front entrance of the hotel, and headed down the beach road a few miles. There was little traffic, and the white sand beach separating the road and Gulf was empty. I fell back some as he slowed, apparently looking for something. A sign said we were entering a little town called Pass-A-Grille, and the Lincoln suddenly swung into one of the metered parking slots along the beach side of the road. I slowed and drove past his car, then pulled the Firebird into an empty slot a few cars down. Antoly crossed the street and disappeared into a restaurant.

I sat in the car for a minute, then climbed out and stretched, feeling the heat of the sun on my face. After five minutes of waiting, I ambled over to the restaurant to get something cool to drink. The sign outside that read "Hurricane Restaurant" proclaimed fine food and drink. Separated from the street by a hedge was an empty patio in front, dotted with stone tables topped with pretty, dark-blue glazed Mexican tile. I opened the front door and stopped in the foyer to let my eyes adjust. The restaurant, too, was quiet. Antoly sat at the bar with his back to me. I walked back outside and found a table that was half in shade. A waitress followed me out and took my order for a tall iced tea.

The restaurant slowly grew busy as a few people came off the beach to cool down, and more touristy types strolled in off the street laden with junk purchased at local curio shops. Some went inside to take advantage of the shade and whirring ceiling fans, and others braved the noon-day sun and sat on the patio. I got up once to check on Antoly again—he hadn't moved, but now had something to eat. He was too calm and confident for a man on the run. Antoly was just killing time. It would do no good to confront him. Frustrated, I went back to my table and signaled the waitress, ordering lunch and a beer. The food was as good as the sign had promised.

When I was finished, I settled my tab and got up to check on Antoly one more time, then walked slowly back across the street. Antoly's car was empty—nothing in sight on the seats, not even an empty coffee cup. I stepped over the low stone wall onto the beach and sat on the sand, willing myself to be patient, watching some children play at the water's edge.

The sound of a car engine starting brought me back to attention, and I turned to see the Lincoln backing out of its parking spot. I got up slowly and stretched as Antoly headed back the way we'd come, then strode quickly to my car and pulled out a few hundred yards behind him. Antoly retraced his route back to Tampa, but this time he took Gandy all the way in to Bay Shore Boulevard and worked his way up around the bay. It was getting to be late afternoon, and I wondered where this wild goose chase would lead next.

He took the short bridge over to Davis Island and wound through the suburban neighborhood just a stone's throw from downtown Tampa. The main thoroughfare circles the island. He turned off on the road leading to the small airport at the southern tip. I slowed and let him pull away. There is nothing at the end of the island except the airstrip and the Davis Island Yacht Club. The road makes a wide, lazy *S* first around the airport, then back the other way around the little bay and into the yacht club. Antoly stopped midway around the *S* and parked on a grassy space that looked across the bay toward the yacht club. This looked more promising.

I followed slowly, pulling off the road a few hundred yards behind him. There was a clear view of the airport off to the left, the Lincoln in front of me, and the yacht club beyond. It was quiet and peaceful. Antoly's car was in the middle of a spit of land jutting a few hundred feet into the water, barren except for a large palm tree and a navigational light at the tip. For a moment, I thought I saw something moving behind the palm. I raised the binoculars, but couldn't make anything out.

I turned my attention back to Antoly. He was out of the car, looking toward the airport. A car pulled out of the airport entrance and slowly moved toward him, then picked up speed as it drove past. Hoping for a better look, I put the Firebird in gear, let it roll another fifty feet closer, and watched him through the binoculars. Antoly raised his arm to look at his wristwatch.

Five minutes went by. Suddenly a car whooshed past, startling me—a silver Porsche 944 with black-tinted windows. Its brake lights flashed as it rounded the curve toward the big Lincoln on the grass, and pulled off the road and onto the grass to the left of Antoly's car. I sat up and looked through the lenses again.

Antoly rounded the back of his car and opened the trunk, pulling out a black case. A man carrying a briefcase stepped around the front of the Porsche, and the two met between the cars. The driver of the Porsche put his case on the hood of the Lincoln and popped it open. Antoly leaned over to look into it, and began fiddling with the contents. A drug deal! Out in the open in broad daylight. It made an odd kind of sense.

There was sudden movement from two other quarters, and I lowered the binoculars to get a wider field of vision. Far beyond, on the other side of the water, a black Mercedes came out of the yacht club and was moving at a good clip around the bay. Off to the right, a lone figure stepped out from behind the palm on the spit of land and was walking purposefully toward the action in front of me. It was another man, a big man. I took a quick look through the lenses—Morgan!

The driver of the Porsche looked up, saw Morgan, and shouted something. Antoly turned, slammed the briefcase shut, and stood his ground, motioning with his hand, palm down, to the other man as though to reassure him. I turned the binoculars back to the Mercedes, barreling around the curve, but the men in front of me hadn't seen it. It was moving too damn fast. Suddenly, a back window went down, and I saw the barrel of a gun poking out. Jesus, Antoly had sent out a press release to announce the afternoon's program. And I didn't like it one bit.

I threw the binoculars onto the passenger seat, rammed the Firebird in gear, and shoved my foot to the floor. The back end slid from side to side as the tires fought for a purchase on the gravel shoulder. The car moved a hundred feet with engine howling and tires squealing when I realized I wouldn't make it in time. I slammed on the brakes and threw open the door. Antoly's attention was on Morgan, but Morgan looked first toward me, then toward the sound of the Mercedes.

I stood up and screamed. "Morgan! Run! Get your ass *out* of there!"

I don't know whether he heard me or saw the ominous black machine pistol sticking out the window of the careening Mercedes, but he turned and ran toward the water. I watched in horror as dark spots appeared like magic across the chests of Antoly and the Porsche driver, jerking their bodies to some wild rhythm and spinning them both around. The staccato burp of the machine pistol reached my ears a second later. The Mercedes skidded to a stop a few feet from the Porsche before the bodies had even fallen to the ground. A man jumped out to grab the briefcase on the hood of the Lincoln, and then the case that lay on the ground next to the bodies. As he ran back to the car, he glanced in my direction, and hesitated when he saw me.

Across the distance, our eyes locked, and his features burned themselves into my memory. He had blond hair cropped close to the skull, a thin, drawn face, and sunken eyes under a sharp brow—a death's-head, grinning in the sunshine of a peaceful Florida day. He shouted something and clambered into the car. The big car spun its wheels in the grass and swerved back around onto the road.

The scene was mesmerizing, but the sound of the Mercedes bearing down on top of me registered, sending a surge of adrenaline through me. I dove headfirst into the Firebird, over the center console and as far onto the floor of the passenger side as I could wedge myself. The whine of the big Mercedes engine grew piercingly loud, and there was a rat-a-tat-tat burst of the machine pistol and the sound of breaking glass in the same instant. Then it was quiet.

There were sore spots on my elbow and head where I'd bumped something hard on my way into the car, but nothing was bleeding. Wriggling out of the passenger seat, I turned around and sat up. The sound of a car engine receded in the distance. I looked around. The windshield and passenger window were shattered. Son-of-a-bitch! They'd used real bullets. Paradise suddenly looked different.

I walked a little unsteadily toward the water where Morgan had disappeared. There was no sign of him. I walked back to the bodies. They lay splayed and bloody in the grass. The incident had not attracted attention. There was no flurry of activity at either the yacht club or the airport, no sirens screaming in the distance. It was a quiet, peaceful, hot summer afternoon. Death had paid a fleeting visit, and life went on.

I looked back at the Firebird. The insurance company would never believe it, let alone pay up, without a police report. I would have to call it in. After using a pay phone in the little terminal building at the airstrip, I drove back to the scene. Antoly looked shrunken, deflated, like a two-day-old balloon. The other man lay sprawled face down in the grass. I had no urge to see his face. Looking at the bodies, I suddenly started shaking uncontrollably, finally realizing how close I'd come to buying it permanently.

Two Tampa squad cars arrived fifteen minutes later, and it took half an hour to answer all their questions. Even then, I had to go downtown and wait while they filled out reports. I told them I'd simply been driving out to look at the yacht club when the Mercedes had driven by spraying bullets. Yes, I'd seen one of the men, and could describe him. But no, I hadn't been able to read the license plate on the big black car. They were polite but thorough, and after they made me go through it three times, they let me go. I made them give me copies of their report for the rental agency.

Sandy was shocked and concerned when she saw the scarred, windowless car pull up to the house. Dave was just as shocked when he came home a little while later. We all watched the seven o'clock local news to see if the media had gotten hold of the story yet. There was a short item about the shooting of two men near the Peter O. Knight Airport. The reporter said that the police had little to go on, but that they were looking into it. There was speculation that the deaths had been drug-related.

Morgan was long gone. Whatever he'd wanted from Antoly was a moot point. He was still on the run, still out there somewhere. And I was back at square one.

VIII

THE RAINS HAD COME. No one could quite explain where they'd come from, or why they lingered, beating heavily against the scorched grass and bone-dry, sun-baked earth. The summer had been so hot that the sudden rains could not soak into the parched soil. Instead, the water ran off into swollen streams and rivers. The weather service issued flash-flood warnings, too late for the grim unfortunates in the northwest suburban flood plains who vainly tried to pump two or three feet of water out of their basements.

O'Hare was even closed for a time, encircled by the rising waters like a castle ringed by a moat. I flew in and drove out only hours before it shut down completely, stranding passengers for almost a day. The heat was gone, replaced by the deluge, giving us all something new to complain about. It took nearly an hour and a half for the cab to make it back downtown. I was glad to be home.

There were no messages on the tape. I collapsed gratefully in a chair. I'd called George the night before to report what had happened in Tampa. I hadn't checked in on Gillian. Subconsciously, I hoped that she'd go away like a bad dream. She was a problem I hadn't wanted to deal with. I would think about her later.

I hadn't been in the chair two minutes when the

phone rang, startling me. It was a Dr. Shapiro from Highland Park Hospital.

"It's Tom, isn't it?" I suddenly felt wooden.

"Yes. I'm sorry, I don't—" He started over. "Mr. Blanchard passed away. About an hour ago."

"Damn. Was anyone with him?"

"No. He never came out of the coma. He just slipped away from us. I'm sorry."

"What about next of kin? Have you notified his family?"

"Uh, no, not exactly." He paused. "He listed you as the contact in case of emergency. There's no mention of relatives on his admittance papers."

"I see. Thank you. I'll make arrangements for the body."

"Thanks." I heard a kind of relief in his voice. "I'm truly sorry. We did everything we could."

I hung up. I didn't want to hear any more. I called Brandt first. He would remember the names of any of Tom's friends that I'd forgotten. Our conversation was cursory, almost curt. I told him that I would arrange a memorial service in the little chapel on Sheridan Road in Winnetka that Tom had liked. Between the two of us, we quickly came up with a list of people who should be told and divided up the calls. Next, I dialed the rectory of the church in Winnetka and managed to persuade the pastor to conduct a short, simple service for Tom at 2:30 on Saturday. I called Brandt back to let him know, then started in on my list.

Tom's father had been dead for years, and his only brother had been killed in Vietnam. I thought Tom's mother was still alive, and remembered that she'd lived in a small town in Iowa. I got the number from information and dialed it. An old woman's voice answered, reedy and thin.

"Mrs. Blanchard?"

"Nope. This is Etta Haskell."

"Is Mrs. Blanchard in?"

"Nope. Miz Blanchard passed away, oh, 'bout seven, eight months ago. I was living with Anne for the last few years. Just kind of stayed on in the house after she passed on. Who's this?"

"My name's Emerson Ward. I'm a friend of her son, Tom. Did Mrs. Blanchard have any other relatives?"

"Not that I know of."

"Thank you, ma'am. I'm sorry to have bothered you." There was no reason to tell her why I was calling.

I felt as sad as the rain dripping from the gutters in a melancholy rhythm. Tom had died an impersonal death, attended by machines, with no human warmth to wish him Godspeed. I made arrangements to have his body picked up and cremated. Then I called his friends, hoping we could make it up to him somehow, let him know that he'd meant something to us. I locked up and left, turning my collar up against the drizzle, walking aimlessly at first, then with purpose up through the park and over to Armitage.

My hair was plastered and my clothes soaked through by the time I let myself into Cat's loft. Startled, Gillian looked up from the book she had been reading.

"Oh, it's you. You're soaked."

"I needed to walk." I moved to the fireplace and started laying in logs and kindling, feeling her eyes on my back. "Are you ready for a home-cooked meal yet?"

"God, yes. I've been starving to death here."

I lit the fire and turned to face her. "You don't look like it."

"How was Florida?"

"Warm, sunny, and unpleasant."

"Did you find your friend?"

"Yes. And no."

"Boy, you're just full of information."

"Sorry." I stripped off my windbreaker and hung it on a poker near the fire, then went to the kitchen. "Would you like a drink?" I called.

"A vodka on ice, please. With a squeeze of lime if there is any."

Gillian followed me to the kitchen and perched on a counter stool. I fixed drinks—a nonalcoholic Kaliber for me—then opened the refrigerator to see what to make for dinner. I pulled out ingredients and rummaged through drawers and cabinets for cooking utensils.

"I *saw* Morgan. I didn't have a chance to talk to him. A bad man in a big black car drove by spraying bullets everywhere before I could get close to him."

"Jesus. Is he dead?"

"No, I think he got away. Two other guys weren't so lucky. One was Morgan's business partner in what I think was a bogus recording studio. I think the killer was a friend of yours."

"What?"

"Thin guy with real short blond hair, sunken eyes, pitted face from acne?"

Gillian paled and whispered, "Digger. How?"

"I don't know." I shrugged.

"Tell me what happened."

I talked as I cooked, looking at her occasionally to see if she was tracking. She wore a grim expression.

"So, Morgan's dropped out of sight again," I finished. "And to top off my week, Tom Blanchard died today."

"The friend who was in the hospital?"

I nodded. "He didn't deserve to die that way." I swiped at my eyes with the back of my hand. "We're holding a memorial service for him on Saturday."

"You should have a wake," Gillian said softly. "A good, old-fashioned Irish wake. Cat remembered Ireland better than me, but I remember Grandma's wake. The men all dressed up in tweed suits, with their rough hands, slicked back wet hair, looking itchy and uncomfortable. The women, sniffling into lace handkerchiefs, dabbing at their tears. And the children—we wanted to burst out of our Sunday clothes. We didn't understand death, didn't understand that Grandma wasn't just sleeping in the casket.

"After the right amount of keening and wailing, the liquor started to flow, and the room grew loud and smoky with the talk and cigars of the men. The women all stayed in the kitchen to finish fixing all the food, and we played, running all over the house until it was time to eat. And through it all, Grandma lay in the middle of the living room, a small smile on her face, as if she approved."

She stared at the counter, a smile on her face as well. "Give your friend a wake. He probably won't give a damn, but it'll make you feel better."

I watched her enjoy the memories, then interrupted her softly. "Come and eat."

We opened a bottle of wine with dinner, and took what was left with us when we finished. We sat quietly in front of the fire, talking some, but relaxed even with the long silences. And when the moment suddenly felt right, I took Gillian into my arms without even thinking and gently kissed her. Instead of haunting me, it felt comfortable. I knew this was Gillian, not Catherine, and I wanted her. Her sister had come to me one night to be less alone. I'd understood. As different as Gillian was, she now understood my same need. She returned the kiss with a soft touch.

We began slowly, holding each other close for a long time, occasionally turning to brush our lips together, increasing the tension between us. The heat shimmered in the air around us, bringing the blood to our skin, making us glow. A light touch became almost painful. I took her hand and led her up the short flight of stairs to the loft bedroom where shadows flickered dimly on the wall. We undressed each other slowly,and climbed naked under the sheet to melt into each other, skin against skin, burning like a brand.

The urgency was suddenly gone, replaced by an easy calm, and a sense that we had all the time in the world. Moving smoothly in unison, we celebrated life and the memories of those we'd loved. She surprised me with her tenderness, showing me a softness under the tough exterior. I'd expected a rough-edged aggressiveness to her lovemaking. Instead, there was a shyness about her that was touching. And when we embraced, I sensed Catherine's presence somewhere down deep under the reality of Gillian.

I sat cross-legged on the bed with Gillian on my lap, facing me, legs wrapped around my waist. We were joined, welded together with moist heat, and our eyes locked. We touched, fingertips tracing outlines on warm skin, and our bodies swayed gently, rocked by the blood pulsing through our veins. With each passing moment, our hearts beat louder and faster. Suddenly, she tensed, and her muscles grasped at me, hungrily sucking me deep into her soul. I took her face in my hands and pulled her mouth to mine. Through the roaring in my ears I heard the quiet, steady patter of rain outside the window.

Gillian's suggestion to hold a wake was a good one. Tom deserved that much, at least, and making arrangements would keep me busy. I ordered food and liquor, ran errands to get ice and more food, and called friends to give them advance warning.

I stayed in constant motion, trying to shut out the bleakness in my soul. There was a nagging doubt in the back of my head that I'd done the right thing by sleeping with Gillian. I'd used loneliness and familiarity as excuses, and she'd already extended an invitation by climbing into my bed that first night. But I wondered what we wanted from each other—or even what we had to give each other. A simple case of post-coital depression, Brandt would say, made a little worse because of my recent withdrawal. He always came up with easy answers to problems that seemed to take me weeks to solve.

On Saturday, I offered Brandt a ride up to Winnetka with George and me, but he said he'd made plans to go with someone else. He was a bit too petulant. I thought he was taking this grudge a little too seriously. But I guess I hadn't been much of a friend to him lately, either.

The service was simple and appropriate, the chapel elegant and beautiful despite the gray day. The foyer was full of flowers from Tom's shop, spreading their cloying scent through the chapel. The pastor read consoling words from the Bible. Blaine Smyth, Tom's friend and manager of the Chicago shop, delivered a short, poignant eulogy.

There were more than a hundred mourners squeezed into the pews close to the front of the chapel—a sea of dark suits and black-veiled hats—and the sound of quiet sniffling and the soft scrape of shoes shifting on the stone floor. Muted light filtered through the stained-glass windows. I felt curiously detached; Tom's death still hadn't sunk in.

The pastor's voice droned hypnotically through a series of prayers asking for Tom's safekeeping during the journey to wherever he was going or had already gone. We all stood to sing a hymn, but I couldn't choke the words out. It was making me feel like there was too little air in the small chapel. The pastor said a benediction, and suddenly, mercifully, it was over.

Outside, leaden clouds hung low like a shroud, closing in the damp, earthy smell that permeated the still air. I straightened and turned as the doors opened behind me and forced a smile for the mourners who emerged. There were no relatives to give condolences to, so we consoled each other, mingling on the steps and the grass, solemnly shaking hands and hugging, and smiling at old friends not recently seen.

While I was talking with a couple I knew, a young man approached, standing patiently off to one side. He looked familiar, but I couldn't place him. The couple drifted away, and the man took a step toward me and stuck out his hand.

"Mr. Ward, I'm awfully sorry about your friend."

I shook his hand, looking at him quizzically.

"Thanks. I'm sorry, I can't remember where we met."

"Bob Webster."

"Oh, right—*Officer* Webster. I didn't recognize you out of uniform."

"The hospital called us when Mr. Blanchard died —it's a felony murder now. The paper mentioned where the service would be, and I just wanted to come by and pay my respects."

"Thanks. I appreciate that."

He shifted his weight, looking uncomfortable. "I also wanted to tell you that we haven't closed the file on this case by any means. We don't have a lot of manpower, but I've been working on this in my off hours. I didn't want you to think we'd just let it drop."

"Any leads yet?"

He looked dejected. "No. But I'm sure I'll turn something up."

"I know you're doing everything you can. I'm grateful." I paused, and there was an awkward silence. Webster stared at his feet. "Look, we're having a wake at my house downtown in about an hour. You're welcome to come down and have a drink."

"Thanks, but I've got to get home. My wife always complains that she never sees me, and I've got some chores to do around the house."

"Well, thanks for coming."

"Sure. I'll be in touch if anything comes up."

He turned and melted into the crowd. I looked around to see if there was anyone else I felt I should talk to before leaving, then decided to find George and head back to the house to get ready for guests. When I turned to go I nearly bumped into a small man nattily dressed in a double-breasted black silk suit.

"Mr. Ward?"

"Yes?"

"I'm John Bailiss, Tom Blanchard's attorney." He put out his hand. It was soft and pudgy, and his grip was slack. He had neatly combed blond hair cut short over the ears that lay flat against his head, smooth features, and a soft body packed into the suit. He appeared to be in his mid-forties, but when I looked closer, the tight skin around the eyes and ears suggested he'd had a face lift to hide the aging.

"I wanted to thank you for making all the arrangements for the service and Tom's cremation. It was generous, and something you needn't have been bothered with. I'll see that you're reimbursed." He stared at me intently with baby blue eyes.

"It was no bother. He was a good friend."

"I can see that. Tom didn't have a lot of friends, but the ones he had were close. They were his family." He paused, his gaze never leaving my face. "The service was beautiful."

"Thank you." I fought the urge to squirm under his stare.

For a moment, he said nothing. "You've never even had the slightest inclination toward your own sex, have you, Mr. Ward?"

"Sorry?" The question startled me.

"That was an observation, not a proposition." He waved his hand. "No matter. I have some business to discuss with you concerning Tom's estate. Are you free on Monday?"

"Yes, I'm sure I am."

"Could you be at my office at, say, nine-thirty?"

I nodded.

"Good." He handed me his card. "I understand you're holding a send-off for Tom. May I join you?"

"Why not?"

"Thank you. I'll see you shortly, then. I'll find my way." He spun on his heel and was gone.

I wasn't good company for George on the ride home. I wondered about the strange conversation with Bailiss all the way, but quickly forgot it as George and I busied ourselves with final preparations for the wake. The first guests arrived only twenty minutes behind us, and we were still putting out food and setting up the bar. I was glad for her help.

"You know, I never realized that Morgan and Tom were that close," I said as we dished out food.

"No closer than you two, I suppose. You know Tom —he was generous. He seemed to like everyone."

"I still don't understand why he would loan Morgan money."

"What's so unusual about it? Wouldn't your friends loan you money if you needed it? I'm sure Brandt would. I know we would." Her voice held a trace of annoyance.

"I suppose you're right."

"I'm sorry. I didn't mean to sound snippy. Besides, Morgan did Tom a favor, and he was grateful."

"What was that?"

"You know how much Tom loved the farm. Well, I guess he was afraid he was going to have to sell it because it was getting too expensive to maintain considering the amount of time he spent there. Morgan suggested he rent it, and even helped him find tenants. I remember Tom mentioning it to me."

The first guests rang the bell before the thought

had a chance to sink in. I hurried to the door to let them in. Early arrivals were quiet and somber, but within an hour, the house started getting crowded, and an hour after that the party moved into high gear, filled with the sound of talk and laughter and clinking glasses.

No one came empty-handed. The McFaddens brought a bottle of Scotch. Greg and Sally Edwards brought wine. Judy Snow brought a casserole. Rob and Lonnie White came in with a whole honey-baked ham. Paul Rivelli was loaded down with a shopping bag full of chips and dips and tins full of nuts. And still the food kept coming. As I circled, replenishing empty plates and glasses, I heard bits of bawdy jokes, raucous laughter, and bright chatter.

Toward nine, when the crowd thinned and more than half the booze had been consumed, it calmed down, and there were solemn toasts and some quiet reflection. The last guests left a little after ten, and Brandt was among them. I'd seen him occasionally through the evening, but hadn't had a chance to talk to him. He lingered at the door.

"Nice party," he said softly.

"Thanks. Tom deserved it."

"Yes, he did. Call me tomorrow if you want help cleaning up." He turned and went down the steps before I could reply.

I didn't even think of facing the mess. I drove over to see Gillian, to tell her how well her idea had worked. She was quiet and thoughtful, but glad of my company, she said. She showed me later when we made love slowly in the dark.

Nightmares fractured my sleep, weaving an endless

tapestry of surreal images that horrified and fascinated me—bloodied bodies hung on hooks like sides of beef, rows of coffins waiting in line for interment. I ran from the images, across a barren plain, but finally, the only escape was into wakefulness. My heart pounded and cold sweat covered me in a thin sheen. I lurched to the bathroom to splash cold water on my face, and hung over the sink breathing heavily, feeling my body tremble, waiting for the wisps of dreams that lingered in my mind to dissipate. Death had won another round, and it wasn't over yet.

The office of Bailiss, Torpin, & Sneed was in a red brick colonial just off Green Bay Road in Glencoe. I arrived a little ahead of schedule, and waited patiently under the watchful eye of a stern-faced receptionist. The interior of the office matched the exterior. It was old school—dark paneling, oak and leather furniture, oil paintings on the walls, and muted lighting from brass table lamps. The wait wasn't long. The receptionist showed me back to Bailiss's office.

"Sit down." He motioned to a chair as he came around the desk.

I sat in one of the leather wing chairs, and he lowered himself into another. There was a coffee table between us with a tray and china coffee service on it. He reached to pour two cups.

"I apologize for the impropriety of my remarks the other day. I'm curious about you, and I let it get the best of me. No offense."

"None taken. You wanted to know if I'd ever been Tom's lover. Why?"

"Blaine Smyth says you did Tom a favor once," he said, changing the subject.

"Friends do that for each other. It wasn't much."

"According to Blaine, you may have helped save the business."

"Tom made the mistake of having an affair with one of his managers—before he hired Blaine. I think he'd really fallen in love with the guy, but he was smart enough to realize that the kid was ripping him off. Tom didn't have the heart to go to the police, so he asked me if I'd help. We figured out how he was doing it, and I shook the kid up some and told him to leave town and not look back. It wasn't that big a deal."

"Let's get right to the point, shall we? I'm executor of Tom's will. As you may or may not know, he had no family. Until his mother died a few months back, Tom's will named her as beneficiary of his entire estate. Tom got around to changing his will only recently. Now it's divided roughly into thirds."

He sipped some coffee. "One would think that with no family, a person would leave things to close friends, or lovers. Indeed, that's what Tom has done. His house and personal belongings are to be sold, and the proceeds given to charities Tom supported over the years. The business is going to Blaine, a loyal and good friend for many years. Blaine will do well with it."

"Why are you telling me this?"

"You're too impatient. Tom's land, house, and property out in McHenry County comprises the final third of his estate. He left this to you."

I sat in stunned silence for a moment. "Why me?"

"That's the question I asked myself. Again, no offense. I didn't know who you were. I thought perhaps

Tom had been conned by some young stud after his money. That also would have provided a motive for his death."

He saw the indignation on my face and raised his hand before I could speak. "I know you had nothing to do with his beating. Your description doesn't match the one Tom gave to the police. And though you could have hired someone, I don't believe you were involved. I've been checking up on you."

"I noticed."

"You have to understand, Mr. Ward. Tom Blanchard was not just a client. He was my friend. I didn't know you, but I think I know you now. I wouldn't tell you this except that what I've learned about you suggests you have a certain, um, sensitivity. I won't apologize for looking out for the best interests of my client. I am sorry for doubting your friendship with Tom."

"What the hell is your problem, Bailiss? Are you having a hard time believing that Tom had straight friends?"

"Not at all. Just making sure who his friends were, that's all."

"So what do I do now?"

"Nothing. It will take some time before the property and business holdings are appraised for estate tax purposes. When it's all settled, you'll receive title to the land. In the meantime, you might want to go out there and take a look at it."

"What the hell am I going to do with it?"

"I guess that's your problem now. Keep it. Sell it. Do whatever you want with it."

I mused for a moment. "Tom was worried about something out there. Have any idea what it was?"

"No." He looked puzzled. "The house is currently being leased. I haven't heard of any problems with the tenants."

"What's the term?"

"It's a five-year lease with an option to renew. The present tenants made him a very lucrative offer to buy, but he turned it down. They've been out there about two years I guess."

"No problems that you know of?" He shook his head. "Damn. I promised him I'd take a look before he died. Now I'm not sure it matters."

Bailiss watched me in silence for a moment, then stood. "Unless you have questions, I'll be in touch when all the papers are ready. In the meantime, rent checks from the tenants will go into escrow. All right with you?"

"Yes, that's fine." I rose to go, a little bewildered.

"Congratulations." He stuck out his hand.

"Thanks." I had a strange feeling, as though someone had traced my family tree and discovered that I had royal lineage, suddenly making me a member of the landed gentry. I couldn't see myself in the part, and I felt uncomfortable with the fact that Tom must have felt he'd owed me for something. If I hadn't run that kid out of town, any of his friends would have gladly done it. And maybe he would have been better off calling in the police and pressing charges. But he didn't think so. He'd appreciated my discretion and the fact that I hadn't passed any moral judgements. But that's what friends are for.

IX

ON TUESDAY, the clouds broke early in the wee hours as a high pressure system pushed in from the west, clearing out the rain. Though fall was officially three weeks away, it was an autumn day—clear and dry and cool. Summer had ended early, and the city seemed to breathe a sigh of relief, released from the weight of the heat and smog that had sat like a woolen cap on top of it for two months. The rains had washed away the grit, leaving everything fresh and sparkling.

The change in the air woke me early, and I padded around the house in the dark checking windows and doors, wondering what had roused me. Deep sleep still came hard after the months of keeping odd hours with a whiskey bottle. I finally noticed the blue-white moonlight falling on the patio, and opened the back door to breathe in the fresh air and look at the clearing night sky. It felt good, peaceful, even normal. I locked up and went back to bed.

When I woke again, it was nearly eight, and I felt refreshed. I pulled on shorts and sneakers for a quick run through the park before breakfast. I jogged easily, trying to limber up and not put too much pressure on the joints. The knees had complained loudly during the brief wet spell. I cut across the baseball diamonds at the south end of the park, and ran up the length of the lagoon, nodding at the fishermen who dangled lines in the water, meeting with an occasional cheery "good morning" as I passed by. I only went as far as Fullerton, then came back past the botanical gardens and the farm in the zoo.

When I rounded the corner toward my house, I saw a dark-clothed figure sitting on the top step. I stopped, startled and wary, then approached slowly as the man stood. There was no mistaking the round face and ruddy complexion.

"Hello, Ward." He came down the steps, hands in the pockets of his dark-blue trench coat.

"Hello, lieutenant. What brings you by?"

"Let's go for a walk." He took my elbow and turned me around to face the street. We walked slowly, shoulder to shoulder, toward the lake.

"Nice to be rid of that damned heat."

"And the rain, too," I said congenially. I would let him make the opening gambit, even if it took him all day to get around to it. This was no social visit.

"Yeah. You didn't get flooded, did you?"

"No. You?"

"Some, but no damage done. I've never gotten around to finishing off the basement as much as my wife nags me."

He led the way into a small playground near the corner of Astor, and motioned to a park bench. He sat on the other end and turned to face me, crossing his legs and draping an arm over the back of the bench. Two youngsters laughed loudly as they chased each other up and down a slide across the way under the watchful eye of a well-dressed young mother.

"What are you up to these days?" He was playing coy.

"Not much. Keeping busy with the usual—a few articles, thinking about starting a new book."

"Oh? What about?"

"I don't know yet. I said I was just thinking about it, that's all."

"How do you come up with ideas?" His interest seemed genuine.

"I read the paper. And just let my imagination run."

"And then you do research?"

"Sure, if I need to. Lieutenant, I know you have better things to do than ask how my writing's going. What's on your mind?"

He looked at me with a peculiar expression, rubbing his chin. "You've got a problem, friend."

"What's that?"

"You called me, remember, for a favor. It made me curious. You should never make me curious. If nothing else, I'm persistent. I checked around. It seems that we got a request from L.A.P.D. recently for a rundown on you. Want to tell me about it?"

"A close friend of mine dropped dead in a hotel room in L.A.," I said without hesitation. "I flew out to identify the body. It turned out she'd died of an overdose of cocaine."

"But you had nothing to do with it."

"No, I didn't."

"Then why did you want me to check up on Peter Harriman?"

"It's difficult to explain, lieutenant."

"Take your time. Like they say in the old country, 'He who made time, made plenty of it.'"

"Off the record?"

He hesitated, looking uneasy. "It depends. Okay, off the record."

"Look, my friend—Catherine McCrae—didn't do drugs. She never touched a line of cocaine in her life. I wanted to know why she had an ounce of coke in her stomach. I still want to know. For reasons I'd rather not go into, I thought Harriman might have something to do with it."

"Does he?"

"I don't know. You tell me if it's possible he *could* have had anything to do with it. I'm still trying to get a take on the guy."

He mused for a moment, staring at an inquisitive squirrel a few yards away. "Peter Harriman has no record. There is no reason to think that he's anything but what he appears to be—a well-known fashion photographer with expensive tastes."

"But? . . ."

"About three or four weeks ago, the DEA picked up a mule in Tucson carrying ten kilos of cocaine. They cut him a deal—lead them to the buyer and they'd go easy on him. The mule didn't know much. All he had was a place and time, no names. The agents figured it was better than nothing, so they flew up to Chicago with the guy to see what would shake loose. The deal was supposed to go down at an airport hotel room.

"It was a bad bust. Harriman was the occupant of the room. He had no money. He denied any knowledge of the deal, said he didn't know the man, and told the agents he was there waiting for a meeting with a client. The feds were left with ten keys of coke, a mule who knew nothing, and egg on their faces. But you think your friend might have been mixed up with Harriman, and your friend died from an O.D."

"Yeah, that's sort of how it goes. Look, I'm still trying to put together the pieces."

"Maybe I can help." He got no response. "You know, you owe me, Ward. I could have locked you up a long time ago when Jack Saldi was killed. The book's still open on that one. I read the papers, too, and I'm smart enough to guess that you know a whole lot more about Bertrand Culbertson's disappearance than the papers ever reported. Now, I don't think you're telling me half of what you know, and I can't help you if you don't help me out a little, too."

His words startled me. He had a long memory and was a lot smarter than I'd given him credit for. "I appreciate that, lieutenant, but I don't think I'm ready to let you in on this one. I really don't have anything to give you. What's the problem, anyway?"

He sighed. "I tried. Right now there is a DEA guy in my office who wants your head. Badly. I cooled him off and said I'd come talk to you. I thought maybe I could find out why everyone is suddenly so interested in you. Maybe I can help take some of the heat off."

"It's not me they're interested in. It's something they think I know, whoever 'they' are. That's why I can't help. I don't know what the hell's going on."

"Then they'll dig it out of you. They'll needle you until you tell them something they want to hear. These fellows from DEA don't have much of a sense of humor. I'm sorry, but I have to take you down to the station."

It was my turn to heave a sigh. "Can I put on some clothes first?"

"Sure. Come on. I'll wait while you change."

The man in Lanahan's office was a dry fellow named Feder. He was tall and thin with a long face and curly dark hair. His gray pin-stripe suit hung in straight, well-tailored lines over a white, crisply starched shirt and red silk tie. Lanahan had been right —he was steaming.

"Put him in a room," he snarled at Lanahan, looking at his watch as we came in. "I want to talk to you."

Lanahan motioned to someone outside the door, and a uniform came in to lead me to an interrogation room with graying, peeling walls, a table in the center under a fluorescent fixture, and four chairs. I took a seat and waited. It was only a few minutes before Feder slammed the door open and stalked in, followed by Lanahan.

"You are in it up to your eyeballs, friend. You better have some answers for me."

"I'm not your friend," I said quietly. "And until you ask the questions, I'm not sure I have answers to anything."

He stared at me for a minute, sizing me up. "You can go, lieutenant," he said, his eyes still on me.

"Uh-unh," Lanahan shook his head. "I'll stay. Your department asked me to cooperate, and I can't do that unless I know what you're trying to find out. Besides, this is my turf, Feder."

Feder looked at him long and hard, then finally shrugged his shoulders and turned back to me. Lanahan straddled a chair at the other end of the table while Feder paced silently for a moment.

"What were you doing in Florida last Tuesday?"

"Visiting friends."

"Who?"

"Dave and Sandy Roberts in Sarasota. Lido Key. You want the address?"

"Why did you meet Raul Gonzalez in Tampa if you were visiting friends in Sarasota?"

"I didn't. I never even heard of the guy. Who is he?"

"You deny being in Tampa?"

"No, but—"

"Who's Morgan?" he interrupted.

"Morgan Grant. A friend of mine."

"Did this Grant fellow have business with Raul Gonzalez?" He kept firing questions to throw me off balance.

"I told you, I don't know any Raul Gonzalez."

"You got a message that this Morgan was in Tampa, and you went there to meet him and set up a deal with Gonzalez, right? Only someone screwed up the deal and killed Gonzalez. Right?"

"Whoa! Hold it right there. You couldn't have possibly known about that message unless you had a tap on my phone. You get a court order for that, Feder?"

His face reddened. "I was told you asked the agency to find out who put a tap on your phone. That's informed consent. I don't need a court order."

"What the hell is this all about, anyway?"

He stared at me. "There may be a major drug war brewing down in Tampa, and I think you touched it off. I want to know what the hell you were doing in Tampa."

"I'd like to call my lawyer."

"We're getting nowhere here," he muttered, turning to Lanahan. "I want you to hold him until I can get an arrest warrant."

"On what charge?" I asked.

"Suspicion of murder. Conspiracy to commit a felony. Whatever I can get."

"Bullshit! You don't have enough to hold me." I thought for a moment. "Your attitude stinks, Feder, but I'll tell you what. Let's start over. We don't need lawyers or warrants. You tell me nicely what you really brought me down here for, and I'll see if I can answer your questions."

His eyes bulged, and his face turned even redder. A vein pulsed in his temple. But he held it all in.

"I'd tell him," Lanahan said quietly. "You can't hold him on the basis of that phone tap. It's inadmissible."

Feder looked first at Lanahan, then at me. Finally, he yanked a chair away from the table, twirled it around, and straddled it, sitting between us with a glum expression.

"You start," I said. "Why am I here?"

He stared at the table for a moment. "Someone at the agency made contact with you. I don't know why. It's an undercover job being run out of the Los Angeles office."

"You people don't talk to each other?" I was incredulous.

"Most of the time, yes. Unfortunately, we get too damned parochial at times. We weren't asked to cooperate on this one." He seemed embarrassed to admit it. "We were asked to monitor a tap on your phone. We found a little voice-activated recorder and transmitter on a pole in the alley in back of your house. We checked it last week. Someone had activated it. The last conversation on the tape was the message that Morgan was in Tampa. Yesterday, someone took the little box off the utility pole. We didn't see who." He said it quietly, with effort.

"I still don't see what that has to do with me being here."

"Like I said, sometimes we do talk to each other. The conversation on the tape meant nothing to us until we got a routine field report from Tampa. The Tampa police reported the shooting to us, figuring the deaths were drug-related. Gonzalez is a heavy dealer in the

Bay area down there. The other man was a fellow named Burt Antoly. We know Antoly dabbled in the business, but didn't think he was well-connected enough to deal with Gonzalez. Our Tampa office sent the report to us. Your name was listed as the only witness. I made the connection.

"Your turn. Who's this Morgan Grant?"

"I told you. A friend of mine. He disappeared a couple of weeks ago. His wife asked me to help find him. When we got the message that he'd been spotted in Tampa, I flew down to see if I could trace him."

"How did you end up in the middle of that shooting?"

"When I was looking for Grant, I saw Antoly. Grant's wife says he may have been doing some business with Antoly, so I followed him. He was the one doing the deal with Gonzalez."

"Jesus. This isn't even close to the report you filed. I don't know what to believe. I think I just wasted my time and energy here, Ward. I think you're a certifiable flake."

"Could be. Fact is, I like to keep a low profile. If I'd told it the way I just told you, the Tampa police might still be holding me for one reason or another. Which wouldn't make it very easy for me to find my friend. Besides, I did my civic duty—I reported it."

"Nuts." He looked at me in wonderment.

"By the way, has anyone matched the description I gave with a name?"

"Not likely. Next time, take a photo."

"Why don't you run the name Stan Graves through your computer and see what you come up with. And while you're at it, ask whoever's running this show in L.A. to check into this guy, too."

"Why should we?"

"Because I think he's your man. And I'd rather you people found him before he finds me. He saw me."

"Ward, you're too small time to worry about. The tap's off your phone, which tells me you're no longer of interest to anyone, including us. On the other hand, maybe this guy wants to cover his tracks. If so, you'll be in a whole lot deeper shit than you're in now. Maybe you should leave town for awhile and keep your nose out of places it doesn't belong. File a missing persons report on your friend and take a long vacation. That's the best advice I can give you."

"Thanks for the vote of confidence."

Feder got out of his chair and walked to the door. "Take my advice, Ward. It might keep you alive."

"He's not a happy man," Lanahan said quietly as the door closed.

"I didn't intend to make him happy."

"What does all this have to do with the woman who died in Los Angeles?"

"Frankly, lieutenant, I don't know. It may not have anything to do with it." His question made me wonder.

He was silent for a minute. "You know, Feder's right. You're playing this a little close to the edge. It could get you hurt."

"Look, I'm just making some inquiries, doing something that you probably don't have time for, anyway. How many runaway kids are you trying to find? How many murders do you have to solve? How many burglaries? I'm simply doing a favor for a friend, trying to find her husband."

"Okay, okay. I think you should go through proper channels, that's all. I can't stop you from asking questions, but we wonder about people who keep finding corpses. It looks suspicious."

"I'll remember that."

I was moderately grateful that Feder had not seen fit to throw me in a cell. But he'd turned me loose on the street with the admonishment that the DEA was no longer interested in me. Which meant that I would receive no help from that quarter.

I took a cab up to Catherine's apartment, but had the driver drop me at a corner a couple blocks away so I could buy a pack of cigarettes. Gillian looked up startled when I let myself in. She was sitting on the living room couch.

"You scared me."

"Sorry. How are you doing?"

"Okay. I'm bored."

"I know, I know. I don't think it'll be much longer, though. I think the DEA, at least, is convinced you're dead."

"Why? What happened?"

"I just had a conversation with a very irate fellow named Feder." I told her about my run-in with Feder down at the police station. "He didn't make the connection with Catherine's death in L.A. Whoever's running this show is keeping everything pretty close to the vest."

"But that cop thinks there's a connection. What's his name?"

"Lanahan? He's okay. He won't stick his nose in it unless he has more to go on. Right now he doesn't know any more than we do."

"You're still the center of attention, you know," she murmured.

"Yes and no. Feder knows that Morgan's partner was killed in Tampa, but doesn't know yet how closely they were tied together. If he finds out about that lease on the loft over on Clybourn, they'll throw my ass in jail. Damn Morgan anyway for putting me in the middle of this." I paused. "Feder also said the tap on my phone's gone. Which means that either someone's convinced I don't know anything, or they found out what they wanted to know." I thought for a moment, then suddenly felt a leaden ball burning in the pit of my stomach. "Shit."

"What is it?"

"The last call I got before the tap was taken off the phone was from Georgia to tell me that Morgan was in Tampa."

"So?"

"So, what would Graves be doing in Florida?"

"I don't know."

"Every run you made was from Mexico, right?"

"Yes." She nervously pulled at her lower lip.

"You were making deliveries to people in L.A. And Steve and Ed said they thought the distribution centers were Los Angeles and Chicago. Why would Graves even think of messing with the families in Florida? The Columbians down there don't take kindly to strangers. It's not Graves's turf. Which means that Morgan was somehow involved with distribution in Chicago. That's the only reason Graves could have been in Florida. He must have been after Morgan for some reason."

"Then he's in big trouble. Digger won't stop until he finds him."

"Maybe. The question is, where did Morgan go? Mexico's the key. It has to be. Tell me again where you went."

"Puerto Vallarta, Tijuana. I don't know—lots of places." There was a note of exasperation in her voice.

"Think, damn it. Go back to when it all started. This is important."

It took more than an hour. Gillian began slowly, trying to reconstruct the blur of parties and contacts and trips south of the border. I made her go back again and again, to pinpoint dates, to try to remember names of people and places, looking for anything, a common thread, that would lead me to Morgan, or Digger, or even bigger fish. I was tired of being paranoid, of living under a big question mark. I wanted to rattle somebody's cage and see what shook loose. I found a pencil and a piece of paper in the kitchen while Gillian was talking and took notes, full of pent-up nervousness. When Gillian was all talked out, I looked at my notes in silence, trying to make sense of it all.

"I think we have another problem," Gillian said finally.

"What now?"

"I think someone's watching the apartment."

"Where? How do you know?" My palms began to sweat.

"There's a guy in a car just down the block, on the other side of the street. He hasn't moved all morning."

"Why didn't you tell me?" I went to the window and cautiously pulled the blinds a fraction of an inch away from the frame.

"I was going to."

There was an old brown Chevy Nova across the street with someone in the driver's seat. I couldn't make out man's face. Smoke drifted out of the car window. Feder may not have made the connection with Cat's death, but Ed would have wanted to check it out, I realized. He would have started to wonder how one woman could lead the kind of double life that Cat and Gillian had led separately. I cursed myself. Feder had probably been told to put a man on stakeout without even knowing why.

"It could be nothing, just coincidence, but we can't take a chance. If the tap's off my phone, then maybe my house is the safest place for you right now."

"And a lot more convenient, huh?"

"Be serious." I looked at her curiously, silent for a moment. "I didn't think you objected," I said softly.

"I don't know." She smiled nervously. "Maybe I made a mistake. You're . . . different. I don't know. Maybe I'm just a little ashamed of myself."

"For what?" She dropped her eyes and wouldn't answer. "Look, I won't push you into anything you don't want. You can have the guest room. I'll be completely honorable. But we have to get you out of here, just in case. Pack your things, okay? I'll be back in twenty minutes to pick you up. When you hear me honk—two short and one long—come out the back door. Got it?"

"Yes. I'll be ready."

I left through the corridor and opened the back door slowly, then stepped through into the sunshine, sauntering away as though the prickling at the back of my neck wasn't really there. I walked a few blocks before I caught a cab. No one followed. Once home, I went out to the garage and started up the motor home. It rumbled grumpily to life, running roughly from disuse. I wheeled it out into the alley, closed the garage door behind me, and drove back to Cat's apartment, pulling up as close to the building as I could. A few moments after I honked, Gillian stepped through the doorway and right up the steps into the bus. She moved back into the interior and flopped onto the banquette at the little dining table.

I drove to the end of the alley and around the corner onto Armitage, heading back toward the front of the building. Driving slowly past the brown Chevy, I tried to get a look at the driver's face. He paid no attention to the bus, but stuck his head out the window, trying to see around us. I didn't recognize him. I pressed the accelerator, and we drove home in silence.

I called Ray on his beeper and left a message. I'd met him at one of the innumerable parties I'd attended, and had found him interesting. We'd spent some time talking, and though he knew I didn't do coke he'd offered to set me up with some if I ever wanted it. He'd also given me his beeper number in case I ran across someone who was looking to score. I was a little dismayed that I remembered the number so easily. He called back within twenty minutes, and I told him I needed to see him.

"I probably can't deliver until later tonight. How much did you want?"

"I don't," I replied hurriedly. "I need to talk to you. Have you got some time?"

"Sure. Business is a little slow right now. I could be at your place in, say, half an hour."

"Not my place. Someplace neutral." I thought a moment, then named a coffee shop up on Clark Street where I wasn't known. He agreed to meet me there.

Half an hour later, I sat in a booth in the coffee shop, watching the door. Ray was late. He was always late, according to his customers. I was nervous, but didn't know why—I wasn't consummating a deal. It was probably the thought of all the stupid things I'd done in the past few months. The waitress came by and took my order for coffee—decaffeinated. I stirred it absent-mindedly and lit a cigarette.

A cup of coffee and twenty minutes later, Ray came through the door. He was a small, wiry man with sharp features and a pencil mustache who drove a new pickup truck and carried a long-barreled .44 magnum. It was hard to tell if he carried it in the holster under the leather airman's jacket or if he'd left it in the truck. Despite the illegal firepower, he wasn't a heavy user or a hardened criminal. The few times we'd met he'd talked a little about himself. Very simply, he was a union laborer who'd been laid off and had fallen into dealing almost by accident, first acting as a go-between, then putting up the money for a couple ounces. He was a pleasant fellow, amiable but quick-tempered, not intellectually bright, but street-smart.

He paused at the door and gazed around the restaurant until he spotted me, then ambled casually back to the table.

"How's it going?" he smiled, sliding into the booth.

"Can't complain, I guess. You want anything?"

"Yeah, I think I will." He waved the waitress over and ordered coffee and a piece of pie. "What did your friends think of that last batch?" he asked when she was gone.

"It was good, I guess. I wouldn't know." I paused.

"That's cool."

"You're not mad that I'm not here to buy?"

He shrugged. "Why should I be? Nobody was forcing you. I been thinking about getting out of the business anyway."

"Why?"

"Too unpredictable. And the hours are terrible." He grinned.

"Business is bad?"

"Nah, I wouldn't say that. It's just changed a lot. It's riskier. Too many crazies now who'd just as soon kill you as look at you. The other day, this young chick I know was so hard up for some blow that she gave me her two-year-old as collateral until she could come up with the money for a half a gram. Can you believe that shit? I took the kid because I thought he'd be better off with me for a while, and I told his mother I wouldn't sell to her no more. I mean, that's crazy." He shook his head sadly. "So what can I do for you?"

"Have you noticed any new competition on the street lately?"

"As a matter of fact, yeah. There's been a lot of stuff around. Good stuff, too. It makes for stiff competition."

He confirmed a hunch. "I need a favor." I looked around nervously to be sure no one was within earshot. "I need to know where you get your stuff."

He gave me a funny look, then shrugged again. "I call my guy, and either he has it or he doesn't."

"Where does he get it?"

This time the look on his face was unpleasant. "What are you after?"

"Look, I'm not trying to scam you, or move in on your business. I really need this favor, Ray."

"I could get into a lot of trouble for asking." He spoke cautiously. "You know how it is. The stuff comes in. Word gets out that it's available. Someone puts a label on it, like 'Peruvian flake,' and I get a phone call from my guy, or I call him if my customers have been asking for it. My guy's pretty reliable, but I try a little and if I like it, I buy enough to fill orders I know I'll get from my regulars. Shit, I don't know where he gets it, and I don't ask. He gets it from some guy, and maybe that guy gets it from somebody else."

"I need to know, Ray. I need to get to the source."

He stared at me impassively. "Why?"

I told him. I told him everything, or as much as I knew, and I told him what I had in mind. I couldn't think of any other way to do it but to trust him and see if he could help. It took a while, and he stared at me wordlessly while I talked, occasionally taking a bite of his pie. He rubbed his chin when I finished.

"You're crazy, you know."

"Maybe. Does that mean you won't help?"

"Oh, I'll help—if I can. I just think you're nuts, that's all." He fell silent for a moment, staring into space. "Okay, here's what you do. Sit tight for a couple, three, four days and let me see what I can find out. I'll call you as soon as I hear something. Don't bother me on the beeper, okay?"

"Okay."

"Thanks for the coffee." He slid out of the booth and stood, then spoke softly. "I think I know you pretty good. You always been square with me. But if this is a setup, I'll kill you myself."

"You won't have to." I watched him go with an involuntary shudder.

It was two days before he called. Gillian was sullen and remote the whole time. I tried to entice her out of her mood with offers to play backgammon or cards, but she insisted on staying cooped up in the guest room reading books and magazines, coming down only for meals. After a day of weathering the frost emanating from her room, I quit trying and gave her a wide berth. I had enough to do without worrying about her change in attitude, but it puzzled me. And I was uncomfortable with the self-analysis my subconscious kept trying to shove in front of my nose.

The phone rang just after dinner on Thursday. "It's Ray," the voice on the line said. "I can do that favor for you tonight. Be at the Logan Square el station at eleven. Take public transportation, and make sure you're not followed. Got it?"

"Yeah, I got it."

"Are you carrying?"

"No." The question startled me. I didn't like the thought of having a gun in the house.

"Good. Don't. Catch you later." The phone went dead.

I finished washing the dishes, then went upstairs to tell Gillian I was going out. She didn't even look up from her reading, so I turned to go. She stopped me.

"Emerson, you don't have to do this, you know." She sat cross-legged on the bed, long hair hiding half her face.

"Yes, I do," I said quietly. "I have to know why she died. There's this gnawing in my gut, this guilt that tells me I may have been responsible somehow."

"Stop." She put her hands on her ears, and her eyes searched my face. When I said nothing more, she took her hands away. "I've been thinking that maybe I could go to the DEA, turn myself in. This has all gone too far. It's gone on long enough. I can't hide forever. Maybe they'll give me a new identity or something."

"And what will you tell them that they don't already know? You don't have anything to bargain with. They'll lock you up and throw away the key. Or worse, turn you loose so Digger can finish what he started. No, I'll do it my way, thanks."

She said nothing, but when I turned to go once more, I heard her murmur softly, "Be careful."

I changed into jeans and a light windbreaker, then killed a little time downstairs before walking out the front door and locking it behind me. At the Clark and Division subway station, I caught a southbound train into the Loop, taking careful note of the passengers who got on with me. Downtown, I took the pedestrian tunnel over to the Dearborn subway, casually looking around to see who might have gotten off with me. I let two trains go by, and when I was satisfied that no one was interested in me, I stepped through the doors of the next train. It rumbled noisily out of the station and into the dark tunnel, its screeching steel wheels reverberating against the close walls.

I found an unoccupied bench on the Logan Square platform and settled in for a wait, lighting a cigarette. It was a little before eleven, and Ray would be late as usual. The platform was nearly deserted, and as trains pulled in and out of the station only a few people disembarked each time. No one paid attention to me. At about 11:20, Ray got off the last car of a Loopbound train. He walked past me without a word, and a moment later I got up and sauntered after him. He led the way up the escalator to the street, disappearing from view. When I emerged into the night air, I looked around to see where he'd gone. He came up behind me silently.

"Got a light?" He held out an unlit cigarette.

"Sure." I dug in the pocket of the windbreaker for a lighter.

He leaned in close, cupping his hands around the flame. "Any problems?"

"No."

"Let's go."

He turned on his heel and started off. I caught up quickly and matched his stride. We walked a few blocks to where he'd parked his pickup truck, and he unlocked the passenger door for me. He climbed in the other side, closed the door, and sat silently, resting his forearms on the wheel.

"Aren't we going somewhere?"

"Nah." He turned to look at me in the darkened cab. "I had to think about this long and hard, man. Like I said, the business gets crazier by the day. Too many people willing to blow holes in you over nothing, man." He paused. "After I talked to you the other night? The union got me my job back."

"Hey, that's great."

"Yeah, so I figured it's about time to get out. I wanted to let you know. I cleared up all my accounts, sold off all my inventory, and then called in all the markers I had coming. If it hadn't been you—if it hadn't been your woman that was killed—I might not have done it, but I figured, what the hell, I'll do this last favor, since I'm getting out of the business."

I started to thank him, but he held a hand out. "Just so you know how it is." He paused. "You want a guy named Harriman."

"How did you find out?"

"Better you shouldn't know, but a promise is a promise." He shrugged. "Word on the street gets out. When the deals are big and the coke is good, the rumors fly about who is supplying it. But I got even more. Like I said, I called in some markers. The stuff is coming in through Mexico."

"How?"

"I don't know."

"Where, then?"

"Slow down. This wasn't easy. I know this guy who's tight with one of the families in town—one of the Bolivians, Juan Carlos Olavarria. You heard of him, right? Who hasn't? The Bolivians run everything, even here. Anyway, this guy, Ramon, he's not really a player, but he trades information. He has a cousin in La Paz, down in Baja who says that there's a lot of stuff moving through there."

"Can I get to him?"

"You really want Harriman bad, don't you?" He looked at me for a minute. "Okay, then, what you do is ask around town for 'El Gaucho.' If he wants to talk to you, he'll find you. When he does, you tell him Ramon sent you. Maybe he'll talk to you. That's all I've got."

I let it all sink in. "It's better than nothing."

"It's a lot." Ray looked at me hard. "Look, man, I told you everything I could get because I want you to know this is it. You don't call me no more, and you leave my name out of it. I'm going back to work, and I'm putting this business behind me. It was fun while it lasted. Now I'm through."

"I understand, and I want you to know I appreciate it, Ray."

"Hey, we had some good times, didn't we?" He punched me lightly on the shoulder and flashed a smile. His face quickly turned serious again. "Good luck, man. I really hope you find what you want. But don't forget, if any of this comes back to me, I'll come looking for you."

"I hear you, Ray. Loud and clear."

I climbed down from the cab, and with a last look, he drove away.

X

"I WANT to go with you."

"You can't, and you know it."

"But I've been there. I could help you find your way around." Gillian lay sprawled on my bed, clad in only jeans and a sweatshirt, watching me pack. She reminded me of a teenager who'd been grounded, pleading with first one parent, then the other, trying to get one to relent by exasperating them both.

"No, it's too dangerous. Draw me maps. Show me pictures. But do it quickly. I have to leave in twenty minutes."

It was early Saturday morning, and I had a reservation on a nine o'clock flight to San Diego. It had been almost one in the morning when I'd eventually found a cab to take me home. I'd slept like the dead for ten hours, then had scrambled Friday afternoon to get airline tickets and cash.

First I checked one of the customized hiding places that had been added to the motor home when I'd had it refurbished. Under the queen-sized platform bed in the master stateroom was a spare fresh-water tank. Hidden catches released a hinged lid on a separate portion of the tank. Most of the cash was gone—not working for six months had taken its toll. I drained the two bank accounts, checking and savings, emptied all the cash reserves from the hidey-hole in the bus, and took the largest cash advance I could on one of the credit cards.

It came to a little more than twenty-one thousand. I banded it, distributing it as evenly as possible inside the lining of a leather jacket. I wanted to keep it as close to me as possible, both in and out of Mexico. I fully intended to bring the bulk of it back, if I made it back. But I thought I might need to flash a substantial bankroll in my newly adopted guise of drug dealer.

"Leave the answering machine on and don't answer the door while I'm gone if you can help it." I zipped the small carry-on bag closed. "If someone does find you here for some reason, I asked you to watch the house while I'm on vacation. Call Brandt immediately if that happens. The refrigerator's full, and I'll leave some cash so you can order in food if you run out. If you have to go out for anything, for God's sake try to cover your face."

"Yes, 'Daddy.' " She looked at me petulantly, her full lips pouting. "How long will you be gone?"

"I don't know. If I can't find this guy, or nothing turns up, I'll be back in a few days. If I get a lead, it could take longer. I'm not sure what to expect." I thought for a moment. "If you haven't heard from me one way or another in two weeks, I'm probably dead. Let's say the nineteenth. Give me until then."

"You want me to stay cooped up here for two weeks?"

"If need be," I snapped. A wave of anger washed over me. Her complaining had become a major source of irritation, and I realized I was tired of playing the parent. My displeasure was quickly replaced by a sad sense of resignation.

"Look, you do whatever you want, go wherever you want. We don't owe each other anything, and if you'd rather be out on the street, that's your business. I thought I was trying to help. I thought I was keeping you alive, but maybe I'm wrong. You're a big girl. You can take care of yourself. Just do me a small favor. If you decide to leave, give this to Brandt before you go." I pulled an envelope out of my pocket and handed it to her. "If you stay, and I haven't contacted you by the nineteenth, give it to him then. He'll know what to do."

She took the envelope from me hesitantly, a look of shock and confusion on her face. Maybe she hadn't realized that she was free to go all along. After all, she'd sought me out. I didn't have time to figure out why a tear suddenly rolled silently down the side of her face. It was time to go. I picked up my small bag and started out the door, wondering if I would ever come back, thinking about the letter I'd written to Brandt. I'd composed it carefully late the night before.

Brandt, if you're reading this, it means that I'm not coming back. I am, or will be, dead, most likely at the bottom of the ocean with my feet chunked into a bucket of cement, or left in the desert somewhere for the vultures to pick clean my bones. It doesn't matter.

The woman who gives you this is Gillian McCrae, Catherine's sister (obviously). She should inherit Catherine's estate, and I know you'll figure out the best way to handle it. She needs a little direction, so I suggest you resist what will probably be her wish to sell everything off and take the money. Make her a manager of one of the stores or something. Put her to work and help her along. Keep an eye on her. She's not a bad sort, but she takes a little getting used to.

I'm sorry I haven't been a very good friend lately.

I'm leaving to try to put a stop to some of the madness that killed Catherine. And I've fallen deep enough into this that I know these people play for keeps. If you're reading this, then I probably wasn't much better at playing avenger than I was at being a friend.

Contrary to what you told me, it wasn't just the drinking. It's something deeper, something that I haven't been able to put my finger on. It has something to do with me, with my sense of self-worth. Life just seems to have lost its purpose. I'm not sure what I want anymore. Catherine was trying to show me, but I wouldn't let her. Her death made me want to live, at least long enough to get even, and maybe I'll have enough time to find out what's off kilter about my life.

I told Gillian to give you this on the nineteenth. If you can get the Mexican authorities to confirm my death, then everything here belongs to you. Mike Lansing has my will. Sell it all—the house, the bus, the Alfa—and use the money to set up a scholarship fund for needy kids or something. I know you'll do something nice with it. And throw a party for me, like we did for Tom, and for Jessica.

The plane descended between the fluffy cotton-ball clouds in a blue California sky and landed in San Diego a little past eleven. But for the breeze blowing in off the Pacific, it would have been as hot as it had been in Chicago a week or so earlier. I took a bus from the airport to San Ysidro and walked across the border into Tijuana, making sure I got my tourist card validated properly. I was still optimistic enough to believe I could make it home. A cab took me to the Tijuana airport where I caught a late afternoon flight to La Paz.

La Paz was warmer still, even as the sun dipped low in the sky, and I finally shed the leather jacket on the cab ride into town. I shunned the bigger beach hotels and went downtown to find a room at the Hotel Perla on Obregon, the main street running past the waterfront and the commercial wharf. There was no problem getting a room. Despite the Labor Day weekend, it was still summer—the tourist season hadn't really started.

I found the room, unpacked, and washed up. Stripping to briefs, I pulled the covers off the bed, lay down on the cool sheets, and let the travel fatigue roll me under into a light sleep. When I awoke, it was dusk. I set my watch back two hours, and dressed in drawstring cotton pants, sandals, and a loose-fitting cotton shirt.

The hotel had a sidewalk cafe. My Spanish is limited to pleasantries, but I can find my way around a menu. The food was plain, but good, living up to the cafe's reputation as the most traditional place in town.

The night was warm, soft, and dry despite the salty smell of sea, and the moon was almost full and brilliant in the clear air. After dinner, I strolled down the waterfront, getting a feel for the place, trying to change gears and slip into the modulated pace of life south of the border. My greenbacks were welcome, but I was still a gringo, and I had to remember that *mañana* was the watchword down here. The town was quiet. A few men milled around the commercial wharf, chatting quietly, and I heard the soft strumming of a guitar somewhere down near the water. The nightlife was probably all at the larger hotels down the waterfront, the Gran Hotel Baja and the Hotel Los Arcos.

A few blocks inland, I stopped in a cantina for a

nightcap. All eyes looked my way when I entered, then turned away disinterestedly. There were a dozen locals at the tables. Empty stools ringed the bar. I hitched myself up on one. The bartender ambled slowly toward me.

"*Cerveca, por favor. Negra Modelo.*" The bartender shuffled away and pulled a bottle out of a cooler, uncapped it, and set it on the bar. As I pulled some money out of my pocket, I switched to English. "I'm looking for someone here in La Paz. He's called The Gaucho."

The bartender looked at me impassively.

"I said I wondered if you know a man named El Gaucho."

The bartender shrugged. "*Yo no hable Inglés, señor.*"

I handed him a couple of singles and took a pull on the beer. I hoped I would have better luck elsewhere, or I would have to find an interpreter. I finished the beer quickly, and went back to the hotel to fall into a deep, dreamless sleep.

Sunday dawned bright and clear, and the azure blue of the Bahia de La Paz sparkled across the way. Street sounds floated through the open window—rumbling traffic, barking dogs, and laughing children. Mountains rose up sharply a little distance to the east and west, rocky and barren, like vertebrae up the thousand-mile spine of the Baja Peninsula.

I splashed water on my face and dressed in sandals, shorts, and a short-sleeved shirt, knowing that the temperature would likely hit a hundred degrees by midmorning. The cafe served dark Mexican coffee and *huevos* for breakfast. Sitting in the morning sun, I realized why the pace was so slow. There was no need to hurry, particularly in the heat. Life was to be enjoyed, savored. Questions that suddenly became important were ones like how blue the sky could get, how white the sand, how big the fish that might be tempted by the lure. Nothing else mattered.

It was mid-morning when I pushed myself away from the table and forced myself to crisscross town methodically, starting at the waterfront. I worked my way inland one block at a time, picking my spots carefully, asking if anyone knew of El Gaucho. I was met with indifferent, impassive faces that smiled politely, but looked at me blankly when I asked my questions.

La Paz is no small town. It's a small city, and by mid-afternoon, I was dog-tired, parched, and grumpy from lack of success. The sun beat down relentlessly, and the straw sombrero I bought at a curio shop provided little relief. A dim cantina and a beer provided a little more. At five-thirty, I quit in disgust, and wandered slowly back to the hotel through the dusty streets, dying for a cold shower.

Monday's luck was not much better. I talked with people in *mercados* and *farmacias*, in *luncherias* and *tortillerias*, in *cantinas* and *taller mecanicos*, businesss-es both large and small, but no one seemed to have heard of The Gaucho. Those who spoke no English gave me a shrug and a "*no comprende*," and those who understood me gave me a shrug and said they didn't know any cowboys except the occasional tourist from Texas decked out in full regalia.

Late Monday afternoon, I gratefully gulped a Corona with lime in the hotel cafe, confident of only one thing. I'd gotten the word out—a crazy gringo was looking for the mythic El Gaucho. If he existed at all, he would hear that I was looking for him. If nothing happened in two days, I would go home with only a little sunburn for my trouble.

One of the brown-skinned street urchins hovered on the sidewalk, his large brown eyes searching among the tables. He was dressed in grimy cutoffs and T-shirt, and his feet were bare. Like the dogs that roamed the city, they were everywhere, flocking around the RVs that trundled slowly through town, offering to wash windshields for a few pesos, or gathered down at the wharf and on the street corners offering to shine shoes, sell trinkets, act as guides, or anything else they could do for a little pocket change.

A waiter tried to shoo the boy away, but he artfully dodged the man's grasp and darted in among the tables, coming straight to me. I reached into my pocket for a coin and flipped it to him. The boy caught it and slipped it into his pocket in a fast, graceful move.

"*Señor, señor,*" he said excitedly. He pulled my arm with one hand, and motioned for me to follow him with the other, glancing over his shoulder. The waiter was fifteen feet away, striding toward the table with an angry expression. "*El Gaucho,*" the boy said, crooking his finger.

He had my attention. "You'll take me to him?" I stood.

"*Si, si!*" He tugged at my arm.

I waved the waiter away, left some money on the table, then followed the boy into the street. He danced excitedly in front of me and began to lead me inland through a maze of city streets. Stores gave way to residences, at first clean and neat, then more ramshackle and run-down as we entered the heart of the city's living quarters. Windowless structures with holes in the roofs and sported clotheslines laden with colorful fabric flapping like signal flags. There were relics in the driveways. I felt a little uncomfortable as we walked down the dirt streets, knowing I stood out like a sore thumb.

It was half an hour before the boy stopped in front of a house like all the rest and pointed at it, motioning me to go ahead.

"El Gaucho," he said firmly.

I fished out a dollar and gave it to him. He took it shyly, then bolted away, disappearing quickly down the street. There was an old Toyota next to the house, with orange tongues of flame painted on the hood. A low wire fence stretched around the yard, enclosing a date palm and little else. A sheet of galvanized steel had been hung over the front door as a porch roof. Like the neighboring houses, the window frames were empty. I pushed open the gate and walked hesitantly up to the front door. Before I could knock, a man appeared on the other side of the screen.

"Come in, quickly." He opened the door, and I pushed past him into the dim interior.

"El Gaucho?"

The man laughed. "José." He was dressed in a blue denim shirt and jeans. Sticking out beneath the cuffs of the jeans were a shiny pair of five-hundred-dollar lizardskin cowboy boots. "You should not have given the boy so much money. Now he will be spoiled. Come and sit. *Cerveca?*"

I nodded, curious. He led the way into a large room that was furnished sparely. I took a seat on a worn couch while he disappeared into another room. I hadn't expected such a friendly reception. He came back into the room and handed me a cold bottle of beer.

"You have been asking many questions about me, *señor*. You must want to see me very badly."

"Ramon sent me."

His eyebrows rose a notch. "My cousin. What is it you wish to see me about, *señor?*"

"Cocaine."

"You have money?"

"Enough to interest anyone who might be selling."

He scratched his head. "Buying and selling drugs is a serious crime in Mexico, *señor*. The penalties for smuggling are very harsh, and our prisons are very unpleasant. I would not do anything so foolish. I am not in that business, *señor*."

"I didn't say I wanted to buy drugs from you. I've heard there are large quantities of very pure cocaine being moved through Mexico, perhaps La Paz. I want to know where it's coming from and where it's going."

"Ah, you want information. I would be happy to sell you information."

There was silence until I realized that he'd cued me. I dug in my pocket, pulled out the cash I had on hand, and peeled off a hundred. He took it from my outstretched fingers and stuffed it into a shirt pocket.

"As I said, the penalties for smuggling are very harsh. There is no drug traffic in La Paz that I'm aware of."

I peeled off another hundred, but when he moved to take it, I held it tight and moved my hand out of his reach.

He looked at me for a moment, then grinned. "We have no drugs in La Paz, but you may be interested in a boat that came into the harbor at Pichilingue, up the road."

"Why?" Pichilingue was forteen miles up the coast. Its harbor was deeper than that of La Paz, so most deep-draft boats docked there, including the ferries from the mainland and most ocean-going vessels. An industrial park had been built there for businesses that needed access to the sea.

"It was a shrimper."

"I don't understand."

"The shrimpers rarely come south of Bahia de Los Angeles, *señor*. One does not see them in these waters. There are no shrimp here."

"You think it may have been carrying cocaine?"

"Hard to say. The shrimpers are all run by cooperatives. The cooperatives, in turn, are controlled by the government. It would take much of *la mordida* for a shrimper to get that kind of cargo past the *federales*. But nothing is impossible, *señor*."

"Is the boat still there?"

"No. It left the harbor three days ago."

"Where did it go?"

"How would I know?"

He'd told me something, yet he'd told me nothing. I pulled out my wallet and found the tattered picture of Morgan and showed it to him.

"Have you seen this man? He's big, bigger than I am."

He took the picture and studied it, frowning. "No.. But he's big you say?" I nodded. "I heard of a big gringo in town lately. I like to listen to the gossip, you know." He grinned.

"Where could I find him?" My hopes lifted.

"There is a *Norte Americano*, a gringo, who works at the Marina Gran Baja. You could ask him. His name is Jack. He may have seen your friend."

I stood up. "*Gracias*, José." I handed him the money. It quickly disappeared into his shirt pocket with the rest.

"I hope you find what you are looking for. Where will you go now?"

"Back to the hotel."

"Let me drive you, *señor*. We don't have much crime here in La Paz, but it's better not to walk after dark. One never knows."

We went out the back door and got into the old Toyota. It rumbled to life with a cough and a snort, spitting smoke, and we rattled back down to the waterfront. He dropped me off at the hotel.

"If I hear of anything you might be interested in, I will find you," he said as I climbed out of the car. He waved and roared off.

I went looking for the gringo named Jack first thing in the morning. The marina was quiet, with a few sportfishing boats getting ready to go out for the day. The bulk of the boats in the slips were small cabin cruisers tied up for only a day or two while their owners replenished supplies and saw the town. There was only an old Mexican manning the gas pumps on the dock. He spoke no English. Through charadelike sign language, he made it understood that Jack would not be there until about ten.

With more than an hour to kill, I walked over to the hotel to find a taxi to take me to Pichilingue. I couldn't make the driver understand that I wanted to find the harbor master, so I looked for a building flying the Mexican flag and had him drop me off when we got there.

The building down near the docks housed *Immigracion*, the ticket office for the ferry, the state fishing license bureau, and other government functions. I wrangled with the language and a host of uniformed officials for nearly an hour before I found one who seemed to know about the comings and goings of boats in the harbor. But when I asked about a shrimper in the harbor within the last week, I was met with a peculiar expression.

"No, *señor*, I do not know of any shrimp boat in this harbor. They are not common here, though as you can see, we have many fishing vessels. Perhaps it was here for engine repairs. If one was here and then left, it probably would have gone north. I don't know where."

Frustrated and hot, I found another taxi to take me back to town. The old Mexican on the pier at the Marina Gran Baja flashed me a toothless grin and pointed off to my right. I turned and saw a muscular blond man in cutoffs and a tank top working on the small beach, hauling windsurfers out of a thatch-roofed shed. He was tanned almost as dark as a native, and his hair was bleached by the sun. I strolled off the pier and onto the beach.

"*Hola. Buenos dias.*"

"Yeah, sure." As I approached, the man stopped, looked up, and wiped the sweat off his forehead with the back of a hand.

"Emerson Ward." I stuck out my hand, but he ignored it. "You're Jack?"

"That's me. What can I do for you?" His voice had a little twang in it.

"I'm looking for a friend of mine. Maybe you can help me."

"Maybe. You a guest at the hotel?"

"No." I pulled out the picture of Morgan and showed it to him. "I heard you might have seen this guy in the past week."

He looked at the photo, then at me, his face impassive. "Nope. Sorry."

"Look again. I'm sure you must have seen him."

"Are you calling me a liar?" His jaw set, and there was anger in his eyes. "Look, man, if you don't want to rent a windsurfer, then get off the beach. This is hotel property." He was too defensive.

He turned away, and I put a hand on his arm to stop him. "This is really important."

He shrugged my hand off his arm. "Get lost." He put his fingertips on my chest, and gave me a little shove.

I took a step backward and planted my feet in the soft sand. "I'm not leaving until you tell me where he is."

He'd had a fight with his girlfriend, or maybe he'd had too much to drink the night before. Whatever it was, he was hiding something and was just itching to take his hostility out on someone. A flicker in his eyes gave him away, and I managed to get my hands and elbows up and my shoulders hunched just before he landed his first swing. He fought like a brawler with big, heavy, wild swings. I took about four or five blows on the upper arms, then saw an opening and jabbed with a left. It smacked him on the bridge of the nose, and he sat down heavily in the sand, his hands going to his face. I stood over him warily, waiting for his next move, tingling with the sudden rush of adrenaline. But he sat there unmoving, tears in his eyes from the pain.

"Shit, I think you broke it." His fingers gingerly felt his nose. There was no blood.

"It'll heal." His pride might take a little longer than the nose. "Now, you want to tell me where my friend is?"

"What do you want him for?" He blinked up at me.

"He's a friend of mine. His wife's worried about him. I just want to talk to him, make sure he's okay."

"Yeah, he was around a few days ago. I ran into him in a bar. I recognized him. At least I recognized his voice. I used to listen to him on the radio back in Texas a long time ago. Called himself J.P. Morgan on the air. We got to talking. He said he was in some kind of trouble, asked me a few questions, and told me if anyone was looking for him I should act like I hadn't seen him. He hung around town for a couple of days, then he split."

"What kind of questions?"

"I don't know. He was looking for someone. It sounded like he was after someone in the drug trade. I couldn't help him. I don't know anything about that shit."

"Where did he go?"

"He said something about Rocky Point. Asked me if I knew it."

"And?"

"Puerto Peñasco, man. It's a little town in Sonora, up north, at the top of the Gulf. I don't know why he'd want to go there. There's nothing there. A few fishing boats, some condos on the beach. Can I get up now?"

I gave him a hand and pulled him to his feet. "How long ago did he leave?"

"Maybe three days. Yeah, I think it was Saturday."

"How far is this Rocky Point?"

"Damn near a thousand miles, man."

"Then I guess I'll have to fly. Know any good pilots?"

"Look, man, you're asking an awful lot." Some of the bravado was back in his voice. "I don't know who you are or what you're after, but there must be something in this for me."

I sighed, weary of pulling money out of my pocket. The whole damn country operated on gratuities. Now I understood why they called it *la mordida*, "the death bite." I came up with about fifty dollars and some change. I gave him the bills. "It's all I've got, pal."

He stuffed it into his shorts pocket without looking at it. "Go out to the airport—to the hangers, not the terminal—and ask for Miguel. He's got a single-engine Cessna, and he'll take you wherever you want to go so long as you're not carrying contraband."

"Thanks." I left him there nursing his bruised nose and ego. My shoulders and elbows ached. He'd had a lot of raw power in his swings. And my knuckles were as sore as his nose, but I felt good. My reflexes were still pretty quick, and I'd learned more than I'd expected to.

I packed up everything, settled my bill at the hotel, and caught a taxi to the airport within forty-five minutes. I found Miguel without too much trouble, and after some dickering, we agreed on a price of a hundred an hour for the plane, half now and half when we got there. It took another forty-five minutes for him to gas the plane and file a flight plan. Finally, he reappeared and said we were ready to go. He climbed into the pilot's seat, and I stepped up on the landing gear, threw my bag in the back, and climbed into the copilot seat, strapping myself in.

"I hope you took a piss," Miguel said, grinning as he fired up the engine. "It's a long flight." Before I could answer we were bumping down the taxiway.

It *was* a long flight—six hours—and the sun was low on the horizon when we circled the airstrip at Puerto Peñasco. I didn't see it at first, then I saw the hanger and a few small planes parked in the sunshine, and the gray tarmac standing out in contrast to the brown desert floor.

The tarmac was like a blast furnace, absorbing the 110-degree heat and reflecting it back, burning through the soles of my shoes. They radioed a taxi from the small operations building while I settled with Miguel. He asked if I minded sharing the cab so he could get a bite to eat while his plane was refueled. He was going to make the return trip that night.

"Full moon," he laughed. "It's going to be a beautiful night for flying."

The ride into town was hot. It was desolate country. Behind us, distant mountains rose straight off the desert floor. Nothing grew for thirty miles to the north but brown, sunburned creosote bushes. The desert did not begin to turn green again until the border at Lukeville —the southern edge of Organ Pipe National Monument in Arizona. Puerto Peñasco was built at the foot of a barren, rocky promontory rising a hundred feet in the air. Beyond was the flat, blue calm of the Sea of Cortez.

I'd never seen a more inhospitable place to live—desert on one side, salt water on the other. The natives were friendly enough, though. The taxi driver wanted to take me to one of the larger hotels in town, but I insisted on something simple. He finally acceded and took me to a little motel on the other side of the harbor. They had a room with a bath. I paid for a couple of days in advance and collected my room key. When I found the room, I gratefully stripped and stepped into a cool shower for a long time.

In the morning, I walked through town to get a feel for the layout. To the west was a gently curved beach stretching for miles and dotted with recreational vehicles and campers, a kind of blue-collar tent city. The center of town lay to the south, on the other side of the harbor. Someone had dredged the channel into the little inlet and expanded the small harbor to a square the size of about six football fields. It contained a hundred or more shrimp boats, all gang-tied together, stretching from the docks out into the middle of the harbor.

The town was sleepy, dusty, and hot. A few green citrus trees, palms, and bougainvillea bushes lent color to the monotonous white and brown buildings. It would have been quaint had it not looked so tired and rundown. Poverty here was closer to the surface than in the city of La Paz. A number of buildings with the names of the cooperatives that José had mentioned made it obvious that fishing was the primary industry. Tourism was the other major moneymaker, and just on the other side of the promontory, modern, white stucco condos with orange tile roofs stretched for miles down the town's other beach, weekend havens for *Norte Americanos* from Phoenix, Tucson, and San Diego.

Most of the shops were empty, but I showed Morgan's picture around anyway. At noon, I found an air-conditioned *luncheria*, and stopped for sustenance —cold beer and an excellent shrimp ceviche. I lingered over lunch, reluctant to go back out in the heat.

When siesta time was over, I mustered the energy to

walk up the street to the Viña del Mar hotel. Morgan hadn't registered. I found a taxi outside the hotel, and spent the rest of the afternoon checking the other hotels and motels in town. Morgan had to be strapped for cash by now, and wouldn't likely be staying in a hotel, no matter how inexpensive, but I went through the exercise.

I finally called it quits for the day and walked down to the beach for a long swim in the warm Gulf. And after an enormous dinner of broiled shrimp, *carne asada*, and lots of beer, I found a deck chair on the motel's courtyard patio, and sat looking at the moon, thinking of nothing.

I roamed the public beach the next morning, kicking along in the sand, asking campers if they'd seen the man in the photo I carried. There were more Mexican families than American, so I was answered most often with a silent shrug and a shake of the head. It wasn't an unpleasant way to spend a few hours—looking at shells, taking an occasional plunge in the sea to cool off, chatting with total strangers—but it was fruitless.

When I trudged back up over the hill, something was different—the harbor appeared empty. When I drew closer, though, I could see the shrimp-boat masts barely sticking above the level of the piers like a forest of toothpicks. The tide had gone out, and with the effect of a full moon, the boats had dropped about twenty feet. Some even rested on muddy bottom close to shore. It was eerie. Suddenly, a light went on in my head.

José had said a shrimper in La Paz was unusual. But it wouldn't be here. Like me, Morgan had gone to

La Paz, but had left a day after the shrimper had left port to come here, to Rocky Point. What better place? It was only sixty miles from the border. Cocaine could be smuggled across in tourists' cars, or flown across in a light plane. A plane could land practically anywhere in that desert. Watch the harbor for a lone, inbound shrimp boat, and I'd probably find Morgan.

After lunch, I took my straw hat, a bottle of sun-screen, and a paperback book to the waterfront, and found a bench in the park between the harbor and shoreline. It gave me a clear view of the harbor entrance and a pretty view of the Gulf and the long stretch of beach to the west. I settled in and got comfortable. Not more than two hours and half a book later, I heard a familiar voice call my name a few feet behind me.

"Hey, Emerson!" I turned to see the smiling face of Morgan Grant. "I heard you've been looking for me."

XI

THE HOT SUN beat down, reflecting brightly off the sea, shimmering off the desert in the distance. It was a foreign environment, and I suddenly realized how angry I was. I jumped off the park bench and squared off in front of Morgan. "You son-of-a-bitch! Come on, let's have it out. Right here, right now!"

He took a step back and put his hands up, palms out. "Whoa. I don't want to mix it up with you."

"Let's go, damn you! I want a piece of your ass, you bastard!"

"I deserve that, but I won't fight you. Calm down."

"Chickenshit." I dropped my arms. The anger started to fade. "You set me up, damn it."

"The lease?" He winced when I nodded. "You weren't supposed to find out about that."

"What did you expect to happen? You set it up so if something went wrong, your name wouldn't be tied to it."

"Nothing was supposed to go wrong."

"Well?"

He looked good, slimmed down some and sporting a healthy sunburn. I'd expected him to look more like a fugitive—wan unshaven face, unkempt clothes—but he didn't. He had on worn jeans, a blue denim work shirt, and leather sandals, and looked more like a native than a tourist.

"Let's sit for a minute," he said, pulling a pair of

mirrored aviator glasses out of his shirt pocket. "Give me your hat. I don't like being out in the open for too long."

I sat and turned to face him. "Georgia's been worried sick about you."

"I figured. But I couldn't risk calling her. I didn't want her involved. How is she?"

"She's fine. Just worried, that's all."

He was silent for a moment. "How'd you find me, anyway?"

"A little perserverance and a lot of luck."

"It's important. I have to know if anyone could be following me." He seemed nervous.

I told him everything that had happened, starting with the day he disappeared, about the phone calls, and the tap on my phone, and Catherine's death. I explained about finding the loft space on Clybourn, and Gillian's sudden appearance, and then the phone call to Dave Roberts in Tampa. He listened intently, a mixture of surprise and concern on his face.

"I was blown away when I saw you in Tampa," he murmured. "I didn't know what to think. I didn't know whose side you were on."

"Yours, of course. I didn't understand it when you dropped out of sight again after the shooting. A week ago, it started to fall into place, and it suddenly seemed like this whole thing with Catherine and Gillian was somehow connected to whatever it is you're into." I told him the rest of it—the meeting with Ray, the trip to La Paz, and the lucky tip that brought me to Puerto Peñasco.

There was a long silence when I finished. Morgan just stared out to sea, and finally heaved a sigh.

"Man, I never thought it would turn out this way. I never thought you'd get dragged into this." He paused, and I held my curiosity in check and let him think it through. "Burt Antoly came to me with a proposition," he started slowly. "He knew that I had connections through the radio station, contacts who could set us up, and he kept bugging me to get into the business. He'd dealt some on a small scale, and he saw a chance to get into it big time. I never trusted Burt. He was a sleaze bag. And I don't know why I listened to him, but something in me told me to go for it. I knew a lot of people in my business who were always looking for a gram or two, and I figured it would be easy to unload the stuff. It seemed so simple, and dangerous enough to be fun. Fun, shit." He snorted, and looked at the ground beneath his feet.

"Anyway, Burt and I set up shop in the loft. We started with small quantities to see how much we could move, and as we built some capital and found new customers, we increased the quantities we were buying. It was easy—no muss, no fuss. Take the stuff, step on it a little, weigh it out, and sell it. The people at the top liked the business we were doing, and we were making money. Then, two things happened. First, our supplier got busted out at the airport. The feds had somehow latched onto one of the mules bringing a shipment up from Arizona. The bust was no good, and they let our guy go for lack of evidence."

"Harriman. So he *is* involved."

"How did you know?" He looked at me sharply.

"He's the photographer Gillian McCrae worked with."

"Yeah, okay. Well, after that the heat started to

come down because Harriman thought someone had set him up from the inside. We were all suspect, and it suddenly wasn't that much fun anymore.

"The second thing that happened was that Burt got greedy. After we built up a reputation with these people, the way we were working it for large quantities was like this. We paid half up front, and the organization fronted us the rest of what we needed. When we sold it, we paid off the other half. Burt decided to go into business for himself and took two hundred thousand—a hundred of theirs and a hundred of ours—and split.

"I knew he'd try to parlay it into more, and I had an idea of where he'd go, so I followed him. I also knew that if I didn't get that money back, I was dead meat. Harriman and his people would never believe that I wasn't in on it. So I left, too. I followed Burt to Tampa and learned he was trying to set up a deal to buy more coke, figuring he could sell it on the street and walk away a rich man. Obviously, Harriman's people found out."

"From the tap on my phone. But I don't understand why you disappeared again. They got the money back, killed Antoly, and ripped off some cocaine in the bargain."

"I told you, Emerson. I knew Harriman would think I was in on it. He was already paranoid that someone inside had set him up. When Burt split, it focused the attention on the two of us. These folks play for keeps. You saw what they did to Burt. I figured the only way out of this mess was to try to trace Harriman's source, see if I could find the pipeline and take Harriman out of the picture completely. It was the only thing I could think of. I'd heard enough to know where to start, so here I am."

"Why not just go to the police?"

"And do time? Come on. I've been running for my life."

"What does Tom Blanchard have to do with all of this? George says you did him a favor."

He thought a moment before answering. "I knew Harriman socially before I got involved with him, before I even knew he was dealing. We were talking at a party one night. I don't remember how the subject came up, but he said he had some friends who were looking for a place in the country, wanted to retire. I knew Tom was trying to figure out what to do with the farm, so I suggested he rent it out, and I put him together with Harriman. I thought that was the end of it. Later, I suspected what was going, and I tried to warn Tom, but he just looked the other way. The money was too good."

"Jesus, you mean the farm is a front for the operation?"

"I *think* so. I don't know for sure. Just like I don't *know* that Harriman is running the whole thing. But it makes sense. And I think Tom had a change of heart. He told me he was going to go out there and find out what was really going on."

"He's dead, you know. We buried him a week ago last Saturday."

"Oh, shit. How?"

"He was mugged. Beaten up. It was bad enough that he just slipped into a coma and never came out of it."

"Or else it was a warning. Damn! It's all gone wrong, hasn't it?"

I let his words sink in. "How the hell did you get here?"

"Stole a car."

"You what?"

"I stole a car in Tampa. Didn't you ever hot-wire a car when you were a kid?" I shook my head. "Yeah, I found an old beater and drove it as far as Biloxi, dumped it, then hitched to New Orleans. From there, I took a bus to Houston. I've got some friends in Texas. They loaned me some money so I could buy some clothes and fly down to La Paz. When I found out what I needed to know, I hitched a ride up to Santa Rosalia, caught the ferry over to Guayamas, and hitched and took buses until I got here. It took me nearly three days."

"Where are you staying?"

"I know some people who use a condo over in Las Conchas. There's a guy in town—Jorge—who manages a bunch of those places for the Americans. I bribed him to open up the condo and let me stay there. And I got him to loan me one of his cars, for a small price. It ain't much, but it runs."

There was a long silence. "So what do we do now?"

"Wait for the shrimper. I think I know how they're transporting the stuff, but I don't know where it's going."

"That's what I figured. It's why I'm parked on this bench."

"It won't come into the harbor during the day. Too many curious eyes." He paused. "Look, why don't you get your stuff from the motel and bunk with me. We can go back to the condo, get something to eat, and take a little siesta, then come back here tonight."

"Sounds good."

Morgan drove the dilapidated car around the block to the motel, and waited while I got my things and checked out. Then he drove us over to the other side of town and out the beach road leading to the condo. It was a different world. Past a security gate, as far as the eye could see, modern white houses were strung down the beach, a line of demarcation between the blue ocean and the harsh desert. It was as if the little village didn't exist. There was no sign of poverty here.

The condo was nice, built in the Mexican style, with dark oak furniture, glazed tile floors, and a pretty veranda overlooking the sea. Morgan said he was going back into town. I dropped my bag in a bedroom and changed into shorts, then went barefoot down to the beach. The sand was almost unbearably hot under the soles of my feet. The tide was on its way out, and I had to pick my way through the exposed rocks to find a place where I could wade into the water. I dove under. It was warm and buoyant, and I swam easily, following the shoreline a half mile or so down the beach, then turned and swam slowly back.

Morgan was waiting on the patio with a cold beer. I rinsed the salt off under a shower by the side of the house and joined him, flopping into a lounge chair. It was still an hour until sunset, but the late afternoon sky was golden and pretty.

"If the boat comes in tonight," Morgan said, breaking the silence, "it probably won't try the channel until high tide. That's not until about midnight. We've got a little time."

I nodded and took a big swallow of beer, smelling the fresh salt air and watching some shell collectors stroll the beach. After a while, I got up and went in the house to change. Morgan had bought fresh red snapper and some other supplies in town. I rustled up dinner and called him when it was ready. We ate in silence.

After dinner, I went back out onto the patio, leaned back in a lounge chair, and watched the moon come up.

The next thing I knew, Morgan was shaking my shoulder, and the moon had climbed high in the sky. My watch said it was about eleven. Creaky from dozing off in the chair, I yawned and stretched, then followed him out to the car. We drove back into town and found a quiet place to park on a street with a view of the harbor not too far from the entrance to the industrial park that bordered it. Morgan cut the engine and the lights.

"We can take shifts if you want."

"I'm not sleepy anymore. I can take the first watch."

Morgan leaned back and rested his head on the top of the seat. "Why did you follow me down here, anyway?"

"I did, and I didn't. I came for the same reason you did—to try to put a stop to all this. Gillian can't hide out for the rest of her life. And I was afraid I'd spend my life jumping at shadows. I want to know who killed Cat. I want the son-of-a-bitch who did it."

He was silent for a long minute. "God, I'm sorry I dragged you into this."

"You should be. Hell, you must have known I'd help George find you." I paused. "How did you know they'd put a tap on my phone?"

"Antoly saw you with the girl—Catherine, I guess—and thought it was Gillian. He'd seen her once in L.A. From what you told me about the DEA, Harriman must have figured she was trying to cut a deal, and wanted to check you out. I just remember him being all upset when he found out you'd been seen with this girl, so I thought I'd try to warn you somehow."

"For chrissake, I saw you the day you disappeared! You could have just told me."

"I didn't want you involved. I really didn't."

I looked out at the moonlit harbor, wondering if Catherine's soul was out there somewhere.

"I'm sorry they killed her, Emerson. I know she must have meant a lot to you."

"It just pisses me off that no one seems to give a damn. Nobody's doing anything about it. Except me. Us. I don't know."

"What about Gillian? Is she a flake, or what?"

"I don't know. I feel something for her, but it's different. More than anything, I think I feel sorry for her. She just can't seem to get it together. But I feel like I owe her something. And Catherine's so much a part of her, I can't help loving her a little."

He didn't respond, so I looked out the window again, and there was silence for a long time. Finally, I glanced at him. I thought he'd fallen asleep, but I saw the moonlight reflect off the wetness of his eye.

"Why did you do it?" I asked softly.

"The excitement, I guess," he said after a moment. "A last chance to live on the edge, feel young. It was like being back in 'Nam. I hated the war. God, how I hated the senseless killing. But there was something about sitting out there in the jungle knowing each breath could be your last that put an edge on everything, gave everything a certain kind of clarity. Dealing gave me the same kind of feeling."

"I don't know why I ever used it the first time. Power is the reason to take the second snort, Emerson. That sense of power is more habituating than the drug, and I didn't think it was a feeling that could be induced any other way. After a while, it doesn't feel good anymore, but it just gets too hard to stop. Now I don't know how I'll put my life back together."

"You'll manage. George will help." I stared out the windshield. "How did you ever convince Tom to invest in drugs?"

He turned his head sharply. "I didn't tell him what it was for. I'm not that crazy. I just needed a little front money for the lease and some of the equipment. I paid him back. Look, I feel guilty. Does that make you feel better? Damn it, you're no saint, either. The only difference between us lately, friend, is the fact that the drug you abused is legal."

I looked at him sullenly in the dark. "Sorry."

We lapsed into silence again, and Morgan drifted off while I watched the harbor. Nothing moved, and the minutes ticked by slowly. The boats in the harbor were gradually sinking below the piers again. After a while, I quietly opened the car door and sat on the ground a few feet away to smoke a cigarette and look at the moon. At four, I finally woke Morgan. He agreed that we probably wouldn't have any luck, so we drove back to the condo as the sky slowly brightened in the east.

We spent the next day sleeping and reading on the beach, occasionally going for a swim to get a break from the merciless heat. It was a Friday, and we were playing vacationers under the Mexican sun. Jorge stopped by that day to check on us and make sure we weren't trashing the place. He acted nervous, and complained about how much trouble he could get into if we were caught using the place without permission. I retrieved some of the money out of the lining of my jacket and gave Jorge a couple hundred, thanking him profusely for his kindness.

Morgan assured him that if the owners had not been unavailable, he would have made sure they called to confirm that we were welcome to stay there. Jorge took the money and left, apologizing for impugning our honesty, saying he was sure that of course we were welcome.

That night, we made our preparations for another long wait down at the harbor. This time, I brought a thermos of dark, strong Mexican coffee, and a bottle of water. The nights were cool, so I wore jeans, sneakers, and a light pullover. As an afterthought, I brought a blanket, too. And then we waited, taking turns dozing, not talking much.

A little before two, Morgan nudged me and pointed out the windshield. I followed his finger with my eyes and saw headlights turning into the industrial park. I sat up and paid attention as they drove around the warehouses to the edge of the docks. Morgan got out of the car, and I followed suit. It looked like a pickup truck, but it was hard to tell from this distance. There was silence as its engine was shut off, and then the headlights were doused.

Nothing moved, and no one got out of the truck. It was nearly half an hour before another engine rumbled off in the distance behind us, and it took a while before I could pick out the running lights of the boat on the water. The dark shape was silhouetted in the moonlight, and it chugged steadily toward shore, finally heading into the channel that led into the harbor.

Men moved on the dock in the moonlight as the shrimper's captain laid it in close before giving it a burst of reverse throttle. Lines were made fast on the dock as two other men scurried on the deck rolling large cylinders toward the gunwales.

"That's it!" Morgan hissed. "Oil drums. That's the shipment."

The big steel drums were offloaded and hoisted onto the bed of the pickup truck in a matter of minutes. Morgan started moving back to the car before I even heard the sound of the truck starting up. I climbed in hastily as Morgan turned over the starter and drove the car up the block to the corner. He stopped and waited. The entrance to the industrial park was now two or three blocks down the cross street to the right. When the truck pulled out of the gate and went straight, Morgan turned the corner and accelerated down the street so we wouldn't lose it. We turned the corner onto the main road through town and saw the truck about five blocks ahead of us.

Morgan hung back, and as the truck got closer to the outskirts of town, he dropped back even farther. There was practically no traffic on the streets. The truck was definitely heading out of town, and as we drove into the desert, Morgan turned onto one of the last side streets in town. I wondered what he was doing, thinking we'd lose the truck, and was about to say something when he killed the headlights, swung the car into a tight U-turn, and pulled right back onto the highway.

The taillights of the truck were more than a half mile ahead of us, but were easy to see on the long, straight road. The moonlight was more than sufficient to see by, and Morgan drove steadily, holding the distance between us and the truck. We drove past the airstrip, heading north into the desert, and it was perhaps another ten minutes before the red lights flashed brightly on the road ahead, then turned left off the highway. Morgan counted softly to himself, and when he reached ten, he turned the headlights back on, peered intently at the instrument panel, and after a moment, slowed down.

I figured out what he was doing. "There," I said, pointing to a dusty side road off to the left.

Morgan killed the lights, then made the turn. Sure enough, the taillights of the truck popped into view again. We slowed down considerably, and the truck didn't seem to pull much farther away. The dirt road headed due west, and we drove for about ten miles before I finally saw the low, spiny ridge of a range of hills rising out of the darkness in front of us. Morgan had let the distance between us grow to at least a mile or more, and suddenly the red lights in front of us veered off to the left and seemed to rise off the desert. I held my watch up to the moonlight at the same time Morgan started to count to himself. He held his speed steady, and when my watch said two minutes had passed, he took his foot off the accelerator, coasting to a stop.

He started again slowly, and in another minute, we found a track off to the left that had been cut clear of creosote bushes. The red lights were still in front of us, but above us now, and as we followed the track, they wound up into the hills. Bouncing and bumping over the rocky terrain at only fifteen miles per hour, we followed the rutted path in the moonlight. The track climbed a little higher, then hugged the base of the ridge that rose up on the left. The taillights up ahead blinked in and out of sight as we climbed up and down the foothills. Finally, they climbed up a high hill and blinked out altogether. Morgan kept driving until we seemed to reach the base of the same hill, and suddenly he let the car roll to a stop.

He put the gearshift in park and leaned over the wheel, resting his forehead on his arms. "I can't do it," he said, turning to look at me in the dark. "I can't go any farther."

"What the hell are you talking about?"

"I thought I could take these people, Emerson, but I am just too damned scared to go in there. If I know anything about these people, it's that they have no souls and they have lots of guns. Maybe I used up all my luck in 'Nam. I just feel like if I go in there, I won't be coming back."

"We're not the Marines. We're just going in to take a look around. Let somebody else take them down."

"I can't do it."

"Damn it, you put me in the middle of this. You say you want to set things straight. Prove it."

"I can't do it. You were right—I'm chickenshit."

I looked at him for a long time, trying to read his face in the dim light. "Well, I have to," I said softly. "I have to know if this is where the stuff is being funneled through. I have to know if this is Harriman's operation. I have to do this for Catherine—and for me. Do you understand?" He nodded. "There's a full bottle of water. It'll last a day. And I can make it back to the main road on foot. Come back to the turnoff at sundown tomorrow. If I'm not there, or you haven't heard from me by then, call in the cavalry. Get the *federales* out here."

I took the bottle of water and the blanket out of the back seat and climbed out of the car.

"Are you sure you want to do this?"

"Yes. Damn sure."

"Okay, I'll see you tomorrow then. I'm sorry, man."

"Don't worry about it. Just make sure you're at that turnoff tomorrow. Now get out of here." I watched as he turned the car around and headed back the way we'd come. When I couldn't see it anymore, I turned and trudged up the hill, following the trail.

The track wound down the hill, around the base of a knoll, and up another hill. As I neared the top of the rise, I heard voices and the rumble of an engine, and I slowed, stepping softly. I moved off the track and into the scrub, watching where I put my feet. There were some large rocks off to the left at the top of the hill. I made my way up to them, using them as cover.

Three hundred yards on the other side of the hill, down in a little flat hollow, were two buildings about a hundred feet apart. Both appeared to be cinder block, but one had empty window frames. The other was smaller but sturdier, more solidly built, with glass-block windows set high up under the eaves, light shining through them with a greenish glow. The truck was parked near the smaller building, and men moved in and out of the open door. I counted five. There was a jeep parked on the other side of the door. Light came from only one of the empty window frames in the other building, dim and yellow, and there was no movement from that direction.

The truck had been unloaded, and there was a stack of oil drums piled off to the side of the smaller building. The sound of an engine droned steadily—a generator toward the back of the building. Three of the men got in the truck, and I crouched behind the rocks as the motor roared to life. The truck swung around in a circle and came up the hill past me. In a minute or so, its lights disappeared in the hills, and the sound of its engine slowly receded in the distance.

The voices below were muffled, then clearer as two men emerged from the door of the building. The lights in the building suddenly went out, and my eyes had to adjust to the darkness again. The two men walked slowly to the larger building and disappeared inside. Their voices drifted out the open windows for a few minutes, then there was silence. Ten minutes later, the dim light went out. I waited patiently for another twenty minutes, watching the little compound for signs of life. Nothing stirred. There were no guards posted, only the two men remained. The silence gave me confidence, so I decided to go down for a look.

I left the blanket and water bottle up in the rocks, and made my way down the hill carefully, as silently as I could. Giving the larger building a wide berth, I circled around behind the smaller building, feeling exposed in the moonlight. I hugged the wall, staying in shadow. The door was locked. I moved back along the wall to inspect one of the oil drums, tipping it gently. Empty. The cap on top was loose and came off in my hands. I bent and put my nose to the hole. It hadn't contained oil. The smell reminded me of nail polish remover, and then I had it—acetone. A sudden click and whir of a motor behind me made me jump and whirl around. It was just an air conditioner mounted in the side of the building.

Moving quietly over to the far side of the jeep, I leaned in to open the glove box. It was empty except for a few tools and a book of matches. There was nothing on the floor or the seats. I wasn't having any luck, so I went cautiously back up the hill, staying low, moving carefully. I found my things in the rocks, took a swallow from the bottle, and went behind the rocks to relieve myself. Then I wrapped up in the blanket, found a spot in the rocks that offered a good vantage point and seemed free of snakes, and settled down for a wait.

The moon had dropped in the sky and was about to disappear behind the ridge on my left. Off to the right was the flat expanse of desert that stretched for miles before any mountains jutted abruptly into the sky. My watch said it was nearly four-thirty, so it would begin to get light soon. By dawn, I might have a plan, I decided. Because if there were only two of them, I was sure I could take them—somehow.

Something hard poked me in the ribs, jarring me out of sleep. I rolled my head off my chest and opened my eyes.

"Real easy, Slick," a voice behind me said. I froze. "This is a .45 automatic I'm sticking you with, and I'm the nervous type."

I nodded slowly. It was daylight, but the buildings in the little hollow were still shadowed, so it was early morning. The desert was orange in the light. I could feel some of the warmth of the sun on my back, but it was overwhelmed by the chill that ran through me.

"Okay, now. I guess you're awake, and I know I've got your undivided attention. I'm going to take one step back, Slick, and I want you to get your hands up behind your head where I can see them. That's it. Easy now. Just let that blanket fall and stand up real slow."

I did as he said, and the gun was jammed into my back. A hand patted me down. I heard shuffling behind me.

"Now turn around slow, and let's see who you are."

I turned to face the voice, and was numbed with

surprise and fear. The man in front of me was Digger Graves. I could have kicked myself. He'd taken me so easily, it made me sick.

"Hey, I've seen you before. Fancy meeting you here, Slick. I think I got me a prize catch. What are you? Vice cop? DEA?" I was silent. "Speechless, huh? Yeah, I can see you're glad to see me, too. Come on, let's take a little walk down the hill."

He jabbered at me as I led the way down to the compound, feeling the gun bore a hole in my back. "What a coincidence, Slick. I was out taking my morning constitutional, like I always do. You know, getting the lay of the land, checking the perimeter. Can't be too careful. I'm out and about, you know, looking around, getting a breath of fresh air, and I see this spot of color up in the rocks. Well, that's peculiar, I say to myself. There wasn't anything up there yesterday. So I climb up in the rocks, and I see this person all wrapped up in a blanket, like an indian shaman or something, sitting out in the middle of the desert. Why, if I'd known we had a guest, I'd have invited you down sooner. How long were you sitting up there anyway, Slick? Couldn't have been more than an hour or two, huh? Otherwise you'd have been snake bit. You know, them rattlers like to find someplace warm to sleep at night. If you'd been there all night, one would've found you and crawled right into your shorts to stay warm. What a surprise that would've been, huh?"

He paused a minute, then shouted down the hill. "*Hola*, Manuel!" He yelled something in Spanish, and in a minute, a young Mexican boy came running out of the house. He wasn't more than ten or eleven. Digger said something else, and the boy scampered back into the building.

"I wonder what we're going to do with you, Slick," he said as we came down onto the flat. "I know. Let's have a nice chat over breakfast, and you can tell me what you're doing here. And then, maybe we can take a nice drive in the desert before I shove this gun up your nose and pull the trigger. How does that sound?"

"Sounds like fun," I croaked.

"So, our guest has a voice after all. I was beginning to think I was talking to myself out here. You know, the desert heat and all." He laughed a sort of guttural chuckle that sounded like he was clearing his throat.

We'd reached the house, and Digger shoved me through the open doorway. I stumbled into a large room and steadied myself, looking around, letting my eyes adjust to the dim light.

"Who the hell is that?" another voice said. A tall, thin man with gray hair and horn-rimmed spectacles stood over in a corner of the room in front of an ancient gas stove, frying bacon.

"A visitor I found up in the rocks," Digger replied. "He's alone."

"Are you sure? Jesus, that's just what we need is some yokel stumbling in here by mistake."

"We'll find out soon enough. Slick, here, is going to tell us how he got in."

"Well, I don't like it. It makes me nervous, and I can't work when I'm nervous."

"Don't sweat it, Charlie. I'll take care of this. You just do your thing." He turned to peer into the back of the house. "Manuel! Christ, where is that kid?"

"*Si, señor!*" The boy scampered into the room carrying a coil of rope.

"Good. Okay, Slick, ease into that chair by the

table." I sat down, and Digger said something to the boy in Spanish. "Arms behind your back, Slick. Manuel's going to tie you in."

"Now that's hospitable," I said. "How do you expect me to eat breakfast?"

Digger laughed. "Good. That's very good." He sat in a chair across from me, and rested his elbow on the table, putting the ugly, silver automatic a foot from my face. The black hole was aimed between my eyes. Manuel tied my hands behind the back of the chair, knotting the ropes tightly, looping some through the slats so I couldn't move. Digger leaned over to see how he was doing, and nodded, satisfied.

"Okay, let's start with how you got in."

"Car," I said simply. "I left it in the hills about a mile back." I needed to buy some time to think. I knew I was in deep shit, here, and my mind wouldn't focus. I was dead unless I could come up with a plausible reason for Digger to keep me alive. He'd want to know how I'd found the pipeline, and he'd take as much time as he needed to find out. I didn't want to think about the methods he might use.

He barked an order to the boy, and Manuel ran out of the house. "We'll see. Now, how about a name, Slick? Want to tell me who you are?"

"Joe."

"Just Joe, huh? Got a last name, Joe?"

I shook my head.

"Tough guy, huh? Well, we've got time." He looked over his shoulder. "Charlie, how's that food coming? I'm hungry."

"In a minute, in a minute."

The older man brought two plates of bacon and eggs

to the table and sat at one end. He had a worn face, and eyes that looked as if they'd seen too much. He avoided my gaze. He wore gray wool slacks, a plaid shirt buttoned up under his chin, and a navy cardigan sweater. It made him look like Mr. Rogers, an incongruous sight in the Mexican desert.

The two men ate breakfast in silence. Digger had put the pistol on the table next to his plate, and occasionally glanced at me with those hooded eyes to be sure I didn't start any trouble. I leaned back and tried to relax and think. It was twenty minutes before the boy came back, bursting breathlessly through the door. Digger turned and looked at him expectantly. The boy shook his head and mumbled something. Digger turned back to me with steely eyes and picked up the pistol.

"You're beginning to make me very nervous, Slick." He stood up and came around the table, glowering down at me. "Let's try again. How did you get in here?"

"I told you."

"There's no car, asshole!"

"Maybe someone stole it."

"You worry me, Slick. You waltz in here like a fucking tourist. No car, no gun. What do you think this is? Disneyland? Who brought you here?"

I set my jaw and glared at him. The glint in his eyes sparked and flamed, and his arm came out of nowhere, backhanding me across the face with the barrel of the gun. Pain exploded in my brain as the force of his blow knocked me over, and I fell with a thud on the floor. Tears welled up in my eyes, and I gasped, biting my lip against the searing pain in my cheek. I felt warm wetness trickling down my jaw and into the corner of my eye.

"Pick him up!" Digger commanded.

Charlie and Manuel came around the table and reached down to grab my shoulders, lifting me and tipping the chair back up on its legs. There was fear on the boy's face, and simple sadness in Charlie's eyes. I could read my fate there.

"Jesus, he's bleeding like a stuck pig. Charlie, get something to clean him up a little." Some of the anger was gone from his voice. "I want him to be able to see me."

Charlie went to the sink and said something to the boy while he wet a towel. He came back to the table and wiped the blood off my face and out of my eye, then held the towel tight against my cheek. The boy reappeared from the back of the house with a first-aid kit, and Charlie took out some adhesive strips and taped them down, closing the split skin on my cheek. I could feel it beginning to swell.

"We can make this easy, or we can make it real hard, Slick. It's up to you." Digger sat down at the table and leaned over, looking at me intently. He reached over with the gun and gently put the barrel on the cut on my cheek, then shoved hard. I gasped. The gun came away with a smear of red on the shiny barrel.

"Okay, okay. We came in last night. Two of us. We waited for the boat to come into the harbor, and when it did, we just followed the truck out here."

"Christ, he knows about the boats?"

"Shut up, Charlie! Go on, Slick. Just two of you? Who's your partner?"

"Go fuck yourself." He pulled his arm back. "Wait! Look, you can kill me, but you're finished here. I told my partner to come back for me today. If I'm not at the turnoff from the main road by sundown, he's bringing in the *federales*. You're through, Digger."

He looked thoughtful for a moment, then he turned to the older man. "Charlie, how much time do you need for this last batch?"

"Two days. I can't do it all in less."

"That's okay. That's fine. Today's Saturday, right? Nobody, not even the fucking president of the U.S. of A., could get the local *federales* out of bed on a Sunday, let alone out here in the desert. And even then, we could probably buy them off. And if they didn't come in here with guns blazing, then they don't know what we're up to. They haven't had a chance to call this in. We've got some time, but I don't want to take any chances.

"Charlie, you're going to have to take the Jeep and go into town to round up Roberto and the boys. Tell him I want him to check around town for any strange gringos. And if he doesn't find anybody, have him make sure he's at that turnoff this afternoon. He can take out Slick's partner, and bury him in the desert somewhere. We'll have to make sure that the plane comes in here tomorrow night. There's still enough moon to bring it in after dark. You got it?"

"No. Not if you want this shipment processed. I'll need all of two days. I don't have time to go running around town. Send the boy."

"The kid doesn't drive, you ass!"

"Then you go."

"And leave you here to watch this turkey? I know you, Charlie. You'd probably start feeling sorry for the son-of-a-bitch and untie him and let him go."

"The boy's got a bicycle, doesn't he? I'm not going, I tell you."

"All right, all right! I'll send the kid. Now get out to the lab and go to work."

Charlie shuffled out the door while Digger jabbered at the boy. Manuel nodded solemnly, and finally, Digger took him by the shoulders, turned him around, and gave him a slap on the ass. The boy scooted for the door and was gone. The house was suddenly quiet. Digger turned to face me.

"We're going to try something a little different now, Slick. I guess you know more about this operation than I thought, and I've got to find out just how much you know. Now, I could take this gun and start putting bullets into you—one in each kneecap, then start with the elbows—but I don't think you'd last too long. I might not get everything. So we're going to take you on a little trip."

He got up out of the chair and walked into the little kitchenette. He opened the small refrigerator and took out a brown paper bag. Then he splashed some water into a saucepan, put it on the stove, and reached into the bag.

"Know what this is, Slick?" He held up a small, round brown thing that looked like a mushroom. "It's a peyote button. We're going to put a few of these in this pan and cook them down a little, so you can take a ride. It'll be fun. You'll see."

He dumped some of the buttons into the saucepan and stirred it over the heat, mashing them down. Suddenly, he swore softly to himself, dropped the spoon, and ran out the door, startling me. He stood just outside, looking up the hill for a moment, then he came back in.

"Too late. The kid's gone." He came and stood over

me. "Your partner's the big fellow, right? What's his name? Grant? He was there in Tampa. He was your inside man. Shit, it's beginning to make sense now. He was the one who tipped you guys off to the ten kilos coming in from Tucson. Well, no matter. Roberto will take care of him. By morning, the vultures will be having him for breakfast."

Digger still thought I was an agent. That was fine with me. I hoped he was nervous. I hoped he thought the DEA was just outside his doorstep. He might make a mistake and give me an opening. He went back to the stove and stirred the brew, humming a little tune. When he seemed satisfied, he took the pan off the stove to cool, and disappeared into the back of the house. When he returned, he was carrying a little satchel. He laid it on the table and opened it up. Neatly arranged inside were plastic packets of white powder, vials, small bottles of chemicals, spoons, blades, needles—all the tools of the trade, a self-contained chemistry set no self-respecting dealer should be without. He broke open one of the packets of white powder, spilled some onto a pocket mirror, divided it into thin, even lines, and snorted it.

"Ahh, that's good," he sighed. "I never touch the stuff unless I'm down here. It's not good business. Know what I mean, Slick? Okay, let's see what we've got here."

He got up and retrieved the saucepan, bringing it to the table. He stuck his finger in the gooey mess, and wiped it on his pants. Then he scooped some up and pushed the spoon toward my face. I turned my head, and when the spoon touched my lips, I shook my head back and forth. He reached over the table and gripped my face with one hand, holding my head steady, squeezing until my lips parted like a fish, fingers digging into my flesh. As much as I squirmed, I couldn't break his grip, and he shoved the spoon in my mouth. Lightning quick, he scraped the stuff off on my upper teeth, got another spoonful into my mouth, then clamped my jaw shut with both hands until I gagged and swallowed. It was bitter and earthy tasting.

"Tastes like shit, doesn't it?" He grinned. "Now we just wait a little while and pretty soon, you'll be floating away. Unless I gave you too much. This stuff can kill you, or drive you nuts."

"You son-of-a-bitch!"

He grinned again, a death mask that mocked me. He calmly tapped more coke onto the mirror, cut it into lines, and sniffed it up. Then he cleared the dishes from the table and washed them in the sink, humming the same tune.

Twenty minutes later, the first rush hit me, an indescribable wave that washed over me, tumbling me under, sending my head spinning off my shoulders. The room wobbled in and out of focus, and nausea gripped me. I leaned over and retched once, then twice, and I hoped that I was getting some of the drug out of my system. My body tingled and vibrated, and I thought I was going to pass out. Digger's face came in close to mine, peering at me. I closed my eyes, and felt my mind battered to and fro like a toy boat in an ocean storm. The tides sucked me under, and I slid down, down, down. I was going to die.

XII

I TUMBLED OVER and over, tossed by giant waves that threatened to smash me on jagged rocks and suck me down into the murky depths. Slowly, the storm abated. I was washed into a pool, rocked gently by the ripples dancing across the surface. My eyes opened slowly.

The room and Digger were still there, He smiled at me from across the table. Everything was the same, yet different. It all had a clarity I'd not noticed before. The heat rose as the morning sun warmed the desert. A frigate bird cried somewhere off in the distance. The comforting muffled rumble of the generator reverberated through the walls of the house. I felt the crick in my neck from dozing off in the rocks on the hill, and the dull ache in my cheek. If this was all there was to peyote, I could handle it.

It wasn't. Suddenly, I noticed movement out of the corners of my eyes, and I jerked my head back and forth, trying to see what was attracting my attention. There must be pack rats in the house, I decided. The walls seemed to tilt, and I looked straight ahead until they came back into place. The floor shifted under my feet, and I looked down to see what was there. Nothing. Things seemed to shift and revolve, but when I looked right at them, they stopped. The whole room tipped on its side, and the table slid away from me, then slid back when I focused on it. I closed my eyes, but that was worse. Everything tumbled and swirled, making me nauseous. Twisting and turning, I tried to get away, working my hands against the ropes that bound me.

Digger was still grinning at me, and as I stared at him, his face melted and slid off, leaving his skull exposed. My mind was playing terrifying tricks, fooling my body into thinking that the world was in motion around me. It was as if an earthquake was shaking the house, threatening to crumble everything and collapse the roof on top of me. The harder I fought it, the worse it became. I saw no fire-breathing purple dragons, but ordinary objects took on a life of their own. The spoon on the table bent and swayed, transforming itself into a tiny adder, hissing and spitting, ready to strike. I blinked again, and it turned back into a spoon. The chair legs beneath me curled like tenacles around my ankles, gripping me and dragging me down into the dirt floor.

I gasped and shook my head, trying to clear it of the demons. I heard Digger laugh, and I looked at him, fascinated by the white teeth that grew into fangs, large and razor-sharp. I closed my eyes and fought it, desperately pushing it all away. But it came rushing back, overwhelming me. I could stand it no longer, and I let go, falling into the whirling maelstrom.

"Go with it," a voice said in my mind. I looked to see who it was. A tall, handsome man stood on a beach, looking out to sea, looking at me. "Don't fight it," he yelled. "Use it! Let it roll you under until you find the bottom, then push off." I was a boy, bodysurfing in the ocean, and the last wave had tumbled me under. I'd struggled, and nearly drowned trying to fight my way out of its grip. It was my father calling to me from my subconscious, startling me, and suddenly causing tears to well out of my eyes. I hadn't thought of him for years. The man ran into the surf to catch the boy by the arm and pull him out of the water, hugging him to his chest. The scene faded away.

I heeded the voice. "This is like bodysurfing," my mind said. "Go with it." Eventually, when the drug wore off, I would climb out of the water, wrap myself up in a big terry-cloth beach towel, warm myself in the sun, and grin at how easy it had been. I let the wave roll me under, felt the sand beneath my feet, and pushed off, bursting through to the surface.

I opened my eyes and laughed. Digger had been right. I was floating, levitating in the chair, inches off the floor. He smiled at me from across the table and started asking questions. I didn't mind. They were incidental. He couldn't reach me where I was now. It wouldn't hurt to answer a few silly questions. "Careful," a voice said. "Don't tell him about Gillian. He'll kill her like he killed your Cat."

I cocked my head, listening to the voice, and suddenly a huge cat loomed in my vision, a mountain lion stalking prey in the desert hills. It stopped, pricking up its ears, sniffing the air. The hairs on its back rose, and the lips drew back into a snarl, a growl that rose up from its belly. It crouched, ready to spring, but before it could move, the hunter's bullet slammed into its shoulder blade, splitting the flesh and smashing the bone to pierce the heart.

No, I wouldn't tell him about Gillian.

"Why are you here?" Digger asked me. His voice was faint, hollow, as though he were in the next room.

"I'm trying to find the meaning of life," I heard my

voice respond. I was engrossed by the picture framed in the doorway. At the top half of the picture was a creosote bush standing on a rise a hundred yards away. It burst into flame, and became the fiery orange headdress of an Aztec god. He'd come to take me out into the desert to learn from a simple indian shaman.

"Who told you about this place?"

"We followed the truck." I knew the voice came from me, but it was as though in a dream.

"How did you find out about the boat?"

"Juan Carlos told me."

"Who the hell is Juan Carlos?"

"A friend of El Gaucho, rodeo champion of all time." I giggled as I thought of José on a horse in his lizardskin boots. The hallucinations were getting mixed up with reality. I knew I wasn't making sense, yet it all made perfect sense to me.

"What do you know about this operation?"

"Your name is Digger." It came out in singsong, like a schoolboy's taunt. "Digger, Digger, Dig-ger."

I giggled again. I couldn't help it. Then the visions took over again, and his voice receded in the distance. I don't know what he asked me or what I told him. I went with the flow, and the hallucinations took me places I never thought the mind was capable of creating, stranger and more vivid than dreams. They went on for hours, swirling in my head, bursting with color, terrifying and wondrous, beautiful and serene. I relived childhood memories that I thought were lost. I saw the future, a crazed vision of man reverting to a more primitive state, living peacefully in small villages, once again eking out an existence by working the land and fishing the sea. I saw old friends, a procession of faces, each trying to tell me something important, yet no sound came out of their mouths.

Slowly, the hallucinations began to recede, and I became aware of reality again. The dirt under my feet was firm and smelled earthy. The chair was hard and made my ass sore. The swelling on my aching cheek was making it hard to keep my right eye open. My wrists were raw, and my hands numb from chafing against the ropes. The breeze blowing through the house was cool, and I noticed that no light came from the windows or door. It was dark outside, but still light inside. I wondered how that could be, still confused by the tendrils of the hallucinations that snaked through my brain. I looked around. There was a single bare bulb hanging over the sink in the kitchenette. The room was empty. No one there asking questions. I closed my eyes again. I was so tired.

Someone shook me, and I stirred out of deep sleep. I felt another nudge, and gradually roused myself. I groaned, stiff and sore, and finally opened my eyes. It was daylight again. Digger stood over me, wearing desert-camouflaged bush pants and a brown tank-top undershirt, holding a plate in one hand, eating a sausage with the other. He put it down and sopped up some of the grease on the plate with a flour tortilla.

"Welcome back to the land of the living, Slick."

"Water," I rasped. "Please."

He set the plate down, then got a bottle of water out of the refrigerator and held it to my lips. I drank greedily, slurping it down. When I was finished, he sat down at the table.

"I think I gave you a little too much peyote, huh? You've been out a long time. Someone else might not have lived through that. Good thing you were tied down. If you'd been loose, you might have jumped off a cliff thinking you could fly." He paused. "You really don't know shit, do you?"

"Guess not." I must have given him gibberish.

"And nobody even knows you're down here." He shook his head. "Man, I gave you guys more credit than that, Slick."

"Well, that's what happens when you go deep undercover. You don't get any support. You're out on your own."

It seemed like the right thing to say. He was fishing. He'd given me too much peyote, and now he didn't know how much of what I'd told him was truth, and how much was fantasy brought on by the hallucinations. He was reconfirming, and I didn't know what I'd said.

"Your friend never showed yesterday. I guess maybe he had second thoughts."

"You don't seem too concerned." I was glad that Morgan hadn't been caught in the ambush, but now I was worried. Maybe the cavalry wouldn't come after all.

"Nah. Like I told you, we'll be out of here by tonight. I've got some people taking shifts watching the road. If your friend shows, he's dead meat. Roberto's men are looking for him. It's a small town. They'll find him eventually. And I'm not worried about the *federales*. I didn't tell you, did I—Captain Arojo's in our pocket. Your partner won't get any help there."

Despite the confidence in his voice, he seemed nervous and fidgety. I squirmed uncomfortably on the chair. The ropes binding my wrists seemed looser, and I cautiously twisted my hands, feeling a glimmer of hope.

"Acetone," I said suddenly. The thought had come out of nowhere. "Why acetone?"

Digger looked startled, then laughed. "You're dumber than I thought. What we do, see, is cook the coca leaves down into a kind of paste. That goes into the acetone, which holds it in suspension, and we ship it that way. If the shipment gets stopped along the way, all they find is the acetone, get it? When it gets here, Charlie filters it, washes it with ether, and does some chemical magic with it to take it out of suspension. He'll probably get about a hundred pounds out of this last batch."

He fell silent, and I looked around, thinking furiously. Judging from the shadows outside the door, it was probably mid-morning. I had less than twelve hours to figure out how to get out of there—unless Digger decided to kill me sooner. The thought made me shudder.

"Where is everyone?"

"Charlie's in the lab. I sent the kid home." He looked at me suspiciously. "What do you care? You're not going anywhere."

I shrugged. "Don't you worry about the boy saying anything?"

"He's Roberto's boy. If he talks, he knows I'll cut out his tongue and kill his father." He grinned evilly, and the hatred I felt began to roil in my gut.

The heat was beginning to rise. Sweat broke out on Digger's face and shoulders. He got up and paced nervously.

"This place is useless to you now, you know." He stopped and looked at me. "Even if you kill me, someone else will figure it out. They know I'm in Mexico, and if Grant and I could put it together, it's only a matter of time before they take you down."

"Name of the game, Slick. We'll just pack up and move on. It's easy enough to set up shop somewhere else."

"Yeah, but your whole operation is blown. We know who's running it, and now we know how it's done. Like I said, it's only a matter of time."

"You're beginning to bore me, Slick. When you and your pal are dead, you won't be able to tell anything to anyone." He walked back to the table, picked up the automatic, and waved it in my face. "Maybe I should do it now, huh Slick? Maybe I should put a bullet in your brain and end it right here."

I couldn't stop the involuntary shiver that ran through me. Digger watched me break into a sweat and laughed.

He pulled the gun away and set it gently on the table. "Nah. Let's have a little fun first. This waiting always gets to me, eats at me. Know what I mean, Slick? I'm a man of action. But since we haven't got anything to do, let's say we get high, you and me." He walked around the table and started pulling paraphernalia out of the satchel, spreading it out in front of him. "Let's try some of Charlie's new batch."

He hefted a plastic bag of coke, then laid it on the table and slit it open with a knife, spilling some onto the mirror. He spooned some up with the blade of the knife and sniffed it. Then he took a small plasticene pouch of brown powder and a metal spoon over to the stove. He turned and held up the little bag.

"Ever done a speedball before?" He tapped the

pouch. "Mexican brown—heroin. It's a little rough, but a pretty nice high. You'll like it."

A chill ran through me. Now he had me scared. I wasn't sure my system could take any more drugs. He tapped some of the heroin into the metal spoon and heated it over the stove. I didn't want to be launched into oblivion again. I needed a clear head if I was ever going to figure out how to get out of this mess. I needed a focus, something that would help me hold onto reality this time.

"You killed the McCrae woman, didn't you?"

He whirled around, startled. "Good. That's very good. Damn, what a rush that must have been. You should have seen it. It hit her slow at first. I could see it in her eyes. She was getting into it, and then it hit her like a freight train. She literally starting bouncing, flopping off the floor like a fish. Man, it was incredible. What a rush! But you want to know the best part, Slick? The look in her eyes just before she started to go out of control, that total awareness that she was going to die. I love them when they look like that."

I wanted to shut the words out, to scream at him to stop, but I listened, feeling the ball of rage burn inside. Digger brought the heroin to the table and started to load up two hypodermic needles. He came around the table and pulled up my sleeve, then knotted a length of surgical tubing around my arm just above the elbow.

"You know," he said, talking as he worked, "the only thing I regret is that I never boffed that lady. She looked like she would have been fantastic in bed." He took a few steps behind me, and when he reappeared, he held an oxygen mask with a length of tubing inserted into it. He clamped it over my face. I struggled, but he pulled the elastic band tight around my head. "I should have screwed her when she was flopping around like that. What a ride that would have been."

The hatred I felt was beginning to consume me. Adrenaline coursed through my system as I desperately searched for an opening before it was too late. I twisted my hands, gritting my teeth against the pain as I rubbed my wrists raw on the ropes. Digger took a small funnel from a drawer in the kitchen, and put the narrow tip into the end of the tube dangling from the oxygen mask. Then he scooped some coke out of the plastic bag with a spoon and poured it into the funnel. My eyes widened with fear, and I shook my head violently. Digger pressed the mask into my face. When I took a breath, the load of cocaine filled my mouth and nostrils.

I shook uncontrollably as the coke entered my bloodstream through the mucous membranes, setting my nerves on fire, causing my skin to prickle. My nose and mouth went numb, and I gagged on the taste as it hit the back of my throat. The rush was intense, exploding through the top of my head, constricting my chest around a heart that hammered too hard and fast. It was more than I could handle, and panic gripped me as I thought my heart would burst. I hardly felt it when Digger pricked the needle into a vein in my arm, but suddenly, the world calmed down, and I felt myself falling into a pillowy cloud.

I don't know if it was the heroin, or if the coke triggered some residual hallucinogen in my system, but the room began to slide and ooze. I went with it, letting it pass, and suddenly everything came back into crystal-clear focus. Digger had tied the surgical tube around his own arm, and was pulling it tight with his teeth. The gun lay on the table between us. The cocaine had given me the strength of ten men. I felt the tendons in my neck knot with effort, and my shoulder muscles burned as I strained. Just as Digger found a vein with the needle, my hand came loose, and I lunged for the gun with a banshee yell.

He was quick, throwing himself sideways to the floor as a bullet thudded into the dirt beyond him. I struggled to shake my other hand free of the ropes, consumed by rage.

"You killed her!" I screamed. "You killed Catherine!" I was out of my head on the rush of cocaine, but I knew I'd made a mistake as soon as the words were ripped out from somewhere deep in my guts. It was too late now.

Digger scuttled toward the door, staying low, and I fired another shot as he disappeared out the door. I hobbled after him, willing my legs to move. They tingled as the circulation started to come back. The sunlight was nearly blinding. Digger ran for the lab, zigzagging erratically, and I fired another shot that ricocheted off the hard-packed desert sand, blowing a little puff of dust into the air.

The ground began to buck and sway as another hallucination started to tear at the edges of my mind. I shook my head and focused on Digger's back. Charlie's head poked out of the door of the lab to see what the commotion was about. He had some kind of gas mask on, and under the influence of the drugs, he looked like a Martian insect. He yanked his head back inside as I squeezed off another round. The bullet spanged squarely into the air conditioner mounted in the wall over Digger's head. As the air conditioner shorted out, fizzling and sputtering, he leapt away and clawed on the ground for the cover of the oil drums. I started to run.

The sudden explosion was tremendous. The air conditioner must have ignited the ether inside the lab. The next thing I knew, I was on my back with bits and pieces of roof raining down on me. I rolled over and got to my knees, frantically looking for Digger. He was still crawling toward the barrels under the falling debris. I fired again and missed, hitting the generator. It, too, sputtered and sparked, and a trickle of gasoline spilled out of a hole in the tank. Digger kept scrambling, his hands and feet scrabbling for a purchase in the dirt.

I was afraid that my mind would succumb to the drugs. I fired wildly—two, three, four times—and the bullets whanged and whizzed off the oil drums like angry bees. Suddenly, there was silence. Digger lay motionless on the ground. I tried to bring the world back into focus, and saw him cautiously raise his head. He looked first at me, a curious expression of annoyance on his face, then the other way at the generator. It smoked and smoldered. Gas poured out of the hole, running in a little rivulet on the hard ground. I watched curiously as another trickle ran down the side of one of the oil drums, snaking along the ground toward the stream of gasoline.

Suddenly, the gasoline ignited with a *whoosh*, and the flames danced on the ground. Digger got to his feet, a look of surprise and panic on his face, and started running toward the Jeep parked fifty feet away. I paid no attention to him at first. My mind was fascinated by the flames, and I watched the burning stream slowly creep toward the other little dark rivulet. They touched, and the flames quickly spread with a little popping sound back toward the oil drums and up the side of the one with the hole.

The second explosion ripped the air with a roar, sending an orange fireball spreading out to engulf the remains of the lab, then up into the air like a mushroom cloud, trailing thick black smoke. I felt the force and the heat blow over my head like dragon's breath, and watched as the firestorm overtook Digger, flinging him headlong toward the Jeep, singeing his hair and his clothes. He rolled over and over in the dirt, then scrabbled to his feet and climbed into the Jeep. He got it started and rammed it into gear, spinning it around, tires spitting sand.

It was coming straight at me, wavering in my vision, but I willed it back into focus. As it barreled down, Digger's face was visible through the dirty windshield, empty of expression now. I sat on my haunches and raised the gun with both hands, trying to sight down the barrel. The Jeep kept coming, relentlessly. I pulled the trigger and saw the windshield star in spreading cracks around a small, neat hole. The Jeep swerved and slid on the sand, then roared past me and up the hill out of sight.

There was a dull buzzing in my ears. I felt myself falling over, rolling onto my back. The blue sky overhead revolved slowly and gradually faded to black, and then there was nothing but the strange visions and wispy dreams that swirled in my head as the drugs raged in my system.

A cool breeze blew through an open window, carrying the lulling sounds of waves rushing and burbling on the sand. A white curtain billowed in the moonlight. I smiled. Everything was all right. I was safe now. I was dead, and this must be heaven. I yawned, closed my eyes, and fell into a deep, dark hole.

When I opened my eyes again, I knew that a terrible mistake had been made. Someone had shipped my soul to hell while I slept. It was hot, and every bone in my body ached, nagging me with pain. The light was too bright, and it burned fiercely through the window. I looked around. The white curtain still billowed in the breeze, and the sound of water was not far off. I frowned, then remembered. Mexico. I sat up, groaning, and wished briefly that Digger had put me out of my misery.

I was in bed, in the condo on the beach. I hurt like hell, but I was alive. Swinging my legs out of bed, I staggered to the bathroom. The face in the mirror looked haggard and wan, a sort of pale yellow under the tan. The hair was tousled, some of it short and blotchy from being singed by the firestorm. The beard was unshaven and stubbly. There was a swollen patch high on the right cheek half-covered by a large Band-Aid. What wasn't covered was a swirl of purple and yellow hues. I carefully peeled back the bandage. Someone had replaced the adhesive tape with small butterfly strips over the one-inch gash on the cheekbone. It would scar, but not badly. The skin on my wrists had been rubbed raw, and now was beginning to scab over.

I smelled ripe—sweaty and dirty. I stepped in the shower and let the water run over my neck and shoulders for a long time, rolling my head to work out the kinks in my neck. After I towelled dry and shaved, I dressed in clean clothes and went out to the kitchen to find something to drink. Dehydrated, I drained a quart of juice. My stomach growled, but food could wait. I pushed open the screen door to the patio and stepped outside to look for Morgan. He was sitting in a lounge chair down near the water's edge, wearing a floppy-brimmed straw hat, reading a book. I plopped down in the sand next to his chair. He was silent for a moment, then he laid the book in his lap.

"Nice to see you up and around. You had me worried."

"Thanks for getting me out of there."

"How do you feel?"

"Like shit." I looked out at the water. "What happened?"

"I had a hunch that we'd gotten in all too easily, so I took Jorge out with me Saturday afternoon. I made him drive. When we got to the turnoff, the truck was there with a couple of men in it. Jorge knew them. I stayed down on the floor so they wouldn't see me. Jorge told me there were more men in town looking for me, so I told him what was going on. I had to. Somehow, he knew we shouldn't go to the *federales*."

He paused and looked at me. I couldn't see his eyes behind the sunglasses. "I figured you were dead, and that's why they were looking for me. But I couldn't just leave without finding out for sure. So I made Jorge take me back out there on Sunday. We parked the car a mile down the road from the turnoff, and Jorge pretended he was collecting cans and bottles by the side of the road. We saw the smoke out there. You could see it for miles. And about twenty minutes later, a Jeep came flying out of the desert. It stopped for a minute near the truck, then the Jeep headed north, and the truck went back to town. We waited a while, then went in and found you. You were half out of your mind. I couldn't figure out what had happened until I went in the house. He shot you up, didn't he?"

I nodded.

"Want to tell me about it?"

"Not yet," I said softly. "I'm still not sure what's real. I have the feeling I imagined the whole thing. What day is it, anyway?"

"Tuesday, the fifteenth."

"You're kidding." He shook his head. "Damn, he could have gotten pretty far in two days. We have to find a phone, Morgan. Now." I got to my feet, hoping it wasn't too late. I had to warn Brandt.

Morgan heard the urgency in my voice, and followed me into the house. He went out to start the car while I got some money, then we drove into town to find the *Larga Distancia* sign to make a call to the States. We found a phone next to a *farmacia* on the main road into town, and I placed the call through the operator. I breathed a sigh of relief when Brandt answered.

"It's Emerson."

"Where are you? I can hardly hear you." The connection wasn't too good.

"Mexico," I said loudly. "Brandt, just listen a minute. We might get cut off. There is a woman in my house. Her name is Gillian McCrae. She's Catherine's sister. Go over there as soon as we hang up and make her pack her things and go home with you. This is important. Promise me you'll get her out of my house."

"What the hell is going on?"

"Promise me, Brandt."

"I promise. Now, what's happening?"

"Look, this connection is terrible. I'll tell you this much. Two days ago, I blew up about two-and-a-half million dollars worth of cocaine in a lab down here. The man running the operation got away. He's the same man who killed Catherine. He's a nasty bastard, very unhappy right now, and he's had two days to travel. He had me strung out on drugs for a day, and I have no idea how much I told him, but he may come gunning for Gillian. Keep her out of sight. I'll tell you the rest when I get back."

"When are you coming back?"

"I don't know. I have to get my head back on straight first. I'll call you. Keep Gillian safe. I mean it — don't take any chances. And Brandt, don't be surprised when you see her. She looks a lot like Catherine."

"Right. I'll wait to hear from you, then."

I hung up, satisfied that he would take care of Gillian, but I was worried nevertheless. The world suddenly began to bend at the edges, and Morgan steadied me as we walked back to the car.

The hallucinations gradually decreased in frequency and strength. I spent a lot of time on the beach, reading or sleeping, and each time I felt myself start to slip off into that strange twilight, I tried to check my watch. After a few days, the visions lasted only a minute or so. At first, coming out of them was like being roused from sleep. Later, I was aware of the little side trips my mind was taking. Reality didn't go away; things just took on a different perspective.

"Are you coming back with me?" I asked Morgan on Saturday morning.

"When are you leaving?" He seemed surprised.

"Tomorrow. Jorge found me a ride. There are some people staying in a place just up the beach who are driving back to Tucson tomorrow afternoon. I thought I'd go with them."

Morgan looked out over the water, squinting in the bright light. We sat on the patio having coffee. "I don't know. I think I might stick around awhile. I need to think about what I'm going to do next. You know, I don't even have a job when I go back."

"I don't think George cares."

"Yeah, I know, but it's more than that." He looked thoughtful. "To tell you the truth, I'm still scared. Digger's still out there somewhere. And Harriman's still in operation. You hurt them badly, Emerson. But they can start over somewhere else."

"Maybe."

"I'm telling you, I've just got a bad feeling about all this. Graves is warped in the head. He'll do everything he can to take you out, and me, and anyone else he thinks is tied to what happened here. You made him look bad, Emerson, and he's not going to take that shit lying down."

"Maybe." His words set off alarms in my head, and I hoped that Brandt was being cautious. "You've got to come back sometime."

"I know. I just need a little time, that's all. Tell George I'm fine. I'll probably be home in a week or so."

"I'll do that."

It was a four-hour drive to Tucson. I never thought I'd be so happy to set foot on U.S. soil again, but when we crossed the border, I could have gotten out and kissed the ground. Even the desert looked more civilized. I had traveled with two young couples who'd spent a week in Puerto Peñasco. It was old hat to them.

They came down often on weekends, they said, to play at the beach. But I felt like I'd been halfway around the world, and was finally coming home after years away.

They were nice people—friendly and cheerful, and they made the drive go faster with chatter, word games, and even a few songs. We stopped for gas in Why, Arizona, and they let me pay, but they wouldn't accept anything else from me for the ride. The long stretch of road from Why through the Indian reservation to Kitt Peak was lush and green with cactus and range grass that covered the desert floor.

We made the outskirts of Tucson a little after sundown, and in another twenty minutes we arrived at the airport. They dropped me at one of the hotels on the airport service road. I climbed out with my bag, thanking them profusely, and they drove off, waving gaily. I checked in, and when I got to my room, I called the airlines and made a reservation on a flight to Chicago leaving early the next morning. Then I called Brandt to check in. Everything was fine, he said, and I told him I'd be back early afternoon.

I ate dinner in the hotel restaurant. The food tasted bland and prefabricated compared to the simple, home-cooked food I'd been eating in Mexico, and I washed it down with a couple of beers. I watched television in the room afterward, and it all seemed so foreign, so mindless. Even the news seemed manufactured for maximum entertainment value, alternating between stories intended to shock and puff pieces that were just plain silly. In the cozy confines of my hotel room, all the news was happening "out there" someplace, and just made me feel dislocated, like I didn't belong.

Finally, I fell asleep, and dreamed of home.

XIII

There was a message from Brandt on the tape when I got home, asking me to call. His voice sounded funny, kind of snuffly, as though he had a cold. The only other messages were two from Officer Bob Webster, which had been left on the tape the previous Thursday and Friday. I jotted down his number and slipped the piece of paper in my pocket, then lifted the receiver to call Brandt. I started to dial, but changed my mind. I wanted to see him—and Gillian.

I took my bag upstairs and threw it on the bed, then washed my face and hands to take some of the smell of the airplane off me. When I was done, I locked up again, and walked down the street to Brandt's house. The day was sunny and cool, a welcome relief from the heat of Mexico. It took him a while to answer the door, and I pressed the buzzer impatiently. My heart dropped into my stomach when he opened the door. His left eye was blackened and swollen shut, and his lower lip was puffy and red.

"I couldn't stop them," he whispered. There was a look of wonderment on his face.

I stepped through the door, and when he closed it behind me, I put an arm around his shoulder. "Let's go sit."

He hung his head in shame and shook it slowly as I led him into the living room. "I'm sorry, Emerson. I just couldn't stop them," he muttered.

"It's okay. Sit down and tell me about it."

He sat, looking miserable, and blew loudly into a handkerchief. It was a moment or two before he found the words to begin.

"They got in early this morning, maybe a little before six. I was up. I'd just made coffee, and was waiting for the paper to be delivered. The doorbell rang, and I thought maybe it was the paper delivery man looking to collect. You told me to be careful, but I guess I just wasn't careful enough. I checked the peephole. I only saw one of them, so I opened the door. He shoved it open in my face, and another one came in right behind him. It all happened so fast.

"The first one punched me twice, then got me in a stranglehold while the other one went upstairs. I couldn't cry out. I could barely breathe. Everything was turning kind of fuzzy." His words came slower now. "When the second one came back downstairs, he had Gillian slung over his shoulder like a side of beef. Her nightshirt was pulled up over her head and tied at the top with pantyhose. Her legs were tied, too. She didn't move. I don't know if she was alive or not.

"He carried her back to the kitchen, and the big guy holding me dragged me along behind. When we got to the back door, the man carrying Gillian turned to say something, then the big man hit me over the head and I blacked out. When I woke up, I was lying on the kitchen floor, and there was blood everywhere."

His voice starting rising in pitch, then broke, and he took a minute to compose himself, sniffling into the handkerchief. "I called Greg Edwards and caught him before he went to work, and he took me to the hospital for stitches—six of them, back here." He turned and pointed to a spot on the back of his head. A clump of hair had been cut short around the ugly gash, black with dried blood and knotted silk.

"What did they look like, Brandt?"

"I only caught a glimpse of the big one through the peephole. He came through the door so fast that his fist in my eye made the first impression. The other one is harder to forget—small eyes set deep under a sharp brow, horribly scarred face, sunken cheeks, short-cropped blond hair like a cap pulled tight over the skull. Digger Graves, I presume."

I sighed. The description was all too familiar. "What did he say? Tell me exactly."

Brandt pursed his lips and frowned, then shut his eyes. In a moment, he opened them. "He said, 'Tell Slick to stay close to the phone when you see him.'"

"That's it?" He nodded. I thought for a minute. "How about a drink?"

"Why not?" He sighed, looking at the floor. "At least I can do that right."

"Stop blaming yourself, Brandt. It's not your fault." I let him sit there while I went back to the kitchen for a couple beers.

"I shouldn't have opened the door," he mumbled when I handed him the beer.

"Shut up, Brandt. It's my fault for putting you in the line of fire. You didn't know what to expect. Forget it."

He looked at me suspiciously, like a small child who's sure that there has to be more punishment coming. "I'm sorry. I'm really sorry."

"You're forgiven. Now, shut up."

"Okay, okay."

I could feel his shame. He lived my adventures vicariously, and the one time I'd given him what he'd thought was an easy job, he'd flubbed it. And he'd gotten roughed up in the bargain. His ego was bruised, and it would take a while before he got over it, despite my reassurances. He fell silent while I nursed my beer thoughtfully, wondering where Digger might have taken Gillian. He wouldn't have killed her. He was more sadistic than that. And she wouldn't have been tied up if she'd been dead.

"Want to tell me what happened down there?" Brandt said softly, interrupting my thoughts. "Gillian filled me in on the background."

"It's a long story." I pulled on my mustache, thinking of where to begin. It took a long time to tell it. Brandt listened intently, stopping me when something didn't make sense to him.

"What will he do to her?" he asked when I was finished.

"Kill her. But not right away. I think he wants me to know about it. That's why he gave you that message. Which is probably the only reason you're alive right now."

"Thanks a lot."

"Don't get me wrong. I'm very happy you're still alive. I'd never forgive myself if he'd killed you."

"Aw, you're just saying that." He blushed.

"I mean it." He turned even redder. "What I'm getting at is that Digger's a little unbalanced. I managed to really screw things up for him. I think he's going to strike back by trying to hurt all the people I love, the people he knows who are close to this thing. And then he'll try for me. I'd rather not let that happen."

"What are you going to do?"

"I don't know yet. You didn't call the police?"

"And tell them what? That two men broke into my house and kidnapped a dead girl?"

I got up and paced. "The first thing to do is get everyone as far out of his way as possible. You know, now, to be extra careful. Morgan's still in Mexico, so he's okay, for now. I'll have to call Georgia, get her to go out of town for a while or something. And he's already got Gillian. Who else is there?"

"You, friend." He said it softly, bringing me up short. "I worry about you. Gillian gave me your note."

"She shouldn't have."

"I think she really cares about you. She asked me a lot about you."

"She's so different from Catherine, Brandt. I don't know."

"Yes, she is. But like you said, she's not a bad sort, just a little confused. I have the sense she's never gotten anything in life without having to give up a piece of her soul. You're different. You didn't try to take anything from her. She was having a hard time trying to figure you out."

"I'm not that complicated a person. Look, I've got to call George, tell her Morgan's all right, and warn her to stay on her toes."

"Sure." He looked at me with a peculiar expression.

I turned away, trying to ignore the sudden guilt I felt, and went into the kitchen to call George. I told her everything, and assured her that Morgan was all right. Then I told her what had happened to Gillian, and suggested she take a vacation from work and find someplace out of town to spend a few days.

"I'll be fine, Emerson, really. I don't know anything, and as long as Morgan's safe, I can't imagine anyone will come looking for me."

"Look, I don't want to alarm you, but I want you to be scared and overly cautious. I don't know what this guy will do. And frankly, if he *does* try to get close to you, he'll more than likely do it when Morgan *isn't* here. It's easier that way. Do you understand?"

There was a short pause. "I just had the alarm system checked, and there are neighbors on both sides. Really, I'll be all right."

"Well, at least tell your neighbors what he looks like, so they can watch for him."

"I will, don't worry."

I didn't like it, but I couldn't force George to leave. I turned away from the phone and rummaged through Brandt's refrigerator to find something to eat. I heated soup and made sandwiches for both of us, and carried a tray back into the living room. Brandt was reading the paper.

"I was hungry, and thought you might like something to eat, too, so I took liberties with your kitchen."

"Thank you. I haven't eaten all day."

We ate silently, and when the phone rang, it startled us both. Brandt picked up the extension, listened, then handed the receiver to me. I knew from his face who it was.

"Yes?"

"Hey, Slick! I see you made it home." The voice was altogether too cheerful. "I guess you know by now that I've got your lady friend. I can't believe my luck. I get to kill her all over again. Who'd have thought they were twins?"

"How much do you want for her?" It was worth a try.

"This isn't a negotiation, Slick." The voice turned hard. "I just wanted you to know I'm still out here. I couldn't believe it when I found out what small potatoes you are, man. It really pissed me off to find out I got taken by an irate citizen. That's my fault for not checking you out in person. I just let them put the tap on your phone. Stupid me. But I've got your number now.

"You wasted a good chemist down there, Slick. One of the best. So, from now on I'm going to be your worst nightmare. I hope you read the papers. That way you'll know I'm getting close to you. First, I'm going to do this lady like I told you I should have done it in the first place. Then I'm going to do your friend Grant and his wife. I think I'll save your best buddy there for last. You'll never know where I am, or when I'm going to take someone out. And eventually, it'll be your turn. There's no place to hide, Slick. I'm going to take you all down."

"Harriman won't like that, Digger. You'll be bringing a lot of heat down on him. If you think the cops don't know who I'm after, you're dumber than I thought."

There was silence for a moment. It had made him stop and think at least. "You don't worry me, Slick. I picked your brains clean, and you don't know shit. I'll let you know when I do the McCrae girl. I'll send you a finger or something to remember her by. See you around, Slick." The line clicked and went dead.

The voice sent a chill through me. I couldn't finish my sandwich. If Morgan was right about the farm being a front for Harriman's distribution operation, then that was where Digger had probably taken Gillian. But how could I know for sure, and how could I get in to find out? The uselessness of it all was maddening. I fumed in frustration.

"What did he say?" Brandt asked quietly.

"He wanted to rub my nose in it. He's going to kill her, then come after Morgan, George, you, and me. And right now there's not a damn thing I can do about it." I paced nervously. "I've got to go for a walk."

"I understand."

"You okay? You need anything?"

"No, I'm fine. Go ahead. Go on home. I'll be all right."

"Thanks. I'll call you later."

I walked down his steps and headed for the lake, then went north. Walking along the beach, I watched the waves break on the shore, trying to remember everything I knew and had heard from Gillian, Ray, and Digger himself. I was still stumped and it was driving me crazy. I couldn't let Digger win another round.

It was well after dark by the time I found myself in front of my house, not even sure how I'd gotten there. I let myself in, poured a stiff Scotch, and sat in the living room, feeling listless and depressed. They'd beaten me this time. There was not enough righteous indignation in the world to save Gillian now.

The phone rang. I ignored it. I didn't want to be bothered. Not now, not ever. It rang again, persistently, grating in the solitude, and it kept on ringing. Annoyed, I finally grabbed it on the tenth ring and answered with a growl.

"Mr. Ward? This is Bob Webster. Did I catch you at a bad time?"

"Oh, sorry. No, as a matter of fact, I got your message. I've been out of town. I was going to call you back."

"That's okay. I just wanted to let you know we found a witness to Tom Blanchard's beating."

"You did? That's great!"

"Yeah, it seems a neighbor kid was riding by on his bicycle, saw what was happening, and hid in some bushes. His parents didn't want him to come forward because they thought it might be dangerous. But I guess they changed their minds."

"Did the kid give you a description?" I idly played with the phone cord, trying to be patient.

"Yes. The kid saw two men. I'm trying to line the kid up with an artist to see if we can't get some sketches."

"It wasn't the houseboy, I take it, from the kid's description?"

"No, I think we can rule him out. It's kind of weird, actually. The kid said that one of the guys was really big, but pretty normal looking. But he said the guy who was hitting Blanchard looked like Skeletor."

"Skeletor? Who's that?"

"A cartoon character. Looks like one of those Halloween skeleton costumes. You know, He-Man and all that stuff? I guess you don't have kids, huh?"

The words kind of trailed off in my mind. I knew, now, where this hand was going to be played out.

". . . Mr. Ward? Are you there?"

"Yeah, sorry. What you said just made me think of something, that's all. Look, I really appreciate the call. Let me know if I can do anything to help."

"I'll do that. Good night."

He was a good, persistent cop, and he'd given me the answer I needed. I went back to the den to find

Bailiss's card in the desk and dialed the number. His service answered. I told the operator I had an emergency, and needed to speak with Bailiss right away. She said she'd pass on the message. It was nearly midnight when Bailiss returned my call.

"Sorry to be calling so late, but the service said it was urgent. I was out to dinner with some friends."

"That's okay. I'm glad you called back. I need to see Tom's property right away. Can you arrange it?"

"Certainly. I'll make the call first thing in the morning."

"Who are the tenants again?"

"Mr. and Mrs. Oates, Benjamin Oates. An elderly couple. Nice people. I'm sure they'll have no problem showing the property on short notice. How's Wednesday?"

"That's fine. Do they know who the new owner is?"

"No, I don't believe I mentioned your name."

"Don't, please. I'd rather they didn't know. Just tell them that I'm interested in seeing the place. As far as you know, I have no intentions of selling the place or making any changes in the lease arrangements."

"As you wish. I'll call you tomorrow to let you know what's been arranged." He didn't ask questions, for which I was grateful.

"Thank you. I'll wait to hear from you."

I didn't sleep well, and when the windows turned gray with the early light before dawn, I padded downstairs to the kitchen and put on a pot of coffee, then went to the den and switched on the computer. I'd given a lot of thought to my options, and decided that going straight in was best. It was a gamble that would get me killed if it didn't work. But I couldn't risk taking a SWAT team in. The farm was Harriman's Chicago distribution center, but I didn't know the lay of the land out there. I needed to go in and take a look before I sounded any alarms. If I called in the feds or the cops to raid the place, Gillian might get killed. If I was caught, then we were both dead, and that was fine. I just couldn't go on with another death on my conscience.

I sat at the word processor with a fresh cup of coffee and began to write, typing out a statement of everything I knew and everything I'd done since the first phone call that August morning a month ago. Brandt would be angry that I'd gone and gotten myself killed without consulting him first. But eventually, he'd admit to himself that this was something I had to do on my own, and he'd forgive me.

It took me most of the day and nearly forty double-spaced pages to get it all on paper. When the last page came out of the printer, I took the sheaf of papers down to a drug store on State Street that had a copy machine. I made two sets of copies, then bought large manila envelopes and stamps, and took it all back to the house with me. I signed each copy, then addressed one of the envelopes to Lanahan in care of the Chicago Avenue police station. I penned a cover note to Brandt explaining how to contact the two government types that had come calling on me, attached it to the original, then stuffed it into an envelope with the other copy for Steve and Ed. I put plenty of postage on each, and sat at the table and stared at them for a long time before getting up to find a beer and some food in the refrigerator.

* * *

Early the next day, I dressed in casual white cotton slacks, a short-sleeved sport shirt, white vee-necked tennis sweater, and comfortable sneakers. After a quick cup of coffee, I took the Alfa out of the garage and drove to a nearby gas station to top off the tank and check the oil. Bailiss had called back the afternoon before to tell me the visit to the farm was no problem, and to give me directions. I read them again as the car was being serviced. It looked to be about a two-hour drive. I paid for the gas and pulled out of the station, making one more stop at the nearest mail box to drop the two large brown envelopes in the slot.

I drove leisurely, taking the Northwest Tollway out far past Elgin before getting off on a country highway heading north. It was a beautiful day for a drive—sunny, clear, and cool. The grass was green again after the rains early in the month, but some of the trees were starting to turn autumn yellows and reds, and the harvested fields of corn were left barren with raggedy rows of shorn brown stalks.

The road led deep into the country, away from the sprawl of subdivisions that radiated like cancer from the outskirts of the city. There was nothing out here but small towns separated by miles of rolling fields of crops and grazing land and tracts of untouched hardwood trees.

The directions took me off the highway onto back roads that wound through the countryside, leading me farther north and west. The farmhouses seemed to be farther apart now. A little while later, somewhere near the Wisconsin state line, I found the turnoff onto the last side road leading west to Tom's place, now mine. The concept was still foreign to me.

The house was set back from the road, hidden behind a thick stand of trees that fronted the property along the road. The driveway wound through the trees, then branched left and right. I took the left fork, and the drive broke into cleared land. The house stood on a neatly manicured lawn of nearly five acres, dotted with tall trees. It was a large, pretty, white two-story colonial farmhouse with a pillared front porch shaded by large leafy oaks. Behind the house I could see the corner of a swimming pool, glinting blue in the sunlight.

I pulled the car up near the front door and got out to stretch. There were two cars parked in the drive—a shiny new silver Cadillac Seville, and a Jeep Wrangler with no top. Fifty yards off to the left was a large garage. A dog barked furiously from somewhere behind the house. The property was situated on high ground, and the view to the west was panoramic. The road running parallel to the property rolled gently downhill for two or three miles until it flattened out on a wide prairie that stretched for miles. I walked up the steps to the porch. Before I could ring the bell, the door was opened from the inside by an attractive, white-haired grandmotherly type in a flowered print dress with a lace collar.

"Why, hello." Her voice was as pleasant as her smile. "You must be the new owner Mr. Bailiss told us about."

"Yes, ma'am. I'm Blaine Smyth."

An elderly man came up behind the woman, put a hand on her shoulder, and reached around her with the other. "Hey, there, young fella. I'm Benjamin Oates, and this is my wife Bernice."

I shook his outstretched hand. He resembled Saint Nicholas without the beard, with snow-white hair, sparkling blue eyes, round cheeks, laugh lines around the eyes, and a round red nose. He was dressed comfortably in baggy beige corduroys, white cotton dress shirt, blue cardigan, and oxblood penny loafers.

"Do come in," his wife said, beaming. I stepped inside, and she closed the door behind me.

"Blaine Smyth, eh?" the husband said, leading me into a bright, cheery living room. "I seem to recall that's the name of Tom Blanchard's business partner."

"His manager," I corrected him. I wasn't sure why I'd chosen to impersonate Blaine, but it had seemed a natural choice. "Though I feel like his business partner now that the stores are mine. I feel like he's just away on vacation, that he'll be back any day now."

"Yes, a terrible thing that happened to Tom."

"We were shocked to hear of his death," his wife chimed in, sitting daintily on the edge of a chair. "We didn't know him well, but he was an awfully nice person. His death was such a tragedy."

"Have a seat, young fella." Oates pointed to a chintz wingback chair in front of a low coffee table.

"Thank you, sir." I sat.

"Call me Ben. No need for formalities out here in the country, boy."

"Coffee, Blaine? May I call you Blaine?" Bernice held a china pot poised over a cup and saucer. I nodded, murmuring my thanks. "Your visit was perfect timing," she continued. "We're having some guests in this weekend, but it was just starting to get a little lonely out here without company." She held out the cup for me to take.

"It's just the two of you out here all alone?"

"For the most part, yes. We have a housekeeper

come in once a week from one of the towns nearby, and sometimes we'll hire additional help when we're entertaining. A landscaping service comes in to take care of the grounds. Otherwise, the only person we see on a regular basis is the maintenance man Tom Blanchard hired to look after the place."

"I take it you're retired." I turned to Oates.

"For some time now. We finally decided to get out of the big city and breathe some country air. We found this place, and Bernice fell in love with it. We made Tom a couple of offers for the land, but he wasn't interested in selling. Perhaps you'll consider discussing it sometime."

"It is a lovely farm," Bernice cut in before I could answer. "We'd be happy to take you on a tour as soon as you finish your coffee."

"Thank you. I'd like that."

"I'm surprised you haven't been out here before."

I shrugged. "Tom and I talked about a weekend out here for years. But the business always seemed to get in the way for me. Between the two stores and being open six days a week, there never seemed to be any time."

"You must learn to take some time for yourself," Bernice said seriously. "Life passes too quickly to spend all your time working."

I laughed. I'd let Bailiss give them fair warning, but they seemed far too normal and at ease to be hiding anything. We chatted idly while I drank my coffee, and they seemed to take a genuine interest in what was happening in town and in Blaine Smyth's life. When I set my empty cup down, they both stood as if on cue, and Bernice led the tour, with Ben bringing up the rear.

The house was big, with living room, formal dining

room, parlor, library, and kitchen on the ground floor. All the rooms were tastefully decorated, filled with lovely old furniture and pretty oil paintings on the walls. I asked about the furnishings. Some had been there, they said, and some they'd brought. Their taste and possessions had blended nicely with Tom's. Upstairs were three baths and four bedrooms. They showed me only two bedrooms, with the excuse that one was theirs and too messy to show, and the other was being painted and papered and was in a shambles. It sounded plausible, even to me.

They took me out the back door onto a broad patio overlooking the pool. There was a gas barbecue and lawn furniture evenly arranged on the deck. Beyond the pool was a fenced dog run, and now I could see the Doberman that had made so much noise when I'd first arrived. He pranced from one end to the other, whimpering and pawing at the chain link. At the back edge of the yard was a split-rail fence half-concealed by a row of tall pine trees. Beyond was open meadow.

"Come on, young fella. I'll show you the rest of the property." Oates led the way around the side of the house to the driveway.

"I'll let you two go exploring," Bernice said as we walked toward the Jeep. "I've got some chores to do. Will you stay for lunch, Blaine?"

"No, thanks. I should get back to the city this afternoon. I'm taking time out from work, you know." I smiled.

She wagged a finger at me. "You remember what I told you. A little play now and then won't hurt you."

Oates was in the Jeep when I turned to climb in the passenger seat. He turned over the ignition and put it into gear, wheeling it around in a tight circle to head back down the driveway. He wound through the trees and turned left at the fork. The drive led through a gate in the fence and out into the open. Just past the fence, the drive turned to a grass track that took us across a field toward some long, low buildings. Halfway across, I noticed with surprise that the grass in the meadow seemed to have been mown. I looked to the left and right. A long, level strip had been cleared, and then I saw the little hooded lamps planted along the edges, low to the ground.

"Landing strip?" I asked loudly over the sound of the engine.

"A lot of our friends have private planes. Used to fly myself, but now I keep a pilot on salary. I'm getting too old. This is one of the lease improvements we put in. It just seems to be the easiest way to get in and out of here sometimes."

Instead of heading for the buildings on the other side of the strip, Oates swung the wheel to the right and nosed the Jeep down the hill to the west. In a little while, we came to a small pond lined with birch and weeping willows. He brought the Jeep to a stop and climbed out. I followed him as he walked in toward the pond.

"Good fishing in here. Keep it stocked with bass and bluegills. This is one of my favorite spots. I come out here a lot in the summer and just lay on the grass and remember what it was like to be young. Brings back old memories."

I stood and watched him as he wandered aimlessly, looking out over the water. Finally, he turned and walked back.

"There's another smaller pond at the back of the property," he said, climbing into the Jeep, "but it's not good for much, and it's not half as pretty."

He gave me a running commentary about the history of the place as we bumped our way up the hill over the rough terrain. We leveled out on top of the hill, and Oates swung by the buildings on the other side of the airstrip. One was newer, built of corrugated steel, obviously a hanger for the plane. The other looked like an old barn or stable. Oates answered my unspoken question.

"One of the old barns. The original owners raised beef cattle, I think. Ground's too rocky for growing much in the way of crops, but I'm sure they probably had some corn and put up hay in the summer. The good farmland is down the hill there, on the prairie. Strange how the outbuildings are so far away from the house. I'll bet the owner's wife had something to say about that when the place was built."

"What's inside?"

"Not much left to look at. A little rickety, in fact. That's why we built a new hanger instead of just hanging new doors on the barn." He didn't invite me in for a look.

There was a stand of trees behind the buildings, and more fields of tall grass beyond that. Oates put the Jeep in gear and pulled away. It was pretty country, but kind of desolate. It would be cold and barren in the winter. The nearest neighbor was another farm a mile down the hill. There was a deserted, ramshackle farmhouse and barn standing a quarter mile to the east. And up on slightly higher ground, a half mile away, a tall microwave tower stood out in a field.

The Jeep rolled across the landing strip and along

the path through the tall grass to the fenceline, then up the drive back to the house. There didn't seem to be much more to say. I'd gotten the nickel tour, had inspected my property, and now it was time to leave. I thanked Oates for his time, and asked him to give my regards to his wife.

"Are you sure you won't stay for lunch?"

"Thanks, but no." I didn't see the sense in prolonging my stay. If they were hiding something, I wouldn't find out anything more in their presence. And every minute I stayed, I took a chance on making a small mistake that would let them see through my charade. No, it was time to go.

"Come back some time for a swim before the weather cools any more. Bernice would love to have you spend the day."

"I appreciate that. I'll call sometime when I have a chance."

I shook his hand and climbed into the Alfa, then waved as I headed back out the drive.

XIV

THERE WAS MORE to the farm than met the eye. There had to be, and I wracked my brain trying to think of anything I'd seen that had seemed slightly off center. Bailiss had given them enough time to cover up, which is what I'd wanted in a sense. I hadn't wanted anyone to recognize me. But they'd been too normal. Nothing had set off the alarms. But Gillian was there. I could feel it. I would have to go back in.

I stopped at the first gas station I came to, and asked how to get to the county seat. That would be McHenry, they told me. They gave me directions. It was a half-hour drive. I found the county building, and parked on the street in front of a meter. I had to ask three people where to find the county recorder, and then I waited in line for half an hour in the basement office.

Finally, an elderly woman offered to help, peering at me through black-framed bifocals. I told her I was looking for a deed to a parcel of land up on the state line.

"Who owns it?"

"I do, but it wouldn't be listed under my name. Try the name Blanchard, Thomas Blanchard."

She asked a few more questions, making notes on a scrap of paper with a stub of a pencil, then shuffled off into the banks of file cabinets behind the counter. It was nearly twenty minutes before she reappeared.

"You want a copy, it'll be three dollars."

"No, I don't want a copy. I just want to know where the property lines are."

She looked at me sternly. "You should have told me that to start with. The deed won't show you that. Wait here a minute."

She disappeared again, and when she returned she held a survey map in her hand. "Okay, now, what you do is pay me two dollars, and I'll give you a map. Let's see what township this is." She unfolded the survey map and looked at it. "Right. I'll give you a map of the township where the property is located, and you can take this survey map and set right over there and mark the property lines on the township map."

I paid the two dollars, and she gave me a new, crisply folded map. I had to borrow a pencil. I took both maps over to a metal table, and sat down to compare them under the woman's watchful eye. The township map, printed in simple black and white, was drawn in substantial detail, and was easy to read. It was nearly three feet square, covering half the table. I found the approximate position of the property, then overlaid the survey map on top to see where the property lines were drawn. I pressed down hard with the pencil to mark the corners of the parcel of land, then lifted the survey map and traced the property lines on my map, connecting the little indentations.

Closing my eyes, I tried to remember all the little details that had formed an image in my mind that morning. The two ponds on the property were indicated on the map. Using the one I'd seen as a point of reference, I started to sketch in the location of the house and the driveway, then the airstrip and outbuildings. I lightly filled in little round squiggles to represent trees and wooded areas. Slowly, I filled in other details as they came to mind—the fenced dog run, the microwave tower, the deserted farmhouse and barn.

The property formed a rough square in the top center of a large rectangle delineated by roads. The township road running east and west in front of the house was the only access to the property. The county blacktop I'd taken north up to the farm intersected the township road about three-quarters of a mile east of the driveway. The closest north-south road to the west was more than a mile from the house. The map indicated that it was unpaved, probably gravel. The property itself ran south from the house about three-quarters of a mile. The neighboring parcel of land to the south was another half-mile deep before being bisected by what the map showed to be a small stream with another unpaved road running parallel to it. It looked like I could get onto the road in back of the property from the main blacktop. If so, I could go in on foot.

I pored over the map for nearly an hour, deciding what to do. I could feel the woman's eyes on me from time to time, looking at me curiously, and finally I got up to leave. I returned the pencil and survey map and thanked her on the way out, then climbed the stairs to the street to look for a place to eat. My stomach grumbled accusingly from not being fed all day.

I dropped more quarters in the parking meter, and found a coffee shop down the street, unchanged since the fifties, its expanses of once-shiny formica and linoleum dulled with age and an uncleanable yellow layer of grease. The cheeseburger and fries were greasy, but good, and the chocolate milkshake was better than any I'd had since I was a kid. When I was finished, I ordered a large coffee to go, paid the bill, and left.

The road south of the property was little more than a one-lane dirt and gravel track that followed the stream bed, meandering through a leafy tunnel of trees. I drove slowly, cautious of the deeper ruts that threatened to catch the low-slung car's underbelly. It was a little after sunset, that shadowless twilight time when it's hard to see. I drove without lights. Through the trees to the right, I could just make out the fenceline of the neighboring property to the south of the farm.

The dirt tracks slid past my vision before they registered. I stopped and backed up to take a look. The ruts ran thirty or forty feet off the road to a gate in the fence. I turned the wheel, eased the car up to the gate, and got out to see if it would open. It sagged, but swung easily enough when I lifted it. I climbed back in the car, drove through, then stopped to close the gate behind me. The car bounced and bumped due north over the field up a hill. There was a copse of trees at the top of the long rise and another fenceline—the back edge of the farm. I drove the car in under the shelter of the trees and killed the engine.

The night was turning black. There wasn't even a farmhouse light visible. I turned on the dome light in the car for an instant to look at my watch, then I settled back in the seat and closed my eyes, slowly drifting into a dreamy state somewhere between sleep and wakefulness.

It seemed lighter out when I opened my eyes, and I looked at my watch to see how long I'd been asleep. The face was readable if I turned it just so toward the windshield. It was after three-thirty in the morning. I quietly climbed out of the car and stretched. There was no breeze, but it was cool, and I shivered. A cold blue half-light reflected off the field beyond the trees, giving shape to the terrain. I walked out into the open. A quarter moon hung in the eastern sky, and the stars shone brightly in the clear air.

It was time to move. I was halfway over the barbed-wire fence when I realized that my white clothes practically glowed in the dim light. Stupid. I sighed and hoofed back down to the road. I scooped up handfuls of dirt and slapped it on my trousers and sweater. It helped, but not enough, so I went down to the little creek and tried mud instead. I sat in it, lay in it, slathered it up and down my legs and chest, and smeared it on my face. It was cold and uncomfortable, but when I was through, I was pretty well camouflaged. At least at a distance I might be mistaken for a piece of a Holstein cow. Up close, I probably looked like a creature from hell.

I turned and trudged back up the hill, climbed the fence, and started walking in the general direction of the woods behind the barn and the hanger, skirting the pond at the back of the property. I just needed to get in and get out. I wanted to find out what was really going on. If I could find Gillian and get her out, so much the better, but I was beginning to think that if I found anything, it would be better just to bring in the troops and hope for the best.

I moved slowly, staying low, hoping I wouldn't attract attention. I was being overly cautious. It was the dead of night in the middle of nowhere. There was no sign of civilization within sight, but I felt naked out in the open fields. Red warning lights blinked monotonously on the top of the microwave relay tower, its skeletal steel lattice outlined against the sky. Reorienting myself, I steered a little more to the left toward a dark patch of trees, moving and waiting, moving and waiting, hiding in the tall grass. In another fifteen minutes, I reached the eastern edge of the woods, and ducked in among the trees, breathing a little easier.

I started to work my way through the woods toward the airstrip. A faint buzzing sounded in the distance, and I stopped to listen. It grew louder, more recognizable. A light plane drew closer, and suddenly blue light flashed on and off through the trees, then on again as the landing strip was illuminated. I crawled to the edge of the woods on my belly, staying under the trees. Peeking over the tall grass, I finally spotted the plane's running lights off to the east. It came in low, turning on its landing beacon not more than fifty feet off the ground, and gently touched down.

The plane sped down the grass runway, gradually slowed, then turned around and taxied back to the barn about three hundred yards off to my left. Light spilled out of the barn and the hanger, shining on the figures moving near the plane. There were no lights visible in the farmhouse. Four in the morning was an odd time to be receiving guests. I wriggled back into the trees, then got to my feet and moved cautiously from tree to tree, working my way toward the faint sounds of conversation drifting in the night air. It was dark in the woods, and I stepped carefully, feeling my way, trying to avoid any twigs. My eyes were attuned to the dim shapes and the little patches of moonlight that filtered through the branches overhead.

I literally stumbled over the first guard in the dark. I was breaking away from the cover of a tree when he stepped out of nowhere. I crashed into him, and we both tumbled to the ground, stunned. He recovered first. I don't know why I hadn't expected some kind of patrol. He surprised me by scrambling over me rather than attacking. I turned and saw the rifle propped against a tree, and the adrenaline started flowing. I rolled and kicked it away from his grasp. He backpedaled, pausing for an instant, and I saw the glint of steel in a shaft of moonlight. He'd pulled a hunting knife from a sheath on his belt, and he lunged, holding it out low in front of him.

My mind started screaming at me, and my muscles quivered as I twisted away from his thrust. The blade slashed past my face, embedding itself in the trunk of the tree behind me. I rolled into his legs, knocking him off balance, then scrambled frantically to my knees, searching the ground with my hands for a branch, the rifle, a weapon of any kind.

Panting, he worked the blade free, and just as he came at me again, my groping hands found the rifle barrel. I rose up on my knees and desperately swung it like a bat. It crashed into his knee, shattering bone, and I swung it back at him as he crumpled. The butt caught him in the throat as he fell, crushing his windpipe, choking off the man's scream before it reached his lips. He toppled with a thud and lay still, sightless eyes staring skyward.

Gripping the rifle tightly, I picked up the fallen knife, then moved away from the body quickly and quietly, running low in quick sprints from tree to tree. Fifty feet away, I stopped and fell into a crouch, trying to get my breath back. My mouth was dry and my arms trembled. I cocked my head, listening intently to see if anyone had heard the fight. For a long minute, I heard nothing but the hammering in my chest. But suddenly, a strange snuffling sound came from the direction of the body. The Doberman!

The dog would pick up my trail in moments. I dropped the rifle and the knife and yanked the sweater over my head, quickly wrapping its bulk around my forearm. I picked up the knife and stepped out from behind the tree, peering back through the darkness. The dark shape moved into view through the trees, then broke into a run when it caught the scent. The dog came silently and fast, and I tensed, waiting for its charge. It would go for the throat, and use its hind legs to rip open my belly. When it made visual contact, it took three bounding steps, then leapt at me with a low growl, leaving the ground ten feet away.

My arm instinctively went up in front of my face, and when the dog's jaws latched onto my arm, I let its weight and momentum topple me backward. Pain shot through my arm from fingertips to shoulder. I slashed up with the other hand, driving the knife into the dog's soft belly under the rib cage, using the force of its charge to lift it up and over my head before its legs could find a purchase. The jaws didn't loosen their grip, and as the dog sailed over me, I yanked my forearm back hard. The Doberman's neck snapped audibly, and the jaws let go as the lifeless body fell to earth.

Blood covered my hand, and the sickly sweet scent of it wafted up to my nostrils. A wave of nausea swept over me. I choked it back, taking deep breaths, clearing my mind. The force of the dog's attack had been ferocious, and I knew that if I hadn't reacted as brutally, I'd be dead. My arm ached with pain as I unwrapped the sweater and gingerly pulled it over my head. The thick yarn had prevented the skin from breaking, but the grip of those jaws had bruised it badly.

Afraid that someone might have heard the scuffle, I started to move away. Suddenly, fuzzy crackling and a tinny voice sounded through the trees where the dead man lay. I swore under my breath and fought back the panic setting in. I ran back to the spot, frantically searching the ground for the body.

The voice crackled again. "Check in, damn it."

There was a walkie-talkie in a holster on the dead man's belt. I tugged it loose and thumbed the switch. "Okay here." My voice was breathy and hoarse.

"What the hell were you doing? Taking a piss?"

"Yeah."

"Okay, but stay on your toes out there."

"Right." My hands trembled as my fingers searched for the power switch. I shut the unit off and dropped it next to the body.

The adrenaline in my system took over, transforming me into a predatory creature of the night. I was aware of heightened perception, as if all my senses had clicked into overdrive. I moved noiselessly beneath the trees, working my way slowly through the woods toward the back of the buildings, circling warily, looking for signs of another sentry.

I didn't have much time. Already, the sky had grown perceptibly lighter. The sounds of activity near the barn seemed to have stopped. Someone would go looking for the dead guard soon. The glow of a cigarette gave away the location of the second guard behind a tree a hundred yards east of the hanger. Silently making my way from tree to tree, I came up behind him. A man sat with his back propped against a tree trunk, legs sprawled in front, rifle on the ground next to him. Some noisy birds masked my approach. I gripped the rifle in both hands, keeping the tree between us. He was flicking the cigarette away when I stepped around the trunk and hit him behind the ear with the rifle butt.

He keeled over soundlessly, and I knelt next to him. I rolled him over and undid his belt, tugging it through the belt loops. The man's breath rasped hoarsely in his throat as I rolled him onto his stomach. I started to bind his hands behind his back with the belt when he gave a shuddery sigh, and the breathing stopped. Pressing my fingers to his throat, I felt for a pulse. There was none.

Some relay switch in my brain clicked when the man stopped breathing, and I knelt over his body for a long time, trying to understand the strange feeling that ran through me. It was a kind of madness, I think. Death had caught up with me, and there was no way to retrace my steps. All I could do was keep moving forward. There was fear in there somewhere—I knew I'd been lucky. I was an amateur, not a ruthless killer like these men, but I'd beaten them at their own game so far. And I couldn't allow myself to think of the distinction between me and them. I shut out the guilt. I had no choice. I had to finish what I'd started, and the odds were against me.

I'd counted four men in the light from the barn when the plane had landed. There could be more. The eastern sky was tinged with pink, and a faint breeze was beginning to stir. Voices from the barn roused me. I looked at the rifle in my hands. It was an M-16, the kind

I'd seen soldiers carry in news clips from Vietnam while I'd stayed safe and protected at college. It looked simple enough, with a little switch indicating three settings for safe, semi-automatic or full-automatic. I set it on full-auto. An identical rifle lay on the ground. I picked it up and slung it over my shoulder, then moved in a crouch to the edge of the woods.

This was like cowboys and indians, or the war games we'd played at camp as kids. Red team, blue team. Capture the flag. Stalk through the woods alone, heart hammering in your chest, with a bag full of little balloons, each filled with water and vegetable dye, back in the days before paint-pellet guns. Find the enemy and get them before they get you. "Get them before they get you."

They were loading the plane. Two men pushed a crate through the cargo door. A third stood nearby. A fourth stood guard at the door to the hanger. I ran in quick sprints along the treeline, staying low in the tall grass, keeping my eyes on the men in front of me. The one near the hanger turned his head in my direction, and shouted in surprise. I stopped and fired a burst at him. The recoil lifted the barrel, and the bullets whizzed over his head. The sudden noise was deafening in the early morning air. The man ducked back into the hanger, and for a moment, everything froze.

"Jackass," a little voice in my head said, "it's like a movie camera. Keep it low and pan slowly." All eyes turned toward me, then one of the men loading the plane slammed the cargo door shut, and he and one of the others scrambled to get aboard. The third broke and ran for the hanger. I fired another burst. "Lead him, you asshole! Lead him!" the voice screamed. I sighted and squeezed the trigger, holding it down too long. The slugs ripped a path on the ground in front of the running man. Panic welled up in my throat. I couldn't seem to get a bead on him. I squeezed off another burst that punched holes up his torso from hip to shoulder, spinning him around and flinging him into the grass. The body rolled over and over as the stream of slugs tattered the lifeless body. It took a conscious effort to loosen my finger from the trigger.

I felt a moment of satisfaction, then panic again as bullets whizzed past me, and the stacatto crackling of answering fire registered on my brain. I dove and rolled in the grass, came up firing, then dove and rolled again, lifting my head cautiously, trying to see where the burst had come from. The plane's engine caught and roared to life as another explosion of machine-gun fire ripped up the ground nearby. I lowered my head and rolled over toward the edge of the airstrip, trying to get a better vantage point. When I looked up again, I saw the man who'd ducked back into the hanger. I got to one knee, sighted and fired, blowing him back through the hanger door in an explosion of blood and rent flesh.

The plane had turned around, taxiing past me toward the end of the runway. I turned to fire, but suddenly the ground in front of me erupted, torn up by a spray of bullets. In panic, I threw myself backward and rolled in the grass, then got to my feet and ran for the cover of the trees. Out of the corner of my eye, I saw a man on the roof of the hanger. He let go another burst, tearing the bark off a tree as I dove behind it. The trees served as cover as I worked my way closer to the hanger, sprinting from one to another.

The pitch of the airplane's engine changed, growing

louder as it accelerated back down the grass strip. "Make a choice," the voice said. I poked my head around the trunk of a tree, and yanked it back. The man on the roof was craning his neck, trying to see where I'd gone. I took a deep breath, burst out of the trees, dropped to one knee, sighted and fired, and sprinted toward the runway. The man fell off the roof, gun chattering, spraying bullets into the sky as he fell.

The plane roared past, lifting a few feet off the ground as I reached the edge of the strip. In slow motion, I sighted carefully and squeezed the trigger, emptying the clip into the plane. It seemed to hesitate, then it swayed and waggled. The left wing dipped low and dragged on the ground for an instant, then leveled again. But it was enough to pull the plane into a lazy turn to the left, and it wobbled into the trees, crashing with a dull *whump* and a screech of tearing metal.

The sudden silence was awesome, filling the air with tension. I stared at the spot where the plane had crumpled like paper in the woods. I felt numb, arms hanging at my side. Curiously, I watched a puff of dirt suddenly rise a few feet away from me and drift in the breeze. It was followed by a rolling, echoing boom that suddenly galvanized me into action. I whirled as the dirt erupted at my feet again, and broke for the hanger, running in a zigzag pattern. The boom that followed sounded like a high-powered rifle. Someone far away had figured out who was shooting at who.

A bullet whanged off the side of the metal hanger as I dove headfirst for the cover of the wall. Where were they coming from? "The microwave tower, silly." I took the second rifle off my shoulder, and crawled on my belly to the end of the hanger. Cautiously, I peeked around the corner, trying to see the tower through the grass. It stood out, framed against the bright eastern sky. It was too far away. A sniper up there could keep me pinned down all day. I got to my feet, pressing my back to the metal wall, sweating with indecision. No guts, no glory.

I took a deep breath, stepped around the corner, sighted high on the tower above a tiny figure silhouetted against the sky, and started firing. An answering shot whanged into the wall a few feet from my head, then another, closer this time. I squeezed the trigger until my finger turned numb, waiting for the slug that would blow me backward into oblivion. I heard two more bullets ping into the wall next to me, then all sound ceased when the clip in my rifle ran dry.

I shook myself, not understanding why I was still standing. There was no more answering fire from the tower, just silence for a long minute. This time it was broken by muted voices and the sound of a car starting. near the farmhouse. I cocked my head to listen, gripped by the fine madness that had taken me over. "No survivors, please," the little voice said. "It would be much too messy."

With curious detachment, a piece of me stood by and watched as my body responded to the voice, grabbing a gun out of a dead man's hands and running across the airstrip. Through the trees, the silver Cadillac started to roll down the driveway. I headed for the gate in the fence, hoping I would make it in time, while the voice willed my legs to pump a little faster. When I reached the open gate, the car was barreling down to the fork in the driveway less than a hundred yards away. I had a clear shot through the wide-spaced trees. I stopped, panting for breath, raised the rifle to my shoulder, and squeezed off a burst. The windshield starred and the car swerved as the driver yanked the wheel. The back end broke loose, and the car went into a full skid, sliding sideways down the drive. It's tires squealed until the wheels caught and the car flipped into the air and crashed on its roof. It moved another twenty feet upside down, the sound of grinding metal filling the air, then stopped.

I walked slowly toward the car, gun at the ready. There was no movement, no sound. The passenger side faced me, tires sticking up in the air like the stubby legs of a giant turtle. Approaching it warily, I crouched to look in the shattered window. Bernice, the grandmother, lay crumpled upside down, wedged up between the dash and the windshield. Blood seeped from a gash in her head. I reached in and found a limp wrist, feeling for a pulse. She was dead.

I stood and walked around to the other side of the car. Oates lay on his back, half out of the car window. The roof had collapsed, crushing him against the door at the waist. I knelt on the ground next to his gentle, harmless face. His eyes were closed. It startled me when they opened, fixing on my face. Oates's lips were pressed tight against the pain.

"I can't feel my legs." The voice was calm. His eyes closed for a moment, then opened again, their blueness searching my face. "So, you came back. Bernice believed you, but I had my doubts. I'm just an old fart now, though, so I listened to her instead of trusting my instincts."

"Yes, I came back."

"And this time you brought in a team."

"A team?"

"I guess I expected this would happen someday. Who are you? DEA? FBI?"

"I came in alone."

"Alone?" There was confusion on his face. "You couldn't have gotten this far alone. We had six men out there."

"I came alone."

He frowned. "Why?"

"To stop some of the madness. The cocaine you're distributing is killing people. It killed my Catherine."

"I don't understand."

"Catherine McCrae was my friend. I loved her. Someone in your organization thought she was a threat to the operation. So they made her eat an ounce of cocaine. It killed her."

"Yes, yes, I know about the McCrae girl. A case of mistaken identity." The voice was impatient. "That's it? You undid years of work setting up this operation because a friend of yours died of an overdose?"

"Yes." It was my turn to be confused. He made it sound like there was more to what he'd been doing. "Where's Harriman?"

"I don't know. I suppose you killed him. He came in on the plane." He closed his eyes for a moment, then looked at me again. "Strange. So very strange."

The eyelids fluttered, then closed forever.

XV

A HIGH-PITCHED SCREAM of terror and pain split the air, muffled but distinct. It echoed dimly in the back of my brain, sending a chill up my back, startling and confusing me. The man at my feet lay quiet and unmoving. The sound had not come from him. A trick of the mind. A little joke, perhaps. Because they were dead, all of them. "You killed them all," the little voice told me. But the scream came again, a yowling that quavered and broke, then faded away with a faint gurgling.

I shook my head this time like a terrier coming out of water. It was a nightmare that wouldn't end, I knew. I only had to wake myself and all this gruesomeness would be gone.

Blood oozed from the mouth of the man at my feet, and a bluebottle fly lingered over the trickle of red that dripped into the dust. Its insistent buzz, droning hypnotically, was the only sound now. It was still early. The sun had been up for only a few minutes. I remembered there had been birds chirping before dawn; I wondered where they had all gone.

Four or five whoops in rapid succession trailed off in a lingering wail of utter despair. I picked up the machine gun and broke into a slow trot up the driveway toward the house. It was quiet now. I stayed close to the trees lining the drive, and slowed to a walk where it opened up in front of the house. The front door was wide open, and there were muffled bumping sounds, as though someone inside was struggling to move a piece of furniture. I was fifty yards from the door, moving slowly, when Digger appeared in the opening, shoving Gillian in front of him, an arm around her throat. He held an ugly, little machine pistol to her head and stopped dead when he saw me.

"Hold it right there, Slick! Move a muscle, and I'll blow her head off!" He stepped onto the porch, holding Gillian in front of him like a shield. "Okay, now, Slick. Put the gun down nice and easy and kick it away."

I raised it slowly and pointed it at his head. "Sorry, Digger. Mexican standoff. Kill her and you're dead."

"You wouldn't dare," he sneered. There was a hint of nervousness in his voice.

"Don't push me, asshole. I've got nothing to lose."

He fidgeted, shifting his weight, trying to decide what to do. Gillian was no help. She was almost dead weight in his grasp. There was a glazed look on her pale and drawn face, and the eyes were dull and lifeless. Her clothes were a mess, as though she'd dressed hurriedly. There was no sign of recognition or hope on her face. They'd put her through some kind of hell, and my heart went out to her. I forced myself not to think about what they might have done. I let the hatred in my gut overwhelm the hurt I felt for her.

Digger started down the porch steps, dragging her along beside him. "Don't move, Slick. We're leaving."

"You'll never get out of here. They'll have roadblocks up by now." I lied, desperately hoping to stall him.

"I've got the girl. I'll get through."

He half carried her across the driveway toward the

Jeep, never taking his eyes off me, keeping the barrel of the gun pressed against Gillian's temple. She had a pained look on her face as she struggled to keep pace with him, moving listlessly. I watched helplessly as he lifted her up into the Jeep and climbed in backward to keep me in his sight. He transferred the pistol to his left hand, keeping it trained on Gillian as she slumped in the seat, and used his right hand to start the engine and put the Jeep in gear.

He popped the clutch, and as he wheeled it around in a circle, I suddenly knew what was going through his mind. I broke into a run as the Jeep accelerated toward me, and dove for the cover of a tree near the side of the drive. Digger sprayed a burst of bullets as he sped by, chewing up the tree above me and the ground around me as I rolled away. Chips of wood stung my face like bees, drawing blood. I caught a fleeting glimpse of his grinning face, then heard the chilling laugh as the Jeep roared down the driveway. I trembled in the grass, wondering when my luck would run out.

He turned west out of the drive, not east. I frowned, wondering what it meant, and suddenly the madness returned, pushing me aside and taking control. He was taking back roads out of the area, avoiding the imaginary roadblocks I'd warned him about. And he had only two choices—due west, or circle back. He would circle back. I was sure of it.

Gripping the rifle in one hand, I started running, past the house, the pool, and the dog run, to the edge of the yard. I vaulted over the rail fence, and settled into an easy rhythm—huff-puff, huff-puff—then increased the tempo. The tall grass whipping against my legs as I ran added a swish-swish to the rhythm.

It was a little more than a half mile to the car, now—an easy run, maybe two and a half or three minutes. I stepped up the pace. There was still a chance to catch him. I passed the woods, turned my head to the right, and looked down the hill for a glimpse of the Jeep. There! He'd done it! The black dot was running parallel to me, speeding south in front of a cloud of dust kicked up on the gravel road. It gradually pulled ahead. I had to pick up the pace.

Strange how easy it had been. They'd all fallen like so many dominoes. Surprise had played a part, and a lot of luck, too. This was the way they did it in the movies. I'm a baby boomer, a part of that generation raised on television. Television had taught me right and wrong, but it hadn't taught me to kill. The Cisco Kid, the Lone Ranger, Wyatt Earp—these had been my heroes. The issues and the people had been cut in cloth of black and white. And the violence had been clean, detached, and necessary. Find the black hats, point the gun, and shoot. The black hats fell in the dust. No muss, no fuss, no blood, and the actors got up and walked off the set. But this was real life. The blood was real, and death was final. "Don't think about that now."

White powder had killed my Cat and had sent Morgan running for his life. Its trail had led us all here —me, Gillian, Digger. Now I was an avenging angel. I was Death dressed in white, a sullied, muddy white that spoke of innocence lost. And I had one more victim to claim. "Don't think. Move!"

My breath started to rasp in my throat, and sweat rolled down my face. It wasn't a long run, but it was cross-country, and I was pushing myself to the limit.

The car sat under the trees where I'd left it, waiting patiently. Vaulting the fence at the property line, my foot caught on the top strand of barbed wire, sending me tumbling into the grass, losing precious moments scrambling for the fallen gun.

Then I was up and running again, pulling the car keys from my pocket. Down the hill still some distance to the west, black flashed in the trees. Time and luck were running out. The Alfa's engine roared to life, and the gearbox ground as I forced it into gear. It fishtailed as I swung the wheel and gave it gas, then found a purchase in the grass and spurted down the hill, bumping over the field. "Set up a roadblock and wait. Wait until you see the whites of his eyes and blow him away. Finish what you started in Mexico."

Through the trees, I caught glimpses of black and sunlight reflecting off glass as the Jeep moved fast. There wasn't enough time to open the gate. I shifted into third and pressed the accelerator, gritting my teeth. The little car slid and bounced over the ground, jarring my teeth, pulling the wheel out of my grasp. The gate rushed at the car, filling the windshield. With a clanking of metal and tinkling of breaking glass, the gate swung half open under the car's onslaught before it groaned and snapped under the wheels. The car slid into the ruts leading to the road, tires spinning in the dirt. The Jeep was coming too fast. I wouldn't make it.

The wheels caught, and the car spurted ahead just as the Jeep came flying by. The nose of the Alfa rammed into its rear tire. There was a quick glimpse of Digger's face turned toward me, mouth and eyes round and wide with surprise. Then the impact yanked the Alfa sideways and pushed the Jeep into a skid. The Jeep's back end climbed up over the hood of the car. It hesitated for a moment, caught between gravity and its own momentum, then flipped in the air. Digger somehow managed to jump clear as the Jeep started to roll, tossed aside by the Jeep's momentum. Gillian was flung to the ground like a rag doll. The Jeep slowly turned over once on its roll bar, rocked precariously, then settled on all four wheels.

I sat in the car indecisively, stunned by the impact. The Alfa was angled toward the Jeep which stood thirty feet away, straddling the middle of the dirt road. Gillian lay motionless on the ground halfway between the two vehicles. There was silence again, then movement from beyond the Jeep. Digger was up, scrabbling toward the Jeep with a limp, favoring his right leg as though he'd turned an ankle or twisted a knee in his fall. I struggled to open the door. Where was the damn latch? Digger had reached Gillian, and he put his hands under her armpits and tried to lift her. Her head rolled on her chest. She was out, dead weight, and he let her slump to the ground.

I found the latch and started to climb out of the car, pulling the rifle out behind me by the barrel. Digger glanced up and saw me, then whirled and looked around frantically. I saw the machine pistol on the ground at the same time he did, and yanked on the barrel of the rifle, trying to get clear of the open door. The shoulder strap caught on the gear shift, and I had to lean in to untangle it. Digger scrambled on all fours toward the gun, rump high in the air, reaching it just as I pulled my head and shoulders out of the car. He rolled and came up on one knee, aiming the deadly little pistol at my middle, a look of sinister triumph on his face. I swung the barrel of the rifle around and pulled the trigger.

I felt the tension in my shoulders and chest as I waited for the spray of hot lead that would rip into tissue and bone. It never came. The look of disbelief on Digger's face told the story. The joke was on both of us. His gun was jammed, and my clip was empty. As the realization slowly sank in, Digger got to his feet and started to hobble away, skipping down the road as he favored the bad leg. I dropped the rifle and followed, trotting after him with grim determination.

My breath still came hard after the long sprint across the fields, but I gained on him steadily. Digger glanced over his shoulder and saw me coming. As I drew close, he feinted left and threw himself right. I got caught up in the move and had to backtrack a step or two to follow him through the trees down to the bank of the stream. He was still twenty feet away, and when he reached the stream, he slipped and slid down the muddy embankment on his rear, disappearing from sight. I charged through the trees and down the bank where he'd gone over. He wasn't where I expected him to be. He'd rolled away, and as I slid in the mud, losing my footing, he threw the machine pistol at my head. I twisted and went down with a splash in a tangle of arms and legs.

Digger was on me in a flash, hands searching for a grip on my throat. The water was shallow in the rocky stream bed, and it gurgled past my ears as Digger started to squeeze. I got a palm up under his chin and pushed, trying to break his grip, but his thumbs dug into my windpipe, choking me. Little pinpoints of light danced in front of my eyes, and the world began to dim. I focused on the face above mine, pushing with all my might. I concentrated on that death's head, the cruel, hooded eyes, the thin mouth, and saw the white crystals frosting the rims of his nostrils. It sent me over the edge. That face represented everything I loathed and feared. I couldn't let him win, not now.

My free hand groped in the water and found a smooth rock the size of a baseball. In desperation, I chunked it against the side of his head. He fell over, losing his grip, and air rushed into my lungs. Gasping for breath, I rolled with him and straddled him, slamming his face again and again with the rock, trying to drive the little flecks of cocaine up into his brain. Tiny droplets of blood sprayed my hands and clothes with each blow, and blood slowly flowed into the stream, the curling tendrils of red whisked away by the current. Sanity returned as the rage ebbed, and my arm fell limp, but my hand still clutched the rock. What was left of Digger's face slowly came into focus—I rolled off him and gagged on the taste of bile as my stomach turned.

Sitting on my haunches in the gurgling stream, I took deep breaths, bringing the world back into focus. I scooped up some of the cool water and rinsed the foul taste out of my mouth. I sat there for a long time, feeling the water burble around me, and when I finally got up, I made my way to the road without looking back at Digger.

Gillian was still breathing, but I had a hard time finding a pulse. The front end of the Alfa was smashed, and the right front quarter panel was crumpled on top of the wheel. Even from thirty feet away, it was obvious that it wouldn't drive. I climbed into the Jeep and turned the key. The engine ground. Cursing, I tried again. This time it caught and rumbled to life. I climbed back down and scooped Gillian up in my arms and placed her gently on the passenger seat, then strapped her in.

It suddenly occurred to me that I couldn't leave Digger in the stream a few hundred yards from my broken-down car. I walked over to the Alfa, pulled the keys out of the ignition, and popped the trunk. In it was an old blanket and a couple of large towels I used for trips to the beach. I threw them in the back of the Jeep and drove down the road to the spot where Digger had gone in the creek. I backed the Jeep up through the trees as close to the bank as I dared, and set the parking brake. I spread the towels out in the back, and laid the blanket on the ground next to the embankment. Then I waded into the stream and dragged Digger's body out.

My feet kept slipping in the mud on the bank as I tried to pull him up. I sweated with the effort, and after five tries, I wanted to cry like a child with frustration. Finally, I sat down in the mud, dug my heels in on either side of the body, and pulled him by the armpits until the gory head was resting in my lap. I scooted my butt up the bank a foot or so, dug in my heels again and repeated the process, trying not to look at my own handiwork. When I found myself sitting on dry ground at the top of the bank, I got to my feet, reached down, and dragged him the rest of the way up and onto the blanket. I rolled him into it, pulled it over to the Jeep, and clumsily hoisted it into the back.

Retracing Digger's route back to the house, I pulled up in front of the porch steps. I carried Gillian inside and up to one of the bedrooms, laying her gently on a bed. Little spots of fresh blood seeped through the front of her shirt. I frowned, wondering where she'd been hurt. I trembled with rage and shock when I undressed her. There were tiny cuts all around her nipples and down her stomach, and more on the inside of her thighs.

Some had Band-Aids stuck on them. Others leaked droplets of blood.

There were bandages in a bathroom medicine chest. I wet a washcloth with warm water, and daubed off the blood where the wounds had opened, sticking bandages on the worst of them. Gillian groaned under my touch, but didn't waken. There was nothing more I could do for her. I found a clean sheet and pulled it up over her bare shoulders. I went looking in the bedrooms down the hall. A four-poster double bed stood in one of the rooms the Oateses hadn't shown me. Knotted pantyhose dangled from all four bedposts. The room reeked of urine, and the bedsheets were stained brown with dried blood. A chair was placed close to the bed, and a little box of razor blades, a styptic pencil, and a bottle of lemon juice sat on the night stand. I turned away, feeling sick.

Shutting the door behind me, I went downstairs to stand outside on the porch for a minute, trying to get the stench of the room out of my nostrils. There was still work to do. I climbed in the Jeep and headed down the driveway, skirting the overturned car, then out across the airstrip. I drove it inside the hanger door and backed up to the wall. I dumped Digger's body onto the floor and rolled him out of the blanket, then pulled the Jeep outside.

The first three bodies were easy. One was already in the hanger. I just pulled his body closer to Digger's. The second was out in the grass. I grabbed his feet and dragged him into the hanger next to the first two. The third was just around the corner. I pulled him in. The fourth was farther away, in the woods. I had to stop twice to rest while dragging his body back.

I took the Jeep to find the fifth, driving along the edge of the woods until I found a spot I thought was close. It took me a few minutes to find him in the trees. I rolled the body onto the blanket, and hauled it to the Jeep. I didn't forget the dog. The Doberman felt light compared to the other bodies. I lugged it out of the woods by its hind legs, then took its forepaws in my other hand and swung it into the Jeep on top of the body. Back at the hanger, I stacked them up in the corner, like firewood.

I didn't even want to think of the two in the plane. Let them lay. Next, I tried the two in the overturned car. Grandma Oates was a little stiff, but I managed to get her unwedged and pull her out the window and into the back of the Jeep. Old Ben was a little more difficult. I got a tire jack up under the door sill next to him and pumped until the car was nearly a foot off the ground, prying the roof loose with a tire iron as I went.

It took nearly an hour, and I caught myself talking to Ben as I worked. I clamped my mouth shut, and went looking for a sturdy branch to use as a lever. I finally got him out and laid him next to Bernice. Strange. One of his shoes was missing. I crawled into the open window to look. It was not there, but there was a briefcase in the back. I pulled it out and opened it up. There was lots of money inside. After putting the briefcase on the front seat of the Jeep, I took one more look for Ben's shoe. It wasn't there. "The damn shoe doesn't matter. Forget it!"

I stacked Ben and Bernice next to the others and took stock. Digger and the Oates couple made three. Three near the hanger and two in the woods made eight. Two more in the plane made ten. I was missing someone.

"We had six men out there," Ben had told me. Six, plus two in the plane, Digger, Ben, and Bernice made eleven. I was missing someone and although I mentally retraced my steps, I drew a blank. Finally, I remembered the shots from the microwave tower.

I closed the hanger door and walked next door to the old barn to see what I could find. The interior was dim and musty, smelling of hay and the faint earthy odor of manure that lingered after all these years. A large room at one end of the building had been fixed up with a new door, replastered and painted walls, rewired light fixtures, space heaters, and an air conditioner mounted in the window frame. The overhead fixtures bathed the room in light when I flipped the wall switch. A counter top ran the length of two walls. Scales and bagging equipment littered the counter along one wall—the distribution center. The other wall was given over to a full kitchen. Steel bunks lined a third wall to accommodate the troops.

I turned out the light and wandered into the main room where the animals had been kept. Wooden crates were stacked neatly on the floor. Curious, I walked over to take a look. One of the lids was loose. I pried it off. Nested within were racks of rifles like the ones I'd used earlier to blow holes in people. A short crowbar lay propped against one of the crates. I used it to pry the lid off another box. This one was full of ammunition clips. A third crate had machine pistols inside, just like the one Digger had carried. There were maybe thirty or forty crates stacked up along the wall, enough to start a small war. The rest of the barn was empty.

I tried the garage near the house next. On the floor behind a riding lawn mower, I found a coil of rope. I threw it in the Jeep and climbed in. At the end of the driveway, I turned right, then right again on the county blacktop. A gravel path led off the main road up a little knoll to the microwave tower. It was surrounded by a ten-foot chain-link fence with barbed wire at the top. I parked the Jeep and got out to take a look. Someone had popped the lock on the gate. I pushed it open and walked through.

The base of the tower was forty feet square. There was a ladder on one of the legs. It rose up through the steel latticework to the first platform of steel grating about fifty feet off the ground. There was a second platform at about a hundred feet. The top was at least a hundred and fifty feet up. I craned my neck to see the round microwave dishes far above. A crumpled figure lay on the first platform. I slung the coil of rope over my shoulder and started climbing.

Out of the whole clip of bullets I'd sprayed at the tower from that distance, one must have gone whanging off the steel struts and hit the man on the tower. He was slumped on the platform, back braced against a strut, legs out in front of him. His shirt was off, and a sleeve was knotted around one arm at the elbow. He hadn't been able to pull it tight enough to stop the flow of blood from the clipped artery in his wrist. His eyes were closed in peaceful slumber, but his face was ashen and lifeless. A big rifle with a scope on it lay on the grating next to him.

I threaded the rope around his chest and under his armpits and knotted it tightly behind his back. Looping the coil twice over a crossbar, I tied it to a strut, then pushed the body out over the edge of the platform until it dangled free. Once the rope was untied, it was an easy matter of lowering him to the ground, letting the rope out slowly so it wouldn't burn my hands. The body slowly spun in the light breeze on the way down. The rope wasn't quite long enough. I had to let him drop the last eight feet or so. There was a dull thud and snap of some bone when the body landed. I slung the rifle over my shoulder and walked carefully back to the ladder. I hoisted the body into the Jeep and covered it with the blanket.

It all had gone pretty smoothly. No neighbors had come to investigate. No one else had been hiding out in any of the buildings. And now I had them all—nine stacked neatly in the hanger and two in the plane. I closed the door on them again, and drove back to the house. There were a couple of loose ends, like my car out on the back road, and the plane in the woods, but I couldn't do anything about it now. I'd cleaned up as well as I could.

I carried the rifle and rope and briefcase into the house with me and put them on the dining room table. I checked on Gillian. She was still breathing, and seemed comfortable enough. Now what? The cavalry was supposed to have done all this, not me. I found a phone in the kitchen and dialed the memorized number. It rang only twice before someone answered.

"Is this Ed or Steve?"

"No, it's not. Who's calling, please?"

"I got a message that Ed wanted to talk to Emerson Ward. Is he there?"

"No, but if you leave your number, I'll let him know that you were trying to reach him."

I read the number off the phone and hung up. Fidgeting, I looked around for something else to do. I stared at my hands. They were filthy, covered with mud and dried flecks of blood. There was a big old tub in the master bathroom. I stepped into the shower, clothes and all, and turned on the water as hot as I could stand it, letting the mud rinse down the drain. Stripping out of my clothes, I plugged the drain and sat in the tub while it slowly filled with steamy water. I soaked for a long time, wishing away the bloodstains on my hands.

The sweater was shot. So were the pants, but they would be wearable when they dried. The shirt was pretty clean. I found one of Ben's robes in a closet, and put it on. It fell a few inches short of my knees, and the sleeves reached only halfway to my wrists. I rinsed out the pants and shirt one more time and took them outside and spread them out on the patio furniture to dry. There was plenty of food in the kitchen, but none of it looked very interesting, so I settled for coffee. I sat at the kitchen table in a dead man's robe and stared at the phone.

It was after three when the phone finally rang. I started out of a daze and snatched up the receiver.

"Hello?"

"Ward?"

"Yes. Is this Steve or Ed?"

"No, but I know what's going on."

"I don't think you do. You people don't seem to talk to each other much." There was a plaintive tone I couldn't seem to keep out of my voice. "How do I know you're not just another bureaucrat like that jackass Feder?"

"Whoa, fella. You called us. If you need to get something off your chest, spit it out."

"Sorry. I'm not tracking well. I think you better get someone out here."

"Where are you?"

"A farm. In McHenry County. About eighty miles from Chicago."

"What's so special about this place that we should

send someone out there?"

"Look, I hope you're taking good notes, because I don't want to have to go through this twice. There's a barn here filled with enough weapons to start a war—guns, ammo, and probably explosives, too. Harriman is dead. At least I think he's dead. And so are ten other people here. In fact, they're all dead except Gillian McCrae. There's another room—"

"Hold it! The file says the McCrae woman was killed."

"That was her sister. She had a twin."

"Jesus! Can you stay there? I want to try to bring those two you met back in on this."

"I can stay. Look, you better get someone here in a hurry. I think Gillian needs medical attention fast. How long do you think it'll be?"

"I don't know. Maybe tomorrow morning. Steve's pretty far away, and Ed's in Mexico."

"Checking out what's left of a cocaine lab near Rocky Point?"

"How did you know?"

"He's a week behind me."

"That was you?"

"That was me."

"Are you okay?"

"Yeah, I guess. I just keep drifting away a bit, like walking in and out of a movie theater."

"Hang on, fella. We'll get someone to you as fast as we can. Tell me where you are exactly."

I gave him directions, noting the landmarks, and hung up. Then I went and checked on Gillian again. She hadn't moved. I rattled around the big, empty farmhouse like a BB in a bathtub, and eventually settled on a couch in front of a television. I watched, trying to pretend life was normal, until the room grew dark except for the blue glow emanating from the tube. I finally fell asleep on the couch, curled up like a child, a cushion cradled under my cheek.

The dull, steady whumping of rotors beating the air broke the early morning stillness. There were five of them on the chopper that floated in from the southeast. I stood out by the pool, waving inanely as it circled over the airstrip, then came in close, hovering over the yard, the downdraft flattening the grass and kicking up dust. It gently touched down, and the whine of the rotors diminished. It was a big bird, painted military green—a Huey Cobra. Steve and Ed were first off, followed by two more carrying a stretcher. They all looked grim.

The two with the stretcher pushed past me. I jerked my thumb toward the house. "She's upstairs."

"Jesus, Ward," Ed said as they approached. "What the hell are you doing out here? You could have really screwed things up."

"Things just started to fall in place. The trail led me here. I've been out here nearly forty-eight hours now. Before dawn yesterday morning I came in just to check it out. I was going to call you guys in, but I wanted confirmation first. Everything just got a little out of hand, that's all. It all moved too fast. I didn't really have a chance to think about it. It just happened."

"You should have called us when you found out the McCrae woman was still alive."

"You knew, I suppose."

"We suspected. There were too many inconsistencies. There were times when she would have literally needed to be in two places at one time. We just didn't have time to follow up. All I could do was have a man watch her place. He never saw her."

"She was right under his nose."

Ed sighed. "Okay, show us what you've got."

I led the way around the house to the Jeep. They looked curiously at the wrecked Cadillac in the drive as we passed, but said nothing. I drove them out across the airstrip to the spot where the plane had gone into the woods.

"I'll stay here, thanks." I stood next to the Jeep. "I can't quite bring myself to go in there."

They nodded and marched into the woods. They were gone a long time. I looked back toward the house. The chopper pilot lounged in the grass a few feet away from his ship. The other two men came out of the house with Gillian on the stretcher and loaded her onto the helicopter. One of them disappeared inside with her. Through the trees, two nondescript sedans pulled into the driveway and up to the house. Two men got out of the lead car and strolled across the lawn toward the chopper. They seemed to be having a short conversation, and the chopper pilot gestured in my direction. The pair walked back to their car.

Voices behind me made me turn. Steve and Ed came out of the woods talking to each other. Steve held a small notebook and a clipboard.

"It's Harriman, all right," he said as they approached. "The guy with him was an Arab, someone who we've suspected for a long time has been involved with arms dealings in the Middle East. The flight logs may tell us more about these people and their operation."

I nodded, even though only half of it made any sense to me. The two sedans bumped their way across the field toward us.

"Good. Here's Chuck." Ed climbed into the Jeep. "Let's go."

I drove them to the hanger, got out, and slid open the big metal door. The sedans pulled in behind us, and three men piled out. They all trooped into the hanger while I leaned against the Jeep and waited. In a few minutes, Steve, Ed, and a third man came out, looking a little green. Steve was talking to the third man.

"Be sure to get pictures and prints on all of them. Run them through the computer when we get back to town—Interpol, too. And send them home the fastest route. We'll need body bags out here and a truck to take them all back. Better yet, we'll take the chopper to town with the woman, then send it back to collect this garbage." He turned to me. "The weapons are in the barn?" I nodded. "Okay. Chuck, take Max and Alex and start cataloging that stuff in there. We'll need a truck to take it out. Unmarked. Clear the driver. See that it goes into classified storage. We'll check later to see if there's anything new there.

"When you're done there, check the house. Turn it upside down if you have to. You're looking for a paper trail, anything that can lead us to buyers and sellers. I'll take the flight log with me. Got it?"

Chuck nodded and went back into the hanger to get the other two. Steve turned back to me. "That's a hell of a mess in there. What happened?"

In as few words as possible, I told them how I'd gotten in, that I'd just wanted to take a look. But once I'd stumbled across the first sentry, there was no turning back. It was difficult to tell it, to describe how quickly it all had happened. When I was done, they looked at me peculiarly, warily, like one would look at a large dog that's just growled and bared its teeth.

"You kind of went nuts?" Ed forced a smile.

"Sort of. It was more like running an obstacle course. Take each barrier as it comes. There was pride, and the knowledge that if I didn't keep moving, one of them would blow my head off. They had the advantage of numbers. But I had the advantage of surprise and a whole lot of luck. I don't know. It was almost as if someone else was telling me what to do."

"But Jesus—eleven of them!"

I shrugged. "I didn't think about that. I just kept moving. And it wouldn't have made a whole hell of a lot of difference anyway."

"What did you think you were doing out here, anyway?" Steve asked.

"I told you. The trail led here. You people didn't seem to be doing a hell of a lot. Somebody had to do something."

"We would have gotten to it. We've got other things on our plate besides this. Anyway, Harriman was beginning to make mistakes. We were onto this place."

"I had my own motivation. Look, I probably did you guys a favor. I tried to clean it up as much as I could. There wasn't anything I could do about the car, or the plane. My car is still sitting out on that back road all smashed up. What the hell am I going to do about that? And the old man's shoe. I looked everywhere for that damn shoe. I don't know where the hell it could have gone." I felt myself starting to slip a bit off center, and heard my voice get shrill.

"Hey, take it easy! Take it easy, now. We'll have

your car towed back to the city, and we'll get it fixed. And don't worry about the shoe. We'll find it."

Ed took my arm, led me around to the other side of the Jeep, and eased me into the passenger seat. Steve drove us back to the house. No one spoke on the way. We pulled up in front of the porch.

"The old man, by the way, was Tommy Reilly," Steve said as we went into the house. "Major arms dealer. You *did* do us a favor. We didn't know he was behind this. He's supplied groups as diverse as the IRA and some of Ghaddafi's death squads. Harriman's cocaine pipeline was funding the arms deals. They were probably shipping the stuff out through Canada. What you did here stopped a major flow of arms out of the country. But we still have to figure out where and how Reilly was getting the big stuff out—rockets and such."

I thought for a minute. "I forgot. There was a briefcase in the car. It's there, on the dining room table. There's probably a couple hundred thousand in it. Some papers, too."

Ed went to take a look. Steve stayed with me. "We're going to have to take you back for debriefing."

"I never really knew what was going on. This is all new to me."

"You have a lot of pieces to the puzzle that we don't. They'll want to get it all out of you."

"I guess I can't object. No drugs, though, huh? I think Digger kind of fried my brains a little down there in Mexico. Things go a little fuzzy on me every once in a while."

"We'll try hypnosis. But once they're through with you, you won't be able to breathe a word of what you've heard to anyone."

"Except Brandt Williams."

"Not even him."

"I owe him that much. And you can't keep me from telling him everything."

"Okay, okay."

"And you'll see to it that my car gets fixed?"

"Yes, and maybe we can see that you get some of that money as a sort of reward."

"What about Gillian? What will happen to her?"

"We'll debrief her, too. And depending on how far we think this thing goes, we'll either let her go or give her a new identity. We don't know how much Reilly's customers know about this operation, or if anyone else is left on the fringes who could identify you two. If I knew for certain, we'd give you a new face and a new name."

"I don't much care anymore, Steve. I think I've been running from myself for too long as it is."

He gave me a strange sideways glance. I didn't expect him to understand. I didn't understand it myself yet. Steve disappeared into the kitchen to make a phone call, then we all trooped out to the chopper and climbed aboard. The engine whined as the big blades turned slowly with a low whooshing sound. The pitch grew higher as the rotor spun faster and faster, until the big bird rocked on its gear and lifted off the ground. As we climbed, the pilot slowly spun it around to face the way it had come, then he put the nose down and left that place behind.

We were on our way home.

XVI

THE LATE AFTERNOON sun shone brilliantly in a clear, deep-blue sky, forming long sharp-edged shadows across the bare, gray cityscape. It was a crisp, cold Sunday in late January. Flames danced cheerily in Brandt's fireplace, casting warmth into the room. A "skins" golf tournament was on the tube, broadcast from someplace much warmer and sunnier, like Hawaii. We had Bloody Marys in hand and sections of the Sunday paper strewn on the table. The section I held told of the warm pleasures of travel in the British Virgin Islands—soft sand beaches, sparkling clear waters, colorful fish and coral reefs, good food, and warm, sunny days.

"I think maybe it's time for a trip." I held up the paper.

Brandt peered at it. "The Caribbean?"

"Tortola, Virgin Gorda. I miss summertime. I hate feeling white and pasty looking. I don't feel healthy. I need sun and sand and water and lots of fresh seafood. Anyway, I've been to St. Thomas and St. John, but not to the British Virgins."

"Sounds nice." He put his nose back into the business section. "But when you've known one virgin, you've known them all."

"Says you."

He looked up again, setting the paper aside. "Heard from Gillian lately?"

"No, not for quite a while."
"Do you think she'll be back?"
"Eventually."
"After all, she has a business to run here."
"She knows."

They let me have one phone call. I used it to call Brandt to tell him I was alive, to burn the package he was getting in the mail, and to make sure Lanahan never opened his. Then they locked me up for weeks on end, picking apart my brain, extracting every shred of information they could. When they finished, they knew every intimate detail of the past year of my life.

It hadn't been too bad. The hypnosis had actually helped me deal with it all in small, but emotionally vivid chunks. The facilitator helped, too. Tim was a nice guy, a shrink in his mid-forties who wore his hair a little too long to really fit in with the other GI-Joe types sitting in on the sessions. They would turn on the big reel-to-reel tape recorder, he would put me under, and then I talked, sometimes for hours. I usually came out of it hoarse and thirsty, not remembering any of it.

They went by first names only. And there were always two of them in the room with Tim and me, not always the same two. I saw Chuck once, and Alex and Max two or three times. Each time I came out of the hypnosis, they rewound the tape and took it off the machine, put a fresh reel on, and left. Tim always sat with me awhile, letting me talk it out if I wanted. He'd done a lot of work with Vietnam vets, and I think he felt a little sympathetic. So he used some posthypnotic suggestion to help me deal with the guilt and the pain. At least some of it.

I saw Steve and Ed only once, toward the end of the sessions. For the last time, they said. They told me that the paper trail had helped lead them to a couple of sellers, and they'd managed to plug a few more holes in the dam.

"It won't stop terrorism," Steve said. "But it slows down the timetables, makes it more difficult for them to set up new sources. Now we're trying to follow the trail the other way to see if we can infiltrate some of the groups that stuff was headed to."

The cocaine pipeline was permanently ruptured, they said. I'd seen to that. They'd cleaned up a few loose ends in Los Angeles. And Chicago, too, with Morgan's help. It surprised me. At my insistence, they'd left him alone. I knew his name would come up under hypnosis. But Morgan had cooperated voluntarily when he'd gotten back from Mexico. I guess he'd wanted to wipe the slate clean and start over. I made them promise to leave Ray alone, too. Hell, if they wanted his sources, they could damn well do some legwork on their own. They'd gotten enough out of me, had exacted their pound of flesh.

They finally let me see Gillian. She looked tired, but healthy—a little fuller in the face and hips than I remembered. They left us alone for a short visit in a small room that reminded me of a doctor's waiting room.

"They're going to send me to a clinic when I get out of here. I'm going to beat this thing." She said it quietly, but with a note of excitement. Then she looked at me strangely with a mixed expression of guilt and accusation. "I'm not as strong as you might have thought, I guess. I need help with this."

"I think that's great," I said gently. "Let me know how I can help. Money's no object."

She hesitated a moment, then her face softened. "Thanks. I appreciate that."

"What will you do then?"

"I don't know. I thought a little about Cat's business. I mean, it's a going concern, right? And if I could find a couple of young designers. . . Hell, I know clothes as well as Cat did. I just don't know how to make them. It might work. I don't know. It's a thought, anyway. Your friend Brandt seems to think I could do it. He said he'd help me."

"It's a good thought. And if Brandt said he'd help, count on it."

"Yeah, maybe. It's pretty scary when I think about it. I mean, I've never done anything like that. Running a business. I'm going to have to get my head screwed back on right first. You know, take it one day at a time."

"It sounds like you're on the right track, Gillian."

She was silent for a minute. "I like him."

"Brandt? There's a lot to like. He really cared for Cat."

"I know. You, too. That's too much for me to live up to right now. That's why I think I've got to try it on my own for a while when I get out. I can't run away from my life forever, I guess."

"I think I know exactly what you mean, Gillian. I really do."

"You're some place else again."

"Huh? Oh, sorry." Brandt's face came back into focus. "Just daydreaming."

"Not slipping away on me, are you?" His face held concern.

"No. It's not so bad these days. Every once in a while, I wake up in a cold sweat, and I can't seem to stop shivering. Sometimes I just can't believe it was me out there on that farm. I keep thinking it must have been someone else."

Over time, I'd told Brandt all of it, slowly working it out, trying to make it fit somewhere into my sense of this Emerson Ward person.

"It's like a bad dream. And I'm trying to remember the gist of it. I feel like a reformed smoker—I can't remember what it was like before I quit."

"Interesting analogy."

"Truer than you might think, Brandt. Sometimes I think there's nothing more obnoxious than a reformed smoker. Their holier-than-thou attitude. They overreact. I think that's sort of what happened to me. I overreacted." I shook my head.

Brandt looked at me for a minute, as though sizing me up before speaking. "I hate to sound callous, but you've killed before."

The comment surprised me. "Not like this. Not so many. Not with machine guns strapped to my back."

"It was self-defense. With no time to think or question the morality of it all. You went to war, Emerson. Like most soldiers, it made you want to puke. It violated every principle you were taught. But you did what good soldiers do."

"I'm not a soldier, damn it! I'm a hack writer trying to figure out where I fit in. And occasionally—occasionally, mind you—I get mixed up in some crazy cause and try to make my mark on the world, to stamp the imprint of my personal morality on everyone I come in contact with. Like some damn reformed smoker."

"Here we go again."

"What's that supposed to mean?"

"What's really bothering you? The fact that you killed some people and rid the world of some garbage? Or the fact that you saved yourself?"

He let the words sink in for a minute. "You feel guilty because you're alive and Catherine's dead. I don't need to remind you that her death wasn't your fault. Bad karma, as they say. She was in the wrong place at the wrong time. But you have this compulsion to shoulder some dreadful burden in life.

"The trouble with you is that you take on everyone else's problems. And yet you move through life believing that you're out there all alone. You can't have it both ways. It's all cause and effect, Emerson. You check my mail and water my plants while I'm away, and I help you hose down your patio. You give me a birthday present, and I remember you at Christmas. Why is it so hard to believe you mean something, you stand for something?"

He paused, but I could see that he wasn't finished with me yet. "You're a throwback, a romantic, a knight-errant. You're not really brave, but you're indignant enough to be heroic, a taker of chances, and that's good. You right wrongs that the rest of us would rather ignore. Maybe your motivation is selfish. Maybe you're still trying to prove your self-worth. It doesn't matter. It finally comes down to the fact that you're not a bad person, despite what you did."

Maybe he was right. The ground I tread is risky. The world in which I sometimes live is shadowy and gray, and it tests my sense of morality. I guess what bothered me most was that I had changed. I was no longer who I thought I was, and I had gone through an unwanted, and unnecessary, rite of passage. But maybe Brandt was right. There was a core in there somewhere that remained constant, and it was time to get on with it.

The bong of the doorbell startled us both.

"Damn, that's Lexi." Brandt hoisted himself out of his chair. "I promised her dinner at the Pump Room tonight. And I've got to get ready for a board meeting at the zoo tomorrow."

He hurried out to answer the door. I had a sneaking suspicion that he was up to something. I waited expectantly, annoyed that I hadn't seen it coming. I heard muted voices in the foyer, then Brandt's voice sounding apologetic as it came closer. He entered the room with a young woman on his arm. I clumsily got to my feet.

She was petite, with delicate features and huge sparkling blue eyes. Deep-red straight hair hung to her shoulders in a soft bob. One side was pinned up with a pretty rhinestone hair clip. She wore a black sable over a dark-blue silk pantsuit. The thin spike heels of the glossy patent-leather pumps elevated her to all of maybe five-foot four. But her presence and the overall package made her seem larger than life. Her beauty took away my breath for a moment. It wasn't a haughty, classic look. It was an aura of innocence in the eyes.

"Alexandra, this is Emerson Ward."

"How do you do?" The soft voice held a trace of an accent I couldn't place. Her slender fingers were warm and dry, her grasp firm.

"Alexandra is from Brazil. She's only been in Chicago a short time, and she's never been to the Pump

Room. Emerson, you're going to take Lexi to dinner in my stead. Lexi, dear, I am sorry, but I really have to prepare for this meeting tomorrow, and cad that I am, I forgot our date tonight. Emerson will take good care of you."

Brandt picked up my coat off the couch and held it behind me. I stuffed my arms in it, unable to take my eyes off her. She smiled at me shyly.

"Emerson, take Lexi home with you and fix her a drink while you change. Reservations are at seven in my name. Be a good boy now, and don't do anything I wouldn't do."

I barely heard him as he hustled me out the door, escorting Alexandra in front of us. We were halfway down the steps before I could even think to object. I turned to protest, but he was already closing the door with a grin and a cheery wave.

I had to smile then. He knew me too well. I turned and took Alexandra's arm, looking into the depths of those enormous eyes, feeling a silly, self-satisfied grin spread across my face.

"Well, Miss Lexi, shall we go to dinner?"

MICHAEL W. SHERER is a marketing communications consultant and freelance writer. A contributing editor of several trade magazines, Mr. Sherer was the 1989 recipient of the Cahner's Publishing Company's Award of Excellence. He resides in Chicago with his family and is currently at work on his fifth novel featuring Emerson Ward.

HarperPaperbacks *By Mail*

If you think you can solve more mysteries...
GET MORE AGATHA CHRISTIE MYSTERIES!
from HarperPaperBacks by Mail

The one and only Queen Of Crime is back with 8 great mystery classics. No one knows how to weave spellbinding plots of detective fiction better than Agatha Christie.

Save when you order 4 or more.

When you order 4 or more books from HarperPaperBacks the Postage and Handling is **FREE**.

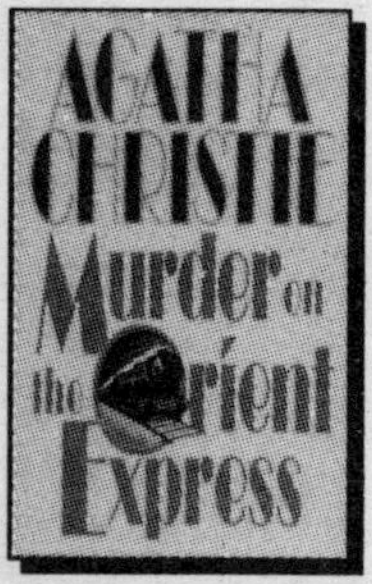

MURDER ON THE ORIENT EXPRESS
Match wits with Hercule Poirot as he tries to solve the murder of a notorious gangster while traveling on the crowded Orient Express—with the killer still on board! (0-06-100274-7)

ORDEAL BY INNOCENCE
Was Jacko Argyle convicted of a murder he didn't commit? Two years after Jacko Argyle died in prison for killing his mother, a stranger stirs up the crime. (0-06-100278-X)

CROOKED HOUSE
When wealthy Aristide Leonides dies under mysterious conditions, the family living under his protection find themselves under suspicion—even the children. (0-06-100277-1)

POSTERN OF FATE
Follow sleuths Tommy and Tuppence Beresford as they stumble across a clue that points to a murder committed years earlier and puts their lives in danger. This is a murder someone doesn't want solved. (0-06-100276-3)

THE CLOCKS

Hercule Poirot has a problem—four clocks, all set to 4:13 were left at the scene of a murder. Poirot must solve this case in time before another murder occurs. (0-06-100279-8)

CAT AMONG THE PIGEONS

Summer school has just started at the exclusive Meadowbank school. In the middle of the night, the gym mistress is murdered... (0-06-100284-4)

THE SEVEN DIALS MYSTERY

A country house guest is found dead from an overdose of sleeping medication. On the mantel, seven clocks are lined up, all ticking ominously. The clues lead to the mysterious Seven Dials Society. (0-06-100275-5)

THE MURDER OF ROGER ACKROYD

No one is sure if Mrs. Ferrars poisoned her husband. Then there is another victim in a chain of death. Follow master detective Hercule Poirot as he takes over the investigation. (0-06-100286-0)

For Fastest Service— Visa and MasterCard Holders Call 1-800-331-3761

refer to offer H0251

MAIL TO: **Harper Collins Publishers**
P. O. Box 588 Dunmore, PA 18512-0588
Telephone: (800) 331-3761

Yes, please send me the books I have checked:

- ☐ MURDER ON THE ORIENT EXPRESS (0-06-100274-7) $4.99
- ☐ ORDEAL BY INNOCENCE (0-06-100278-X) $4.99
- ☐ CROOKED HOUSE (0-06-100277-1) $4.99
- ☐ POSTERN OF FATE (0-06-100276-3) $4.99
- ☐ THE CLOCKS (0-06-100279-8) $4.99
- ☐ CAT AMONG THE PIGEONS (0-06-100284-4) $4.99
- ☐ THE SEVEN DIALS MYSTERY (0-06-100275-5) $4.99
- ☐ THE MURDER OF ROGER ACKROYD (0-06-100286-0) $4.99

SUBTOTAL .... $________
POSTAGE AND HANDLING .... $________
SALES TAX (Add applicable sales tax) .... $________
TOTAL: $________

(Orders of less than 4 books, please include $2.00 p/h. Remit in US funds, do not send cash.)

Name ____________________

Address ____________________

City ____________________

State ________ Zip ____________

Allow up to 6 weeks delivery.
Prices subject to change.

H0251